THE PASSIVE VOICE

THE PASSIVE VOICE

G. C. Scott

CARROLL & GRAF PUBLISHERS, INC.

NEW YORK

Carroll & Graf Publishers, Inc.
260 Fifth Avenue
New York, NY 10001

ISBN 0-7867-0381-4

Manufactured in the United States of America

CONTENTS

THE PASSIVE VOICE

1

BEGINNINGS

'Mailing yourself to Howard on his birthday is an unusual idea, but consider the cost – not to mention the practical difficulties. Suppose, for example, that you got lost in the mail. Such things do happen, you know. And with depressing regularity. Or you might simply be delayed in transit and get hungry or thirsty, or have to go to the toilet. Imagine what the Post Office would do if they found themselves lumbered with a large and unwieldy package standing in a tell-tale puddle. And you'd have to have a lot of help with the packaging and addressing. A delivery service might undertake the job, but you would have to be certain that Howard was at home to take delivery when you arrived on his doorstep. Otherwise the aforementioned problem might still arise.

'Better forget it. I have a better idea – or at least a more practical and lasting one. The novelty of the mailed girlfriend would soon be forgotten, or only told as an amusing story to friends later on. Suppose, instead, that you showed up at his place under your own steam (in several senses of the word) with a padlock through your labia. I'll bet he would remember that a lot longer.

'You could have each lip pierced with a stainless steel ring and then fasten the rings together with a tasteful (or at least corrosion resistant) padlock. You could post the keys to him in advance, and he could open his present himself on the big day. That's a lot less trouble and certainly a bit more fun because he can keep the keys and open his gift again and again. If you like the idea, I know

1

just the place to get the job done – clean, reasonable and discreet. Satisfaction guaranteed.

'Think about it and let me know, but be sure to allow a fortnight or so for healing before the unveiling. You can even get a gold-plated padlock engraved with his name or an appropriate sentiment if you want to go that far.'

That, as they say, is how it all began – a casual jocose conversation with a friend who probably knew me better than I had admitted to myself. I was taken with the idea of turning myself into a locked treasure chest for Howard to open. I knew that he was interested in bondage because I had seen some of his collection of erotica, in which this theme seemed to predominate. And I can see now how far I leaned in the same direction by my own ready acceptance of the suggestion.

In due course she took me to visit her 'reasonable and discreet' contact with the surgical skills. As she had predicted, the job was done well and quickly: no mess, very little pain – like having one's ears pierced – clean, surgical steel rings on each side and with the recommended lock. The healing was quick, and I was able to present Howard with the keys on the day.

The idea of posting the keys to him had been rejected after some consideration. It occurred to me that things really do get lost in the post quite often, small things no less than large ones. If those keys had gone astray, I would have had a difficult and embarrassing time getting myself unlocked. After all, it isn't quite the same thing as locking oneself out of the house or the car. There would have had to be more explanations than I was prepared to give. Imagine the scene if I had had to call in the police or the fire brigade to unlock me. Not exactly the sort of thing I'd relish.

A word of advice to anyone who reads these notes: if you plan to get into the bondage game, don't let your partner lose the keys when you are locked up. You will have to be very careful about that if you want to avoid the kind of awkwardness I've just mentioned.

Well, anyway, I presented the keys to Howard on his

2

birthday, and that day led to the present moment. I don't often regret that day, except sometimes on nice days like this when I might like to go out and do some shopping or lie in the sun. But it's something I freely chose to do, and I've learned to live with Howard's whims.

He will often leave me bound and gagged while he goes out on an errand or with some friend, and when he goes to work he usually puts these leg-irons on me before he leaves. Then, of course, I can't go out, or even answer the door unless I know who it is – someone who knows about our games, I mean. On those days I have to depend on visits from those of our friends who are in on the secret. If no one shows up, I can at least compose my memoirs. I am always interested to learn how others got into bondage games, and I imagine it might be interesting for them to hear my story.

Howard has other ways to keep me indoors which he sometimes uses. Some are more comfortable and some less so than these leg-irons. On those days when he doesn't keep me at home, he will lock my rings together before I dress. He uses the same lock I gave him for his birthday. I can feel it there all day as I go about the town. And it's there whenever we travel together.

I don't want to give the wrong impression. Howard isn't a sadist, or at any rate he is no more 'sadistic' than I have indicated I can accept. But he does keep control of me with his bondage devices, and the threat of heavier punishment is always there when I am helpless. That's a turn-on in itself.

Generally I am content and willing to play these bondage games with him. I must have had something like our present arrangement in the back of my mind when I gave Howard that fateful birthday gift. I just had not thought it through. In recompense for having to stay indoors when I would otherwise like to be out and about, Howard is usually more attentive and sexy when he gets home. He is turned on by the knowledge that I am locked up at home waiting for him. It's a good arrangement that has given us both a good deal of enjoyment.

3

Beginnings are by turns difficult and easy. It is necessary to overcome the embarrassment and to find a point in time to which to refer whenever necessary – a base to touch. My base is the day I presented Howard with those keys to myself. Naturally he was mystified at first, but I told him that he would find his gift later that night when we came home.

We went out for the evening and all through dinner I could feel the small uncompromising weight in my flesh, lying in my lap as I sat or bumping gently against the insides of my thighs as we danced or walked. And throughout most of the evening I remember feeling a hot flush of anticipation.

Of course I wondered what his reaction would be. He was casually expecting to have sex when we got back to his place. I was agreeable, as I usually was – and more than casual. In due course we found ourselves at home, and not long after we found ourselves getting undressed and into bed. We both had a good head of steam up when his fingers first encountered that small, warm lump of steel between my parted thighs. He registered surprise and reached out to turn on the light. Then, as in every good story, all was revealed.

I said softly, 'Happy birthday. Aren't you going to open your present?' Then the light dawned and he got up to search through his clothes for the keys. As I lay there all warm and steamy, he blundered through into the darkened living room. There was a thump, a muttered 'Damn!' and he came limping back to bed.

'Stubbed my toe in the dark,' he said.

Without more ado he unlocked me and entered by the front door. The flavour of novelty might have made that time better than most, but I can't be sure. We usually have good sex anyway, and that night was one of the more memorable.

When we were finished and rested, Howard got up and rummaged about under the bed. With a soft clinking he emerged holding a light silvery chain. He passed the staple of my padlock through the last link and then locked my rings together, leaving me chained to the bed by my cunt.

I asked him in blurry bemusement, 'Do you do this often?' He seemed unusually well prepared for just such an eventuality.

'Now and again,' he replied. 'You'll get used to it. Thank you for the birthday present. I think I'll keep it for a while.'

And so we went to sleep. I remember thinking as I drifted off that I really must ask Howard where he got the idea for the chain, and who else had been fastened by it, and when, and how often, and whether he intended to use it again on her or them, and so on. But that could wait until morning.

When I woke up the next morning he was already up and there was no response when I called him. I wanted to go freshen up and use the loo. I pulled at my chain and found that there was quite a lot of it. I gathered a bight of it in my hand and set out in the direction of the bathroom, hoping that there would be enough to reach. There was. That set me to thinking anew about how he came to be so well supplied with leads for his female companions, but there was no way to find out at that moment.

Anyway, I finished up my morning routine and made my way back through the bedroom towards the front room door, being careful to keep a grip on my chain in case it came up short. It did – just a few steps into the living room. However, I was able to see that he was not in the flat, and since I had discovered the extent of my freedom I went back to the bed and lay down. There seemed nothing else to do, and so I dozed off to sleep again.

Some time later the sound of the front door closing woke me up. I guessed that it would be Howard. It had not yet occurred to me that anyone who opened the door could come in and find me, that there was no escape for me. The fantasy of being found by a stranger while in bondage can be a real turn-on. I don't know what it might be like in real life. I suppose that would depend on the stranger.

But it was Howard this time. He came into the room and asked me if I had slept well. He fished the keys out of his pocket and set about unlocking me. When he had taken the chain off he hesitated with the lock in his hand.

'Are you having second thoughts about your birthday present?' he asked. 'Do you know what you are doing?'

I was not at all sure that I did know. The idea had come at me full blown from my friend. It was not something which I had thought about. Even then I didn't consider what I was doing. All that came much later, and in bits and pieces as Howard taught me the implications of my gift. I told him that I had intended to give myself to him in several senses of the word. Now I realised that I was responding to some deep need.

He nodded his acceptance and gave me a quick kiss. 'Thank you for the present then,' he said, and passed the lock through my rings and clicked it shut.

From then on he kept the keys with him, and I began to learn the implications of my impulsive gift. Some of the lessons were tiresome, but more often than not they were pleasurable. It takes a certain bent and an active imagination to pass whole hours and sometimes days bound and gagged in the house. If Howard simply handcuffs me or puts leg-irons on me, I can get about and do a surprising number of things that need doing about the house.

On the other hand, if he leaves me tied hand and foot, or handcuffs my wrists behind my back, I can't do much more than try to be as comfortable as possible. I can only wait for him to come back and do whatever it is he had in mind to do to me when he left me. Thinking about the 'whatever' is about the only activity I can manage, but that is often enough to arouse me and to pass the time as well. That's what I meant by having an active imagination.

Howard has never inflicted more pain on me than I indicated I could accept, and most of the pain I have suffered seems to be inextricably bound up with pleasure. I'll have more to say later about the relationship of pleasure to pain, but now I want to get on with the early stages of our relationship.

When he drove me back to my place later that day he kept the keys to my lock. I went inside with my rings still padlocked, feeling just the slightest bit tingly with the idea of our little secret. Before he left Howard made a date for

6

drinks and a show next evening. Then he left me alone to get used to my new status. I hardly thought of it as a status at the time, but it was. Someone else's mark was on me even though it could not be seen.

I bumped around my flat for the rest of that day and most of the next, going out once or twice down to the shops or to the market. Even though one has embarked on a new adventure the mundane details of living have to go on. While I was down at the shops I noticed a new type of tights – new to me at any rate. Perhaps the fact that I noticed them just then was a sign that the lock on my cunt was having an effect on my thinking. A case of matter over mind.

The tights had no crotch or sides to them. Very convenient, I thought, and bought several pairs. Was it my imagination that the shop girl gave me a most knowing look as she rang up the purchase, an I-know-what-you've-got-in-mind glance? Probably. But the small weight between my thighs seemed to grow heavier just then. The imagination plays some amazing tricks on us. I left the shop feeling quite the scarlet woman. Not an unpleasant state.

On the way home I decided to wear my new tights when Howard and I next went out. If at the same time I wore no pants the lock would dangle free, and the area of operations would be clear for some of the other things I had in mind. That was a happy choice. Howard liked them too when he saw them. A great improvement, he said, and I've worn them quite often since. If one is going to be provocative, one has to have the right gear.

Most of the time I waited around in the flat for Howard to call, and as I waited I realised that he was very much on my mind, as the song has it. Not anxious or unpleasant. Rather tingly, in fact. And I made other discoveries while I waited. I discovered that I could go to the loo easily enough, and also why the lock had to be corrosion-resistant.

In time the call came. Howard asked me to meet him at the Duke's Head in Mayfair. Eight-ish, he said. From there he suggested we could take in a cinema or a concert. It was

7

the last night of the Proms, and a friend of a friend had a pair of tickets he wouldn't be using. I suggested the concert and spent the rest of the time deciding what to wear and what to do with the rest of my week's holiday before the ugly spectre of work loomed once again.

At the appointed time I met Howard for a pre-concert drink, before we set off for the Royal Albert Hall. The last night of the Proms may be corny with all that Land of Hope and Glory and Rule Britannia stuff, but that doesn't stop me from enjoying the noise and the crowds and the singing. Nor did it deter the endless queue of hopefuls waiting for a last-minute vacant seat or place. Queuing may be the national sport, but it was nice to be able to walk past the great unwashed and take our places.

The concert and the singing took the usual course, and as I stood there in the crowd I was conscious of the small weight dangling between my legs. I had an exciting secret which the rest of the audience didn't share. Doubtless they had their own secrets and wouldn't care about mine, but I enjoyed that small, unobtrusive weight. And the enjoyment was heightened by the expectation of a good screw when we got to Howard's place. He had something on for part of the next day, and I reasoned that it would be easier if I spent the night there. He could easily drop me off at my flat the next day.

But when we got back to his place he suggested an early night. Rather disappointed, I began to undress. That was his first glimpse of me in my new style tights. When he saw me standing there with my bottom sticking out at the back and my bush in front, he asked me to wear them to bed. I thought he had changed his mind. But instead of coming to me he went to the bureau, from which he produced a pair of handcuffs and the leg-irons. They were brand new. He told me that he had bought them for me just that afternoon. Accessories for his birthday present, he called them.

He handcuffed my wrists behind my back and locked the irons around my ankles. Then he told me to get into bed. As he went to put out the lights I caught sight of myself in the mirror wearing my new tights and chains. Nice.

Howard too paused to admire the view before switching off the light. I jingled and clinked my way to the bed and he came to tuck me in. I was quite unable to do it myself. He brushed his hand across my thighs and belly. A probing finger found the small, warm padlock between my legs.

'Nice,' he said. 'You'll keep for a while, and then we'll see how you feel after a night of waiting. Some things are better for being postponed. Sleep well.'

With that he turned over and went to sleep, leaving me very much to my own devices and at the mercy of his. Handcuffs, I discovered, have no mercy, and are hard to sleep in. But it never occurred to me to protest. I had begun this arrangement the day I got the rings and padlock. This was just the next stage of my transformation.

So I slept that night in chains, the first of countless similar nights. Naturally I didn't sleep very well. Sleeping while chained or tied up is a frequent fantasy among hard-core bondage devotees, but it takes some practice to get a reasonable amount of sleep. I recall reading somewhere of a girl in Germany who slept in bondage every night (it would have to be Germany – they do really weird things there). That's a bit much for me, but the experience can be quite erotic from time to time. In this case I woke up randy in the morning from lying all night in chains. When Howard unlocked me we were both on the boil.

Since then we have had both good and mediocre sex with me either in bondage or not. Bondage is not a surefire way to good sex. That still depends on mood and on foreplay. But more often than not I find that I'm in the mood after being tied up. You might say that bondage itself is a kind of extended foreplay for those who enjoy it.

It need not be a matter of leg-irons. Sometimes it's merely the thought of being made helpless that turns me on. At other times I feel my small padlock as a weight and feel it slide between my thighs as I move around the house or while I'm shopping or visiting. Then I notice my breath getting short and rapid – not always an easy thing to conceal from the public.

I don't regret my 'gift' to Howard. We have both gotten

9

a great deal of enjoyment from it. Howard didn't ask me to marry him when we began the game. Nor did he suggest that I move in with him, though he probably would not have been averse to such an arrangement if I had brought it up. I didn't. That came later and formed another stage in our relationship. I suppose that he wanted to see how we would fit together before taking any major step. I hadn't given much thought to the matter.

I am not wholly a creature of impulse, but I act impulsively more often than Howard does. He had obviously given some thought to the logistics of keeping someone a prisoner in the house: witness his chaining me to the bed on the very night I gave him his 'gift'. I hadn't given any thought to such matters. I was just surprised that he had the chain ready. There is a surprising number of new things to consider when keeping someone a prisoner, albeit a willing one, for any length of time. He had thought this out beforehand.

I am certain that Howard is glad I acted on impulse in giving him his present. He still takes pleasure in locking me up, and I still enjoy the idea that a secret part of myself is locked away from me as I go about the town. Even when I am wearing my leg-irons about the house, as I often do, my rings are locked too. Sometimes Howard will leave me tethered by my rings all day, and then he will have me when he gets home.

He did that just last Saturday. He got up early and went out, saying he had to do some errands in town. I think he just wanted to enjoy being out and about while I was chained to the bed waiting for him. He has often told me that he enjoys the thought of me waiting at home for release – in several senses of the word. Whatever his reason for going out, I was ready for sex when I woke up.

When it became clear that he would be out for some time, I began to prepare myself for his return. Since my chain reaches the bathroom, I had a long shower. I did my nails with red nail varnish and rouged my nipples because we both like the effect. A wispy push-up bra came next, then stockings and suspenders. Even my crotchless tights were out of the question while I was chained. I chose a pair of my highest heels because they show off my legs nicely. When I had brushed my hair and applied a little perfume here and there I was ready for action. Nicely packaged, as the advertising types have it. I sat at the dressing table getting hotter and hotter. My little lock was getting heavier by the minute. When he came back, key in hand, the dam burst.

Howard paused only long enough to take in the effect, which was thoughtful of him. Even we scarlet women like to be admired now and then. Especially when we have taken the trouble to dress the part. Howard didn't spoil the effect by undressing me. He unlocked me quickly and had me from the rear. Grand, that was. Lots of heaving and panting and cries of passion which, freely translated, meant, 'MORE! MORE!'

After we had galloped over the finish line more or less together there was a pause while we thought about the next move. Soon enough Howard showed me that he had already made his plans. I've already said that he is more the planner than I am. He got up to fetch some rope while I caught my breath. It looked as if there was more to come – not that I minded. When he got back he took off my dress but left the stockings and suspenders. He likes the effect. Then he tied my hands together behind my back. With some short pieces of rope he bound my breasts so that the rouged nipples stuck out quite aggressively. As a final touch he gagged me, and we were ready to begin again.

Since my breasts were bound, they were more sensitive than usual. So the nipples sprang erect almost as soon as he began to tease them. I gasped and grunted to express my pleasure and to encourage further experiment. Howard seldom needs to be encouraged. Soon after he was using his tongue and hands to good effect on my tits and I was groaning and heaving in a most satisfactory manner.

Then he began to explore my belly and thighs with his tongue while a finger dived between my legs. I found myself wanting to say things like, 'More!' and 'Yesssss!' and

'Ohhhhh!' but all that came out was 'Gnnnggg'. I felt a bit like a bottle of champagne being shaken. The gag acted as a cork to keep the bubbles in and I felt as if I would burst with the sensations spreading from my breasts and crotch. I did indeed burst several times, figuratively speaking, before he decided to enter me. When he did, I exploded firework fashion (if you will forgive the mixed metaphor).

With my hands tied I was unable to guide or prevent him – not that I wanted to do that, and the gag limited my verbal contributions to the odd 'Ynnnghh'. Howard took this to mean, 'More of the same, please'. That's what it meant to me at any rate. He was glad to oblige, and I was glad he did. When we finished this time I felt as limp as a wet string. Wet I certainly was. Our mingled sweat had run down onto me. Of all the ways of raising a sweat, this one is my favourite. We disengaged and lay side by side catching our breath. Howard held me in his arms as I slowly came back to earth. It didn't seem necessary to ask if it had moved for me.

When Howard got up it was to get more rope from the closet. There seemed to be an endless supply there. He used it to tie my legs at ankles, knees and thighs. I didn't resist. Then, as they say in all the best romantic novels, he left me lying in the disordered bed and went off to do whatever he does when I am tied up.

I don't know how long I lay there. After my earlier exertions I kept drifting in and out of sleep. Not surprisingly, my dreams or reveries were of the erotic variety. Howard woke me when he came back to untie me. I didn't have pins and needles in my hands as sometimes happens when I have been tied too tightly or left too long. Howard always takes pains with my bonds. He doesn't want to hurt me, nor does he want me to be able to wriggle free. For my part I enjoy the sense of helplessness when I know I can't get free. Sometimes I can bring myself off by struggling for freedom, and Howard enjoys watching me writhing and jerking vainly at my ropes. So I usually put a good deal of effort into this mutually enjoyable activity.

Getting numb is one of the hazards of the bondage

game, but on the whole I like the feeling of helplessness and confinement I get when tied up. The tightness of the ropes is a turn-on in itself. With handcuffs and chains in general it's different. They don't have to be tight to hold you securely, and you can wear them indefinitely. So far the longest time I have worn chains is one week, when Howard and I spent some time at a friend's summer cottage in Wales.

Friends with secluded cottages are nice to have if one is interested in outdoor bondage games. We are lucky in having such friends. Their retreat stands in an extensive woodland which screens the occupants from most prying. Its remoteness is also nice. Our arrangement with them is based on house swapping. When they want to wallow in town life they use our place, and we move into their cottage for the duration. This all requires prior arrangements and considerable consultation, but then so does almost everything else. Matter and reality are really quite intractable. That's one reason we prefer fantasy. Unfortunately we must live in the real world, but with some care and arrangement we can contrive a short escape from time to time.

We escaped in late August during what turned out to be a long spell of decent weather. Miracles sometimes happen, even in England. They wanted a spell of town life and the reassurance that the rest of the world was still more or less intact. We were in need of a retreat from it. I am essentially a townie at heart and I suspect that I would be at a serious loss if forced to live the bucolic life for any length of time. The lowing of cattle and the bleating of sheep is all right in moderation, but they keep such unsocial hours. And as for planting and growing: I have the blackest of black thumbs. Any plant that comes under my care is under a death sentence. So these retreats are more in the nature of idylls than a serious attempt to get back to nature or the earth.

We arrived at the cottage mid-afternoon after a longish but restful drive through drowsy villages and green country lanes. Peace seemed to settle upon us from the very air –

helped no doubt by the long and lazy pub lunch we had shared back in the last village. Howard put the handcuffs and leg-irons on me as soon as we got inside. It was going to be that sort of holiday. On the bright side, I didn't have to worry about doing the shopping. By putting me in chains Howard had taken that task upon himself. At the same time, there was nothing to prevent me from unpacking our things and getting us settled in for the siege. I saw Howard off from the cottage door, giving him a cheery two-handed wave before clinking back to the job in hand.

That pretty much set the pattern for our stay. I was the prisoner and he was the jailer and errand boy. I spent most of the time there in chains. Sometimes I was tethered inside the cottage. Often he chose to keep me chained to the bed. My rings came in handy on those days. At other times we went for walks in the woods, me trailing along on a lead or in my chains. These walks were both exciting and scary. I expect that the excitement came from the possibility that someone would happen upon us in what could only be called awkward circumstances. Though the place is quite remote, I could never be certain that we were unobserved.

Despite the awkwardness of the situation, the possibility of encountering a stranger aroused me. By now you are probably asking yourself if there is anything that doesn't arouse me, but that's what this tale is all about. In this respect I resemble those people who reputedly enjoy having sex on the Underground. They are turned on by knowing that they might be surprised at any moment, though what would happen then is difficult to say. I'm almost certain that any witness would be too embarrassed to call attention to the situation. And suppose we tried to drive sex off the Underground? Would it then surface more readily?

On one occasion Howard asked me to put on a nice dress with my tights and heels. Naturally enough I assumed that we were to go into the village for the day. I prepared myself for some shopping and socialising, but I knew that was off when Howard handcuffed my hands behind my back and replaced my leg-irons. He reached up under my skirt and locked a light, silvery chain to my rings. It was the type of chain used on dog leads. Then he gagged me. During all this he didn't say a word about his intentions. When he was done Howard picked up the free end of my lead and tugged gently on it. I followed him outside.

I thought it was going to be another walk in the woods, and I wondered why he had asked me to wear my good clothes. On the other occasions I hadn't worn any particular outfit. I felt a hot flush wash over me as I thought he was taking me to meet someone. My earlier fantasy of meeting a stranger was about to become reality. Or so I thought in my confusion.

'Gnnnngg?' I said questioningly, but Howard said nothing. He simply led me into the woods towards a small stream we had found on an earlier excursion. After about a quarter of an hour's walk I began to hear the sound of moving water, and soon afterwards we came out into a clearing beside the stream. It was a fine sunny day with a hard, high blue sky, almost cloudless. In the still air the rush of water was the only sound. Our passage through the woods had temporarily silenced the wildlife. In other circumstances I thought the little glade would make a fine picnic or trysting place. Yes, I know, I'm going on about sex again, but bondage and sex are inseparable for me. But there were other things in prospect just at that moment, though I couldn't guess what Howard had in mind.

He led me into the clearing and dropped my lead into the grass – a bit like ground-tethering a horse. I dared not walk about for fear of stepping on the chain. That could prove painful. I didn't have any place to go in any case. Howard was searching for something in the grass nearby. I looked around apprehensively at the trees. What if there were someone lurking in the shadows?

Having found what he sought, Howard returned to pick up my lead and tug me forward a short distance towards the stream. What he had found was an iron ring, set into what looked like a rock buried in the earth. Without ceremony Howard fastened the free end of my chain to the ring, then tugged on the chain to show me that the ring was firmly set into the ground. It would serve no purpose if I tried to wander away. Since such things as iron rings set into rocks do not occur naturally, I was forced to assume that either Howard or our friends from the cottage had put it there.

Afterwards I found out that it was our friends. Apparently they too were into bondage. You can never tell what people are really into. We groupies don't exactly go about with a scarlet 'B' embroidered on our clothes. But at that moment I was occupied with a mental picture of myself in my good dress and my chains and gag. My lead was a slender silver snake running over the grass and disappearing up under my skirt. I wasn't left to contemplate it for very long, however. Howard stepped up behind me and blindfolded me with one of my own scarves. When he was satisfied that I couldn't see, he told me – rather superfluously, I thought – that I should wait there and be quiet. I heard his footsteps receding and I was left alone, staked out, before I could say more than, 'Nnnnnnnggh!' The foot-falls diminished into silence. I couldn't tell if he had merely stopped and was watching me, or if he had gone away and left me all alone and helpless. Gradually the stillness began to fill with bird calls and small rustlings among the trees.

As soon as he had gone and I was alone I began to imagine that the woods were full of staring eyes. I was staked out in the midst of a clearing with no cover. It felt like standing on a high hill with flat land all around. I didn't want to sit down on the ground in my good clothes, and besides I was wearing no pants. I became quite nervous and very conscious of my chains and vulnerability. The chain which was my tether seemed to grow heavier by the minute, obdurately holding me down to the earth.

All around me I could hear bird cries and small animal noises and other unidentifiable sounds which were nevertheless beginning to sound threatening in their alien multiplicity. I was on the verge of a major flap. Come on, I told myself. Get a grip on yourself. Vainly I tried to find refuge in the sentimental notion that the thing to do when thrust

16

into the great outdoors is to listen and observe and somehow see myself as part of this sylvan scene. No use. I am a complete townie and don't understand the workings of the countryside. Understanding does not come in a moment, nor does it come just because it might help with a momentary problem like mine. I wanted to think of lambs playfully gambolling over the fields. What came to mind was tigers prowling the forests of the night.

Blindfolded as I was, observation was impossible in any case. The only images I had were mental ones. And what flashed into my mind's eye was another panic-making picture: a field mouse might appear from nowhere, as mice are wont to do, and decide to see where my tether led after it disappeared up my skirt. I clenched my thighs together until they hurt. In retrospect it's funny. It reminds me of those adverts for rat poison that used to run in newspapers. They showed a panic-stricken woman standing on a chair with her legs clenched together and both hands tugging her skirt down while mice ran gaily around on the floor. Presumably, if one bought the poison, there would be no more mice to send one screaming up the nearest chair.

If my hands had been free I would doubtless have been tugging my skirt down for all I was worth too. But they weren't. I tugged futilely at my handcuffs instead. The thing about handcuffs is that they only come off when unlocked, but in the panic of the moment I wasn't thinking about that. You could argue that I wasn't thinking at all. My mind was full of tiny mice with malevolent grins running up my tether. Panic does funny things to you.

Exactly what the hypothetical mice might do when they reached the centre of things I don't know. I suppose that on a deep instinctual level we think of them running into the nearest hole for shelter. Hence the clenched thighs. In my rational moments I doubt that a mouse would even approach a human being if it had any choice. But try to tell yourself that when you're staked out in a forest clearing with animal noises coming from all around. As if I needed it, there came the alarming thought that Howard might decide to leave me here after dark. If I was sweating in the bright daylight, the darkness would bring sheer terror.

Of course I knew (didn't I?) that he wouldn't abandon me. After all, I was playing a game with my lover. I was not the victim of a psychopathic kidnapper. Nevertheless it took some time for that comforting thought to calm my fears. But eventually I began to unclench myself and lose some of the panic. However, I was still on a hair trigger. Almost anything, I knew, could send me off the deep end.

I don't know how long my ordeal lasted. It must have been several hours if I judged by the fatigue in my legs. I didn't dare sit down. When you're blindfolded you lose not only sight but the senses of time itself. You have none of the usual visual clues such as the movement of shadows and the position of the sun in the sky to help you judge the passage of time. All quite disorienting. And of course the unexpected can come upon you – well, unexpectedly.

I had just about convinced myself that I was safe from assault by demented rodents and the odd prowling carnivore when I heard the rustling of fallen leaves. Footsteps or the wind? I went all hot and cold as the earlier panic flooded back like a dark tide swamping my cooler self. Then came silence. Had whatever it was gone away? Was I being watched by burning eyes? Was I about to be devoured by an improbable tiger of the two or the four-legged variety? *Tyger! Tyger! burning bright* . . . No, this is silly, I told myself. My legs were getting tired. I had been standing virtually motionless for a considerable time.

There was another rustling of leaves and I was on the verge of jumping out of my skin yet again when Howard spoke. I was so relieved I went limp and almost fell over. His quiet, 'It's me,' had never sounded so welcome. When he removed my blindfold my eyes were dazzled by the sudden light. He set about unfastening my tether while my vision readjusted itself.

Howard gave a gentle tug on my lead and I followed him back to the cottage. He took me inside and removed my lead, though not the handcuffs or leg-irons. Nor did he

18

remove my gag. That's one of the main excitements of bondage: you never know when you will be free. You are governed by the whims of another and are helpless without his intervention. Howard went outside again and I was on my own. There was nothing else to do except wait for him to make up his mind about me. I managed to turn on the telly and settled down to watch.

It wasn't until later that I learned what Howard had been about while I was staked out in the woods – aside from testing my nerve, that is. For part of the time he had been making a video of me as I stood in the clearing. He showed it to me when we got back home and he admitted that he had spent some of the time simply admiring his captive beauty. That's me! I thought, pleased by the compliment. And the video was also in the nature of a demonstration tape in case he decided to rent me out later, he said. That turned out to be one of his jokes, though I know of one couple who do just that and seem none the worse for it. When we have a bondage evening in our group they often entertain us. Some people are hopeless exhibitionists.

I watched the telly for nearly three hours before Howard rejoined me. I was getting thirsty by then. The gag kept my mouth open and blotted up the saliva, so I got a bit dry. We have a large medicine dropper that Howard uses to water me. He produced it soon after coming back inside. I had been half-hoping to be set free, but when I saw the dropper I knew it wouldn't be very soon. My arms were getting a bit cramped but I could put up with it.

When he was finished, Howard put the things away and came back to sit beside me. He pulled me over to him and began to feel me up in a desultory fashion. His main attention seemed to be on the programmes. He made remarks about them and I grunted in reply. But I was not fooled or offended by his casual approach. It was his way of prolonging the warming up process. When he wants to reduce me to a quivering heap he spins out the warm-up for an hour or more. We reached the serious phase when he lifted my skirt and began to pay attention to my thighs and clitoris. I followed the advice my mother didn't give me. I lay back and thought of sex.

I got slowly more frantic as Howard continued his teasing. He brought me to the brink of orgasm and stopped just this side to get a drink. I simmered in my own juices until he came back and began again. Once again he brought me to the edge, and once again he stopped short. I don't know how many times he repeated the act. I felt as if I had been teetering on the edge for hours. I was writhing and heaving on the couch, trying to plead with him through my gag to finish me off. Instead he pulled my skirt down and told me that that was enough for the present.

The exasperating man got up, saying that it was time to feed me. I had a full head of steam up and nowhere to go. If my hands had been free I would have plunged a finger into my swimming cunt. But all I could do was squirm and twist and try to squeeze my thighs together about my melting centre. That didn't bring much relief. I hadn't yet learned to bring myself off by squirming and struggling against my chains. Later that same evening Howard showed me how to rub myself on the couch or bed while trying to get free. I do it regularly now. When he wants to torment me Howard will tie me to a chair or a post so I can't squirm and rub.

When the food was ready Howard removed my gag and fed me. There was wine with the meal. He held the glass for me. But there was another important item on the menu. While he fed me and plied me with wine, Howard kept one hand busy between my legs. It was a novel experience. I didn't know whether to eat or come. I solved this most pleasant dilemma by doing both, spilling a glass of wine over my dress at the end as the long-delayed orgasm shook me. When I had finished heaving and moaning Howard wiped my lips with a napkin and replaced my gag. He said that he was going into the village to get a surprise for me. I knew that he was playing with me again as he had done earlier in the woods, leaving me helpless while he was away. But I had chosen to play the same game, and there was the promised surprise to look forward to. Howard locked me inside the cottage and drove off into the night.

As the sound of the car faded into the distance I found myself once again wondering what I would do if someone got in while I was helpless. The answer, of course, was nothing. I could neither scream nor escape. Nor could I defend myself in any way. I began to fantasise about being raped by a stranger who had broken in. That made me very warm once again. A real rape would be scary at the least. It could be a good deal worse than that. But the fantasy is a fairly common one. On a later occasion I actually did think I'd fallen in with a gang of rapists. That turned out to be a put-up job, but I didn't know it at the time. However, in those circumstances a would-be rapist would have found me difficult to access. My rings were locked together and Howard had taken the keys to the kingdom with him.

Between my erotic fantasy and my would-be erotic twisting and heaving I managed to make myself hot and bothered and unable to resolve the matter. For that I still needed my hands. In the end I had to give up and try to enjoy the television. It had been a long day, and the telly was as soporific as always. Not to put too fine a point on it, I drifted off to sleep. And not surprisingly my sleep was enlivened by more lurid fantasies.

Howard woke me when he came back. He came into the room carrying a small parcel and wearing a large smile, both for me. Without ceremony he removed my gag and unlocked my handcuffs and leg-irons. I was glad for the chance to stretch my cramped muscles. I made off in the direction of the bathroom for a wash and a pee. I hadn't had the chance to freshen up since that morning. My dress in particular was showing signs of hard usage. It was wrinkled from my gymnastics and damp with sweat. I took it off intending to deal with it in the morning, but we all know what the road to hell is paved with.

Nude and refreshed, I went back to see what Howard had in mind for the rest of the evening. I was hoping it was me. He wasn't in the living room and the TV was off, so I headed for the bedroom. There I found that he had laid out a black panty corselet and black tights for me to wear.

21

The choice of colour was a bit conventional. Most men associate black underwear with sex, but I was mystified by his choice of costume. I had become accustomed to wearing crotchless tights or stockings so as to leave the area of operations free for Howard's attention. This was, comparatively speaking, the equivalent of a chastity belt. But that was what he had chosen. Far be it from me to argue.

He was occupied in opening the parcel he had brought back with him. He said nothing as I came in, so I said the same. I sat on the bed and began to put the tights on. The parcel contained two vibrating dildoes, one about normal – that is to say, big – and the other somewhat slimmer. About then I began to see what he had in mind. I had once read of a woman who claimed that she regularly inserted a vibrator in her vagina and then put on a tight panty girdle to hold it in place. Howard had apparently read the same article or had arrived at the same idea independently. She claimed that she particularly enjoyed going out to shop with her secret friend buzzing away. I surmised that I was about to discover how much fun this was. My guess was accurate enough in outline, but Howard had thought up an interesting variation as he so often does. There's nothing like an inventive man to keep one interested in new games.

Howard inserted the batteries in the vibrators and tested each one. Besides being the strong silent type, he is also very thorough. When he was satisfied he came over to sit beside me on the bed. I had put the tights on and was about to get into the corselet. He stopped me there and asked me to stand up. When I had complied he rolled down the tights far enough to let him reach between my legs and unlock my rings. That looked promising. He inserted the larger of the two vibrators into my front entrance and switched it on. Then he had me bend over and touch my toes. When I did so he lubricated the smaller of the two dildoes and slid it up my backside so that I was penetrated fore and aft. He helped me pull my tights back up and handed me the panty corselet to put on.

As I was struggling with it he got a tin of what looked like talcum powder and sprinkled it liberally over my belly and bottom and breasts. After that the corselet slid on more easily. It held my plugs in place and exerted a pleasantly insistent pressure on them, which boded well for the immediate future. Before I covered them up, Howard bent over to tease and cup my tits. The nipples obligingly stood out. I noticed that he was standing out as well, so I knew he was interested in the show. My breath began to come short. Seeing that I was becoming aroused, Howard stopped to pull up the top of my corselet and help me settle my swollen breasts comfortably in the cups. Then he went to the bedside stand for the rope.

I stood beside the bed while Howard tied my hands together behind my back. He left a longish piece of rope trailing from my crossed wrists. My elbows came next, pulled towards one another and tied. The trailing rope he brought up between my legs and tied around my waist after pulling it tight. It pulled my hands downward and against my bottom. If I pulled on the rope in any way it worked into my crotch and pressed the dildoes further in. This seemed promising. I pulled a bit in an experimental way and was rewarded by a general warming of the affected areas. Indeed almost any movement served to remind me of my twin penetrations.

But there was no time just then for further experiment. The gag came next, the same old friend I had worn all day. Howard gestured for me to sit on the bed so that he could tie my legs together at ankles and knees. When he was done I sat and waited for the next development. Now that there was time, I pulled a bit more on the rope running between my legs and felt the movement inside me. This was indeed my first lesson in auto-eroticism – how to bring yourself off to the unliterary – while tied hand and foot.

Howard sat beside me on the bed and began to play with my tits through the corselet. It was all a bit like those frantic petting sessions we had as teenagers, when almost any touching was okay so long as it was done through the clothes. I had had my share of that in the back seats of cars, though no one had suggested then that I need be tied up. Even though I felt the first stirrings of arousal, I

23

thought that there must be more to it all than mere petting. The preparations were too elaborate. The vibrators buzzed away inside me and I was feeling warm under my costume. Howard moved on to caress my thighs and the all-important junction thereof. This did not make me any calmer. Like the proper Victorian lady, I was beginning to glow.

Along with the glow there came a faint itching sensation around my belly and bottom where my corselet was tightest. Not long after my tits began to get warm and itchy too. About then I remembered the powder which Howard had applied to those areas. Itching powder! I thought, and so it was. As if the realisation were a trigger, I felt the sweat break out all over me and the itching suddenly seemed to get much worse. Get out of this corselet now! was the first thought I had. Howard had to let me loose. I said, 'Mmmmmmmf! Nnnnngggghh!' and other pithy things to the same effect. Howard made no move to untie me. I was beginning to prickle all over. Later I discovered that the substance we call itching powder is derived from a plant – or rather its seed pods – which grow in the West Indies and in many other tropical regions. In the eastern Caribbean they call it cow itch. In its concentrated form it irritates the skin terribly. In the domesticated or joke shop form it is cut heavily with such things as talcum powder. That is why I thought at first that Howard was using ordinary powder on me.

Horses and cattle can twitch their skin to frighten off insects. I would have liked to have had a similar capacity. Instead I squirmed and twisted frantically from side to side in a futile attempt to scratch against my tightly fitting second skin. No good. Howard was now watching me with a faint smile. He had moved around to stand in front of me to see better. In the mirror across the bedroom I caught a glimpse of a red-faced woman with wildly flaring nostrils. She was jerking spasmodically against the ropes that held her prisoner. A sinister looking man watched her struggles. A scene from a melodrama starring yours truly.

As the itching spread and intensified I pulled and jerked at the ropes around my wrists. The thought uppermost in

24

my mind, indeed the only thought, was to get my hands free somehow and scratch that almighty itch. Jason must have felt the same way in his shirt of fire. I merely succeeded in driving my twin plugs in and out in time with my jerks. At the same time I became more aware of the gentle vibration inside me. It was a nice balance between my attempts to escape the itching and to relish the erotic effect of that stimulation.

Though I was too busy to think about it at the time, this was what Howard must have had in mind. Through the combination of sensations I was driving myself to orgasm. Or, if you prefer, you could say that I was being driven to orgasm. It's a nice distinction, but I was much too busy then to analyse it. The body had prior claims over the mind, which is only another way of saying that sexual stimulation can blot out even the deepest philosophical questions. Unlike the saints and philosophers, I find myself undismayed by this state of affairs. The furious itching of breasts, belly and bottom made me squirm frantically, while the action of the dildoes made me frantic in a different way. The combination of irritation – I can't say pain – and sexual arousal drove me wild. What started as a struggle to free myself and scratch the itch imperceptibly became something else.

Sometime in the course of my gymnastics I lost my balance and toppled over sideways onto the bed. I almost slid off onto the floor, but I braced my legs and managed to keep myself from falling. From there I was able to heave myself fully onto the bed and begin to rub the itchy bits on the bedspread. That helped scratch the itch, but my heaving also caused the rope to saw into my crotch and created what the sociologists call a state of heightened awareness of my two plugs and the erotic possibilities of my situation. Not to put too fine a point on it, I came. And then I did it again, just to prove that the first one wasn't a fluke. I can't recall the reason for the third and the successive orgasms. They just seemed like a good idea at the time. The combination of relief and pleasure was an entirely new experience for me. I heaved and thrashed about for a fair old time. The gag filling my mouth choked back the noises I was making.

It was a highly satisfying but thoroughly unladylike performance. When it was all over I was sweaty and exhausted. Howard let me cool down and come back to earth before he untied me. When I could move again I headed for the bathroom, shedding my costume on the way. I took a long shower and washed away all traces of the itching powder and sweat. My skin was a rosy red from the irritating powder, and there were random itching sensations for most of the night before I got back to normal, if you think that's the right word for people like me. Towelling myself dry, I went back into the bedroom. Howard had tidied up and the bed was looking inviting. It had been a very long day, but I wasn't complaining. Neither the moments of terror in the woods nor the itchy session just ended could make me forget the erotic experiences I had had.

Howard didn't ask me if I had enjoyed myself. It must have been obvious that I had. I have never been one to hide my feelings behind a cool façade. We spoke easily of the day's events as he remade the bed and I brushed my hair. It had been a rather one-sided day. I mean that Howard had arranged several things for my enjoyment and had taken his own from seeing my responses. Now I was tired and ready for some sleep. He didn't complain about being neglected like other men I have known. On the other hand, I would have made one more effort if he had indicated that he wanted me. But he knew I was tired and so he didn't ask. He put the handcuffs and leg-irons on me and we went to bed. I went to sleep almost at once, the result of long practice.

Harriet Jones, about whom more later, claims that sleeping while tied up is a deeply rooted fantasy. She says it has something to do with surrendering yourself completely to another, an abdication of responsibility for choosing. You are not only unconscious as in normal sleep; you are also incapable of independent movement. In short, you are about as helpless and vulnerable as you can be. Harriet may be mistaken in her claim about the general prevalence

26

of this particular fantasy. She belongs to our circle of bondage freaks, so the sample group on which she apparently bases her conclusion is both small and quite untypical. But almost everyone dreams of surrendering all responsibility for their acts to someone else at one time or another. The I-was-only-following-orders argument is a common justification for doing what we like, especially if what we like is not normally done.

There are all sorts of variations you can try. For instance, you could add a gag, or a blindfold. Or both. You can sleep nude, or in any sort of erotic costume you fancy. Wear the kind of fancy dress you would never wear in public and give your fantasy free rein. Once you explore your preferences and get settled in you can vary the menu to suit your tastes. All good clean fun.

I enjoy all that now, but I spent many restless and uncomfortable nights getting used to my new status. I had given over the control of my body to someone else. That is the ultimate meaning of my 'birthday gift' to Howard. His wishes largely control what I do and set limits to my freedom. I have learned to accept and enjoy that constraint. And paraxodically I am free because I don't have to decide what to do. Howard decides if I will be able to go out on a certain day. When he chooses to keep me at home, he has to decide if I am to be able to move about the house or feed myself or go to the toilet. If he wants me to be silent, he gags me. Or he might blindfold me, or plug my ears. There are so many combinations of dress and restraint he can impose on me. I can leave all that up to him.

I enjoy being left helpless in the house while Howard goes out. It is tremendously exciting – arousing, if you will – to be under someone else's control and at the mercy of chance. Not knowing how long you will be left there adds to the excitement. The first time it happened was relatively easy on me. Howard merely neglected to remove my chains when we got up in the morning. On that occasion I was sleeping in the raw and my wrists were handcuffed together in front. I was wearing my leg-irons as well. That day was simply a continuation of my nightly bondage. He got dressed and put the keys to my chains in his pocket. We kissed goodbye and he locked the door as he left. As there is a deadbolt on both doors, I was effectively locked inside my flat. I think it's a good idea to have a deadbolt or a security lock fitted to your doors and windows if you are to be left alone while tied up. You won't be going out, but more important you don't want anyone to get in while you are helpless. You can fantasise about that if you like, but reality is another matter.

By taking both sets of keys Howard had doubly confined me to the flat. He didn't say when he would be back, and as it was a Saturday I couldn't judge his return by the usual working hours. Luckily I had got my shopping in on the day before. There was no real reason for me to go anywhere, but the moment he was gone and I realised I *couldn't* leave, I discovered six different and compelling reasons why I had to go to town immediately. As any philosophy student can tell you, this is a corollary to Murphy's thirty-sixth theorem: you never discover what you want to do until you can't do it. From the bondage freak's point of view this would be restated: you only start to itch in inaccessible places after your hands have been tied behind your back.

At first I expected Howard to come back quite soon. But one hour became two, then three, and soon it was early afternoon and still no Howard. By evening I was still wondering when he would come bearing keys. During the day I had managed to feed myself, and I had passed some of the time watching the telly. You have no idea how much rubbish there is on daytime TV until you have to watch it. That sounds Murphy-ish, doesn't it? I shall have to remember it. This was the first time I had had to feed myself while handcuffed. It was a bit awkward at first, but I learned the trick after a few false starts. Walking was awkward too. I had to learn not to step on the chain connecting my ankles. A few short trips taught me that.

And of course I couldn't dress myself properly. With the handcuffs I couldn't get my arms through the sleeves of anything. I could have managed a skirt, but it hardly seemed worthwhile. In the end I gave it up. In any case it would be more provocative to welcome Howard home in the nude. But it got later, in fact towards bedtime, and there was still no Howard to be welcomed. Finally I went to bed alone.

And woke up alone. It looked like another day as prisoner. Waiting is fun, but there are limits. As the hours of the second day passed I became more and more conscious of my condition. I was Howard's prisoner. He could do what he wanted and I could do nothing. Going out was impossible. I couldn't answer the door. No company was possible. I was in solitary confinement and at the beck and call of the man whose chains I wore. That is, as the advertising types say, the down side of the relationship. On the positive side I was living out in real life the adventure-story role of the captive beauty. Of course in the proper adventure stories the dashing hero rushes in to save the girl from, what the last century called (with no evidence I can think of), 'a fate worse than death'. I was not waiting for rescue. Nor was I persuaded that death was preferable to what Howard would do to me when he finally got back. Rather late in the afternoon of the second day Howard came back and unlocked my chains. He wanted to know if I had enjoyed the experience. I said yes, and we got down to enjoying ourselves some more.

That became the pattern for all the times later when Howard left me alone and bound. The basic idea is that I am left more or less helpless while locked in the house. I never know beforehand how long I will have to wait for him. When we began to live together and before our 'marriage' (I'll explain the inverted commas later), he frequently left me in chains while he went to work. On those occasions I could guess roughly how long I would be locked up. Before I began to work at home I had to call in sick from time to time, being careful not to let my chains rattle when I was on the phone.

Some of the couples – and singles – we know are deeper into bondage than we are. Bill and Victoria Simms have built a cell in their basement. He says his next project will be a mini torture chamber. He may not be just playing with words.

We don't have much of a cellar, but Howard has converted one of the upstairs closets to hold me. The closet door is heavier than it looks. There is no handle or keyhole on the inside. Not much light gets through the cracks, and the light switch is outside where I can't reach it. Howard put the ringbolts into the floor and ceiling. On the day he finished the modifications he took me up here to show it off. He put me inside and had me sit cross-legged on the floor. With a short chain he connected my rings to the ringbolt in the floor. When he closed the padlock, I was left chained to the floor by my cunt. He pulled my hands around behind my back and tied them together. Then he locked the door and switched off the light.

Time gets very distorted when you are shut up in the dark. I don't know how long I waited there. As I sat there helpless in the dark I began to get warm in all the right places. What made it more exciting was the fact that I daren't move very much because of the short chain connecting me to the ringbolt. When Howard eventually got back and opened the door the light dazzled me. While my eyes were adjusting Howard fell to work on my helpless body. He probed my crotch with a finger and found me warm and damp. The finger slipped inside while he used his other hand to tease my tits. I felt faint.

It was a scene right out of the very worst romantic fiction: the captive beauty swooning with desire as the rough hands bring her to climax half unwilling. Except, of course, I was by then co-operating wholeheartedly. Howard stopped to take off his clothes and I could see what I would shortly be co-operating with. He unlocked me from the ringbolt and helped me to my feet. We made our way to the bed where he laid me down and then laid me in the other sense. Skyrockets and random earth movements ensued, and a good time was had by all.

Howard keeps the bondage gear locked in a cupboard, so I can't get at any of it. All the keys are locked inside when Howard doesn't take them away with him. I seldom know if the keys to my chains are here or out with him. In either case the keys are inaccessible to me. I dare say I could find a key to my handcuffs or my leg-irons if I could get into the store. Those keys are fairly standard. Sometimes the only thing you need is a spanner, but if it is locked away, or if you are chained to something immovable, that knowledge won't help you get free. And as I have said, being an actual prisoner is exciting when there is a good chance that there will be a sexual twist to the prison term when the jailer gets back.

After we'd been at it a while, I was able to make an educated guess about how long I'd be held. The yardstck is how much freedom of movement Howard gives me. For instance, if I'm merely handcuffed, I'm probably in for a long session. A day is not uncommon. If he uses rope on me, the time will probably be relatively short. Tight ropes can cut off circulation if you're left too long. Another part of the game is not knowing when you'll be put in bondage. Howard often says nothing until I am fully dressed. Then he lets me know I am to be confined at home.

I know he likes me to wear tights or stockings whenever I'm tied up, so I do it. He is pleased and I am happy to do what he likes. My leg-irons are smooth on the inside so that they won't snag or ladder my tights. Of course if I wear them long enough there's a certain amount of wear around the ankles. Some women have ankles small enough to wear handcuffs there as well as on their wrists. And others have to have regular leg-irons.

Howard has several sorts of leg-irons for me with longer or shorter chains connecting them. He often leaves me in short leg-irons with my hands behind my back in handcuffs. That's the way I sleep most times. The element of surprise is a large part of our games. Sometimes Howard will let me get completely dressed before I find out that I won't be going anywhere. Last Saturday I had got to the point of putting on my make-up when he came into the bedroom dangling my chains. When they were locked on, he gagged and blindfolded me with two of my scarves. He carried me over to the bed and laid me down on it. Before going out he pulled my skirt up around my waist to bare my legs. He enjoys the view and I enjoy the helplessness.

I could hear him moving about the house and the garden but he paid no further attention to me for some time. There was nothing I could do but wait for him to come back. When he did he began to stroke the backs of my thighs. I could feel the roughness of his palm through my tights. And I could also feel the familiar warmth spreading through my belly and down between my legs. I expected him to roll me over so as to get at my front – something I looked forward to as well. But instead he had brought a riding crop with him, as I discovered when the first stinging blow landed across the tops of my thighs.

The pain was not that great. Howard was not using his full strength on me. He rarely does. But the surprise was complete. I bucked and thrashed on the bed as he continued to lash me and I couldn't escape. He was trying to drive me to orgasm through a combination of bondage and pain and surprise. It worked, as such things almost always do with me. Gradually I became aware that I was spending more time rubbing my belly and tits on the bed than I was in trying to escape the lash. It was a variation of the itching powder episode I described earlier. I heaved and groaned as the waves of pleasure washed over me again and again. I lost track of how many times I came. When it was over Howard simply stopped lashing me and left me lying on the sweaty bed. I lay there for a long time, dozing and waking. When Howard eventually released me it was late afternoon. I had spent most of the day in my chains. I was stiff from my long confinement, but I had also discovered yet another way to enjoy the sex experience.

2

SOIREE

Since I've been in the bondage game we've had one or two social evenings. As you might expect, they are rather small gatherings. The number of bondage devotees is not that large, and of those, the number who dare, or choose, to meet openly with others is still smaller. We know three or four other couples and some singles of both sexes. These occasions are something of a fashion show for the women. Everyone tries to come in something daring and eye-catching. For the first one we held Howard got me a French maid's costume: short skirt, lace cap and apron, high heels and stockings. The sort of thing you see in those adverts for 'exotic' lingerie. He said that the hostess should look the part. The outfit invites pinches and gropes. I got several on the evening, but I didn't mind all that much. It doesn't hurt a girl's ego to know that she's attractive to others.

From my end the logistics weren't too bad. There was simply the usual frantic scurrying around to organise the drinks and snacks for the onset. For our guests there was the somewhat knottier problem (if you'll pardon the outrageous pun) of transporting a bound, and daringly-dressed, female to our place and getting her inside without calling any undue attention to the proceedings.

The protocol for these events calls for the relevant people to arrive in bondage in order to lessen the embarrassment of anyone who still harbours any. It's like a fancy dress party where everyone is supposed to arrive in costume. If the bondage or costume needs alteration during the evening, there is the bondage freak's equivalent of a

33

visit to the powder room. Other rooms were set aside for dalliance. Since bondage is erotic to us devotees, it would be strange if there were no sexual encounters. The thoughtful hostess will make sure that the doors can be locked when necessary. Though many of us exotic types don't mind witnesses or extra participants, there are some who object. We leave it to the people involved.

On that first evening Howard helped me get things ready. When the food was laid out, I got into my maid's outfit. He helped me with that as well, though his help was mainly in the form of rude remarks about my appearance. It's just as well he stayed to talk to me, for I was getting the jitters about the party. Was there enough food and drink? Would they like what I had prepared? Was the house clean? If he had not steadied me, I would have run off in five different directions on last-minute jobs which didn't need doing. My jitters must have been apparent to Howard, because he took me aside for a prolonged grope which did wonders for my nerves and my ego, but didn't help my make-up all that much. When he was done, I made the necessary repairs while he put the leg-irons on me.

That had the effect of calming me down. The handcuffs came next, and I was ready for the evening's activity. I jingled and clinked around the sitting room making my last checks on the preparations. I tried hard to settle down before the guests began to arrive. Howard didn't say anything. He believes in action instead. The next time I came around he stopped me and asked me to raise my skirt. It was so short that raising it was the merest of formalities, but I did as he asked when I saw that he was holding my lead. He locked the chain to my rings and tethered me to the newel-post near the front door, then left me there while he went to get a drink for me. I stood awkwardly sipping it while we waited for the others.

Soon enough the front door bell rang. Action stations. Howard unlocked my lead from the post and refastened the free end to my handcuffs so that the light silvery chain led from my wrists and disappeared into the mysterious regions under my skirt. As I walked to the door I could feel it slapping gently against my inner thighs and pulling gently on my rings.

We had left the outside lights off so that the neighbours couldn't see our guests arriving. We had also turned out the lights inside the door and hall so as to avoid compromising silhouettes in case anyone was walking the dog. Just another tip to bear in mind as you rearrange your life around bondage games. I have often wondered what I would do if I went to the door in my chains expecting a kindred spirit and was confronted instead by a stranger who had stopped to ask directions. On that evening, however, I could be certain that it would be another *aficionado*.

It was a couple actually -- Peter and Janet Cousins, whom we had known for about a year. They had run an advert seeking others interested in bondage, and we had replied. You can find these ads in lots of specialised magazines. There are risks in both running and answering such ads, but you can lessen them somewhat. The most obvious precaution is to meet for the first time at some neutral place for drinks and a mutual looking-over before getting down to more interesting matters. We had hit it off well enough, and had made several visits to their place; and they came to see us a couple of times before we were both satisfied and could drop our guard.

Peter did something clever with computers and Janet helped out with marketing and advertising which she usually worked up herself. He was quite tall but not particularly handsome. With his sandy hair and casual dress he looked rather nondescript. Not ugly. Just someone who would not stand out in a crowd. Janet was striking rather than beautiful, a redhead with very clear skin. She always said that she considered herself lucky to have escaped freckles. When we knew them better Howard asked Peter if he had picked Janet because of her legs, which could only be described as sensational. They were long with well-rounded thighs and calves and sturdy ankles. Not the stick insect legs so fashionable among models. Peter agreed, adding that he had thought she would look well in leg-irons. And she did.

But not this time. She was draped in her travelling cloak which came to just above her knees and would conceal any bondage gear she might be wearing under it. Which she often did. Peter would often handcuff her wrists in front and throw the cloak over her shoulders before taking her out in the car. If they went to the cinema the cloak let her get in without being noticed so long as he played the gentleman by holding the door for her. Once inside she could sit in the dark with the garment thrown over her handcuffs and no one would be the wiser. One warm night they had strolled into the theatre with the cloak over her clasped hands and no one had given them a second glance. Arm in arm they went, Peter said. Janet looked demure. They both agreed that such outings made them randy, so that sex was more than usually enjoyable after they had got away with the escapade.

I learn of new things to try from talking to people like Janet and Peter, and the occasional bondage evenings may offer a new idea to keep us from going stale. On that evening, for instance, Janet's cloak was worn over a really stunning black leather slimming-suit as they are sometimes called. Her newest frock, she called it. It consisted of a single leather garment that fitted her like a dancer's leotard up to her waist. Above that it was armless, so that her arms and hands were confined inside it behind her back while her tits stuck out prominently.

I guessed that there must be a stoutly constructed and heavily wired brassiere built into the suit to make her stand out so well under the heavy leather sheath. The suit was closed by a long zipper up the back, which of course she couldn't reach. There was also a wide, heavy leather waist belt which served to nip her in and to confine her arms to the top part of the garment. In addition to the suit she was wearing black tights and a pair of high-heeled shoes. Since she couldn't use her arms to help her balance, she tended to teeter when she walked. Peter steadied her inside.

We exchanged greetings and compliments on one another's outfits. I was really taken by hers. There's something quite sensuous about the smell and feel of leather.

36

Her body suit was so tight it creaked slightly as she moved. Peter noticed the chain disappearing up under my skirt and asked me where it went. He seemed very interested when I raised my short skirt to show him. That broke the ice, and conversation flowed more freely. Howard joined in with an account of the birthday present. I was pleased that my impulsive gift had been noticed by someone else who liked it. Peter said that he would seriously consider having Janet erotically pierced now that he saw how fetching it looked on me. If imitation is the sincerest form of flattery, I could consider myself well flattered. I intended to return the compliment as soon as I could get my hands on an outfit like Janet's.

Howard led them through into the sitting room while I went to get the drinks. It was just as well I was dressed for the part. I came back with drinks to find Janet seated on the sofa, propped in a corner to keep her upright in case she lost her balance. I gave both drinks to Peter and he held Janet's while she sipped at it. If the woman is bound hand and foot, the man has to wait on her hand and foot. We have to look out for one another.

As I sat down opposite Janet I noticed an electrical lead coming up from somewhere inside her suit. It emerged from the neck at the front and terminated in one of those multiple sockets one so often sees on daunting electronic equipment. One (this one, I mean) could not help but be intrigued. So I did the polite thing and asked about it. Peter, equally politely, told me that it was connected to various parts of Janet inside the suit and was intended to shock her in various erotic ways. The explanation intrigued me even more. I resolved to borrow the suit at the earliest opportunity so that Howard could try it out on me. As it turned out, Janet was the one who tried it out on me, but I am getting ahead of myself again.

We talked of the things people normally do on a social evening: car troubles, funny things that neighbours do, complaints about our work or the troubles that accompanied the latest DIY project. While the conversation ebbed and flowed I was concentrating mainly on Janet. She

37

didn't have much to say. I wondered if she was thinking about the shocking things that Peter had mentioned so casually. She caught me staring at her and gave a small smile. When I asked her quietly if she was all right, she nodded but seemed preoccupied. From time to time her glance fell on a small canvas holdall that Peter had brought with him.

When Janet had finished her drink, Peter moved to fetch the small bag. She drew in her breath as if the dreaded moment had finally come. From the bag Peter took some rope which he used to tie her legs at the ankles, knees and thighs. He pulled the ropes so tight that they sank into her flesh a little. No chance of them slipping off. Like most of us bondage freaks, Janet has a bit of the masochist in her. She enjoyed the tight ropes around her legs. After giving them an experimental tug to see how well she had been tied, she relaxed. Before gagging her, Peter asked Janet if she would like another drink. She shook her head, no. He gagged her. It was a leather strap with a wedge of rubber that fitted into the mouth and filled it pretty full. He removed it from time to time to let Janet eat or drink or greet the other guests, but for most of the evening she was bound and gagged.

As the rest of us continued to chat, Peter produced an electric lead from the holdall. It had a socket on one end that matched the one on Janet's suit. There was also a compact box with four switches and a numbered dial. Peter connected all this up to Janet's suit and turned back to us; he was obviously pleased by our interest in his gadget. Now that Janet was all wired up he took the time to explain the operation. The little black box was a combined battery and control box. There was a fuse to prevent dangerous voltages. The dial turned out to be a rheostat with which he could vary the current to Janet's suit.

Peter continued the explanation by showing us how the various switches worked. Two of them controlled the electric vibrators in Janet's rectum and vagina. They were held in place by the tight-fitting crotch of the leather suit. There was also, Peter said, a special bra built into her suit which was both uplifting and electrified (not to say electrifying).

The bra had a network of electrodes covering the breasts and nipples. He showed us the switch that controlled the current to this device. The fourth switch controlled another set of electrodes covering her stomach, lower abdomen and bottom.

I noticed that Janet's eyes followed Peter's hands as they moved over the control box in explanation. Her glance was filled with a mixture of anticipation and a certain amount of trepidation. I gathered that she had already had some experience with her electrical gear. Her eyes widened slightly when Peter explained that the current could be varied from a gentle tingle to a muscle-twitching jolt. This, he said, should not be sustained too long but rather applied judiciously according to the wearer's tolerance and the type of response the controller wanted.

Later, Peter went on, he planned to blindfold her and offer the control box to anyone who wished to have a go at her. In that way she would have no way of knowing who was controlling her or when they might choose to switch her on. He added rather regretfully that she would have to remain gagged throughout these proceedings lest her cries attract the neighbours' attention. She was, he continued, rather demonstrative when in the throes of her orgasm. I asked Peter if he would give us a small demonstration right then. My voice must have betrayed some eagerness, because both Peter and Howard looked sharply at me. I was imagining how I would feel in Janet's place, and I was finding it a little difficult to breathe normally. There was a tightness in my stomach and I was definitely beginning to feel moist and warm in critical areas. I suspect that my voice may have been just the least bit unsteady as well.

With a smile Peter came over to my chair and placed the control box on my knees. 'You do it,' he said. He suggested that I set the rheostat just below the middle point. A good average current, he said, which should produce a good average response. The dial was numbered from nought to ten. With fingers that trembled ever so slightly I set the pointer to four. Peter suggested that I first switch on the vibrator in Janet's cunt. I moved the appropriate switch and looked across at Janet to see what she would do. She jumped slightly and her eyes widened momentarily. Then she settled back in her seat. I looked questioningly at Peter – had the box gone wrong, or had I done something wrong?

He motioned me to come across the floor to Janet, and when I did he took my hand and placed it between her legs. I felt a gentle vibration emanating from her crotch. She squeezed her legs together over my hand as she smiled up into my eyes. There was a faint buzzing coming from the same area. Still smiling, Janet nodded her head at me. I took this to mean that she was all right. Reassured, I went back to my seat and continued to watch Janet's reactions. When I looked up I noticed that Howard was watching both of us closely. For some time there was no visible result. I made as if to increase the current, but Peter restrained me. 'Wait,' was all he said.

Obediently I waited and watched. But you know what they say about a watched pot. Janet seemed to be taking an unconscionably long time to come to the boil. There weren't even any signs of a good simmer. From time to time she shifted her position, and once she let out a short, low groan which was barely audible through her gag. She might simply have been trying for a more comfortable position. Peter appeared neither alarmed nor impatient, so I decided to leave things as they were. He and Howard went to get a drink on the other side of the room, leaving Janet and I on our own. We were linked by the wire which snaked from the control box in my lap, across the intervening space and disappeared down the neck of her suit. As I imagined where the wire went from there, I felt a shiver of excitement wash over me. There was a sympathetic twinge where my rings were locked together.

As if that had passed down the wire that linked us to one another, Janet shifted her position once again. She raised her hips, as if to thrust against the intruding device inside her. It occurred to me that I was controlling her with the black box, making her respond as a lover would. I don't know where the idea came from, but gradually it took hold of me and I began to grow more excited. On an impulse I turned on the second switch, the one controlling the vibrator in Janet's backside. She jumped in her seat and looked directly at me, as if to show that she too was now aware that I was manipulating her. I could hear the redoubled buzzing from where I sat. This time it was evident that Janet was feeling some effect. Her hips were moving gently to a rhythm of her own devising. I let the second one work on her for a few minutes and then switched it off. The sound subsided, and Janet too seemed to subside on the sofa.

I thought that the best course was to experiment and see what results I could obtain. Peter had said that the controls had a built-in safety fuse, so I would be doing no harm to Janet by trying whatever came to mind. After watching for a few more minutes, I again switched on the second vibrator. Janet's body stiffened in response. She apparently liked what I was doing to her if I judged by the renewed thrusting of her hips. She appeared to be trying to dig her bottom into the cushions, and then she would give a little jerk forward as though thrusting against the dildo in her cunt. Her stomach muscles were clenching and relaxing, as were those in her legs. I could see how the ropes bit more deeply into her thighs as the muscles bunched and then relaxed. I could feel my own stomach tightening in response.

I began to flick the switches off and then on again, watching Janet's body respond to the controls. She was a puppet whose strings I held. As I moved a switch on or off, she jerked about more, or less. Then, too, as I manipulated her, Janet began to moan softly but continuously through her gag. When I turned the second switch on again, the moan changed pitch slightly. I looked up to see her eyes on my face. Our eyes caught and held. Hers were fixed on mine, only widening momentarily as I turned a switch on or off. My hands seemed to be moving of their own volition over the switches. Janet's face was becoming a mottled red and her nostrils were flaring widely as she sucked in air. With a start I realised that she was in the grip of what the romantic writers call a rising ecstasy – rising, I might add, from the buzzing devices which plugged her twin orifices.

I can be facetious now, after the fact, but at the time I was caught up in the drama we were playing out. I had forgotten that we were not alone. As Janet's eyes held mine, the rest of the room seemed to fade away. Peter and Howard receded into somewhere else. My fingers continued to move of their own volition: on, off, on, off, one switch or the other, transferring the sensations from Janet's belly to her bottom or to the two at once. Like touch typing – never looking at the keyboard that was writing the expressions on Janet's straining body and reddened face.

As her arousal progressed, Janet took to squeezing her eyes shut and then opening them again, keeping them always fixed on mine, as though she were urging me on, encouraging me to drive her struggling body to yet greater heights. During one of the intervals when her eyes were closed, I let mine stray to her body. Bound as she was, she couldn't move very much, but she was jerking and writhing in her seat as much as she could. Her threshing legs straightened out stiffly and then slowly her knees flexed again as though she were contracting about her throbbing centre, holding the sensations in the smallest area possible.

My eyes returned to her face. Janet's eyes were open once again, and once more our glances held. Without looking down at the control box I groped for the knob and turned it up one more notch. The effect was immediately apparent on Janet's face: a grimace which accompanied the heightened buzzing from her crotch, and a long-drawn, low-pitched moan of what sounded to me like great pleasure. There was no sign of alarm on her face or in the eyes that held mine once again. As before, she seemed to be urging me on, challenging me to wring further responses from the instrument of her body. In my preoccupation with Janet's throes I forgot completely about the other people who were to come that evening. I forgot that I was dressed in my skimpy maid's costume and was supposed to play the hostess. I forgot my handcuffs and leg-irons. The control box sat on my knees and my manacled hands played over the switches and knobs.

Janet sat across from me, connected to me by that slender electric wire. We were alone in the way that lovers are alone. As I wrung her body, I imagined how it would feel to have my own so wrung, bound and helpless and under the control of one who would drive me wild with ecstasy or pain or both. Janet was the victim, I the torturer, imagining also what the torture would feel like. I'm sure that Janet's responses were heightened, given an extra *frisson* if you will, by her very helplessness in the hands of someone who had so often been helpless herself. I know that my own sense of excitement came from seeing Janet straining in her bonds while I spurred her on. I discovered then a vein of hitherto-unsuspected sadism in myself, who had before then been almost wholly passive. It came as a shock.

I was moved by what I had already done to Janet, but there was more to come before our inspired duet was over. Up until then I had only tried to give Janet pleasure with the vibrators. I had forgotten the other switches which, broadly speaking, were designed to give the opposite. It is difficult to tell where one leaves off and the other begins, especially with someone like Janet. And with myself and other bondage freaks. We're a queer lot.

Keeping my eyes on Janet, I turned up the knob once more. Her moans were merging into a long low humming sound which was interrupted only when she drew breath. I suppose she was having minor orgasms practically the whole time. Her eyes told me to go on. I did. I had never thought of stopping. My fingers found the third switch, flicked it on and held it for a long moment. The effect on Janet was, if you'll pardon another dreadful pun, electric. The effect on me was pretty electrifying too. As the current hit her belly and bottom simultaneously her eyes flew wide open. The cry she would have uttered was muffled by her gag and emerged as an explosive nasal grunt. Her body jack-knifed, bending at the waist until her face nearly touched her knees. Her bound legs drew up as the muscles clenched. It appeared to me that she was trying to curl herself into a ball, presenting the smallest possible area to the current, trying to draw her body away from the closely-fitting suit which both confined and tormented her.

Startled by the results, I hurriedly turned the switch off, but in doing so my fingers inadvertently brushed the fourth control, sending another shock through her specially wired bra into her tits and nipples. Janet straightened up with a jerk and reared back in her seat. Her legs shot straight before her. She threw back her head and arched her back. Again I had the impression that she was trying to draw away from the current. But of course the tightly-fitting suit clung to her outraged breasts and gave her no respite.

She would have cried out, or at least grunted, if she had been able to draw breath after the first shock. But the second one, coming hard on the heels of the first, caught her breathless. Her face was a fiery red and her nostrils were flaring as she struggled to breathe. She twisted wildly from side to side, trying to shake free of the torment. I switched everything off at once. Like a puppet with the strings cut, Janet's body slumped down into the cushions and she began to draw deep whistling breaths through her nose. Her breasts were heaving as she filled and then emptied her straining lungs again and again.

The tension slowly left her muscles. She sat for what seemed hours with her eyes squeezed shut. But when she opened them they were once again staring straight into mine. There was a new awareness in her eyes. She knew that I was enjoying her ordeal. There was no reproach in her glance – just awareness. With a further tightening of my own stomach muscles I realised that I was enjoying her torment. And I liked being the one who was putting her through it.

Seemingly of their own volition my fingers once again closed on the switches controlling the current to Janet's vibrators. As the buzzing and throbbing recommenced, she continued to hold my eyes with her own. She nodded to me, drawing me into her experience and bidding me to do more; to stretch her body out yet again on the rack of pain and pleasure. Now I leave it to you to guess how much instinct and how much will guided my fingers as they once again grasped the switches that controlled Janet. How much was consciously willed, and how much came from somewhere deep inside my unconscious? I am not sure myself even now.

But those are thoughts after the fact. At that moment I was concerned with the way in which I was conducting Janet's ordeal. She was once again turning inward as the dildoes brought her to the point of orgasm. At the time I had no way to be sure whether she was coming or not. I hoped that she was. When I had the opportunity later to speak to her, I learned that she had indeed been climaxing. She added that she had been on the verge of an orgasm several times when I had seemed to sense this and had stopped her with a shock. This had had the effect of postponing her climax as the pleasure was set off by the pain. When she regained the peak after a shock, the orgasm was shattering.

I was not conscious of this at the time. What I was doing was experimenting, and it was sheer good luck that my bent went along with hers. We were attuned to one another on a basic level. Janet grew aware of this as I was turning her on and off, and she admitted that she had been trying to tell me with her eyes to go on. Later still she took her revenge, if that is the right word to describe the way in which our roles were reversed, and it was Janet who used the black box against me. Then it was my turn to heave and struggle in my bonds while she watched and manipulated my body. But that came later.

Janet was sitting across from me and slowly approaching a climax. Once more she was emitting a low humming sound through her gag. Her hips began to thrust slowly backwards and forwards as if she were making love to the dildoes that plugged her front and rear. Her legs began to flex and then straighten as they had before. The humming became more broken, interrupted by little explosions of sound which she perforce had to channel through her nose. These small sounds were coming closer and closer together and rising in pitch.

Throughout all this her eyes had been holding mine, but

she suddenly closed hers to concentrate on the interior sensations, which must indeed, have been sensational. She went rigid where she sat, and then her body began to jerk and heave as her climax washed over her. The low humming became a nasal squeal of pleasure which went on for a surprisingly long time. I knew it was finally over when she lay back against the sofa and her breathing became gradually slower. I noticed that sweat had begun to stain her tights, especially between her thighs where the ropes held her legs tightly together. Her temples and forehead had a light sheen of perspiration too. She seemed to be dozing, or perhaps dazed.

I shut off the current so that she could regain some badly needed composure. I was still oblivious of Peter and Howard, and they remained silent as well, waiting to see what Janet and I would do next. My whole attention was fixed on Janet, silent and still now in her seat, her eyes closed.

My fingers closed on the two 'pain' switches. I knew that the dildoes wouldn't bring Janet back round as I intended her to come back. I switched them both on and held them for a frozen moment: wake up, Janet. I'm still here. I have further designs on you. You can rest later. The shock brought her up with a jerk. Her eyes flew open and she looked wildly about the room before once more settling on me. She knew then that there was more in store for her. It's difficult to say what was in her glance – fear, anticipation, excitement. All three seemed to be there.

I turned off the current and she relaxed fractionally before I switched the two dildoes on again. No rest for the weary, Janet. She looked down at her lap where once more the vibrators were buzzing deep inside her and shook her head in disbelief. She looked across at me with a question in her glance. I nodded, answering her: yes, we are going to do it all over again. To concentrate her attention I grasped the switch connected to her bra. I gave it a quick flick on and then off again instantly. The quick shock brought a gasp from her.

Janet's eyes left my face and became fixed on the box in

46

my lap, where my fingers rested on the pain switches. She was obviously trying to guess when I would use them, as if anticipating the shock would make it more bearable. To test her I moved my hand very quickly, but not to turn the current on. She went rigid at the movement, anticipating a shock that never came. When nothing happened she relaxed slowly and looked up at me accusingly. This time, when she was relaxed and looking at my face, I *did* turn on the current to her belly and bottom. Quite the little torturer I was becoming, using psychology on poor Janet like that.

As before, her body jack-knifed, so that she lost her balance and began to tip over sideways. Unable to use her hands to catch herself, she continued in a gradual fall to the floor. She didn't hit hard. In fact she seemed to tumble in slow motion, her fall broken by the sofa. She ended up in a tight ball at my feet.

I changed switches quickly, shocking her across the tits. Her body jerked out straight, straining tautly. Janet rolled over onto her back and began to fling herself from side to side as she attempted once again to rid herself of the bra which was cruelly assaulting her nipples. She was no more successful than she had been earlier. I began to flick rapidly back and forth: first her breasts, then her belly and bottom, then her breasts again. Janet was rolling and jerking and heaving herself about as if she had fallen into an ants' nest. Her face was reddening again, and she was gasping and grunting through her gag as she fought for breath.

After a minute or so (which must have seemed like an age to Janet), I turned all the pain switches off and let the dildoes work inside her. When I turned the current off she happened to be lying on her side, her body arched like a method actor's who was trying to emulate a bow. As she relaxed she rolled over onto her stomach. Her hair, which had begun to come undone during her struggles, slid forward over her face, hiding her features from me. The hair was matted with her sweat. The backs of her tights were dark in patches where the perspiration had run down her legs.

As Janet lay inertly at my feet, I took the opportunity to

study her outfit in greater detail. I noted the heavy zipper running up the back of the leather suit, and the bulge made by her arms confined inside. From what I could see her arms were crossed behind her back as if they were folded. The waist belt kept her from straightening her arms down alongside her body. She was thus deprived completely of the use of her hands and arms. As I had discovered, you can do a certain amount for yourself if your hands are tied behind your back. You can get about and open doors and even go to the toilet, albeit with difficulty.

But Janet could do nothing. Her arms were encased inside the leather suit and held firmly across the small of her back. Even if her legs had not been bound together I doubt if she could have got up unaided.

Not that she showed any signs of wanting to get up. During the few minutes it took for me to look her over the two dildoes were beginning to have an effect on her. The first sign was a low groan which was muffled by her gag and the carpet. Then she began to grind her hips and belly into the carpet, thrusting against the twin plugs inside her. I watched as she worked herself up to another climax, knowing that I could stop her at any time with one or both of the pain switches. Once again I was about to play upon the instrument of her body with my new-found expertise.

Soon enough, Janet began to make the noises of someone approaching climax as she continued to writhe and twist on the floor. The soft moans rose in pitch and became more broken and explosive, as if they were being forced out of her. I continued to watch as she worked herself up to fever pitch. She was in almost continuous motion as she thrashed about, oblivious to everything except what was taking place between her straining thighs. This time, when I judged that the time was right, I sent the current flashing through her breasts, knowing that they would be pressed against the floor as she rolled about on her stomach. The chorus of whimpers was cut off abruptly. Janet let out a strangled noise and heaved herself over onto her back with a convulsive jerk.

She tried, once again unsuccessfully, to fling off the electrodes that were shocking her. From her waist to her neck she did a sort of shimmy as if she were trying to slide her tits out from under the bra. Despite all the frantic movement nothing moved. I reflected at the time that Janet's tits must be incredibly firm because there was no wobble in them. When it was my turn to wear the suit, I found that it was a combination of her and the tight leather bra which supported her. I held her there for a few moments while her back arched and she rolled from side to side. Her face got very red and snorting noises came through her gag.

As soon as I switched off, the taut bow of her body relaxed and her bottom touched the floor. That was the signal for me to shock her there. As if stung, she heaved herself over onto her stomach. But that was no help because the electrodes were then pressed tight against her straining belly. Her body leaped again. As I had done before, I switched back and forth, keeping Janet in motion until once again she was gasping in distress. Then I let her relax once more. She needed time to regain her breath after the latest shocks.

As before, Janet lay still for a time as her breathing slowed to near normal. I had left the vibrators switched on. As her distress subsided, Janet began to respond to their gentle massaging of her sensitive areas. Once again her hips began to thrust up and down. As they say in the romantic novels, the tides of pleasure were sweeping her away. Couldn't have that. I switched back to the shock mode and shot her down. Surprise, as they say, was complete. Distress was almost the same. There were more frantic jerks and heaves as the current swept through her. No rest for the weary.

If I was relentless, Janet was seemingly indefatigable. As soon as I switched off the current she began to respond to the vibrators. The alternation of pain and pleasure must have sharpened her responses. Practice makes perfect, as they say. This time I let her come. There were the same nasal squeals and whinnying I had noticed before; apparently Janet's characteristic pleasure noises. She flung herself about on the floor with great verve and enthusiasm.

When she finally subsided I turned everything off and let her lay in a sweaty, untidy heap on the floor. I guessed that Janet was worn out, at least for the moment. I had no idea of what her recovery time might be. In the stillness which followed the violent storm I sat looking at my victim lying at my feet.

I was brought abruptly back to the present by a scattering of applause. Looking up, I noticed for the first time that I had an audience. Peter and Howard had been joined by two more couples. I had not heard the doorbell or seen Howard let them in, so intent had I been on my manipulation of Janet. They were all applauding the show Janet and I had put on. My face flushed hotly and embarrassment made me speechless in front of the guests. I had been deeply and privately involved with Janet when I put her through her paces and had not thought how it would all look to outsiders.

I gradually recovered my composure as they greeted me and congratulated me on the performance. I realised that they had genuinely enjoyed the show. Like a conductor after the finale, I tried to direct some of the applause to the other half of the act. I gestured at Janet as she lay on the floor where she had finished. Peter and Howard came over and together they lifted her back into her seat on the sofa. We left her there to finish her recovery.

While I had been preoccupied with Janet, James and Helen Samson had come in, followed shortly by Victoria Simms and Bill Mason, her live-in lover. Helen is what they call a statuesque blonde. She is something of a fitness freak (in addition, of course, to being a bondage freak) who loves showing off her body. She was showing off that night in a flesh-coloured body stocking with matching tights. The sheer nylon covered her completely yet left her bare. There was no doubt that she was in marvellous shape. She stuck out where she should have, and went in in all the right places.

Her full bosom was on display through the nylon. Her nipples were erect; firm red cherries under the cloth. It looked as if she had been aroused by the performance just ended. Her flat belly and light pubic hair – our Helen is a natural blonde – could also be clearly seen. She looked more naked under her outfit than if she had been truly nude. Good clothes should do that for a girl. I wondered if she had driven over in that outfit. Besides being a bit on the chilly side, the costume simply invited stares. There was also the possibility of an accident or breakdown to add the spice of danger.

Like mine, Helen's wrists were handcuffed together in front of her. She also wore thumb cuffs. Her leg-irons had only a foot or so of chain between, much shorter than mine. A chain connected her handcuffs and leg-irons so that she couldn't raise her hands above her waist unless seated. When she walked, she was forced to take very short steps. She looked as if she would need help with eating and drinking – not that she did all that much of either. Helen often said that she had only to walk through the kitchen to put on five pounds. She liked to be as thin as possible (don't we all?) but with her body type she was never going to attain the stick-insect look so popular among fashion models and victims of malnutrition. Indicating her handcuffs, Helen said that she had enjoyed the performance and would have applauded if she could.

When I turned to Victoria she expressed her approval of my outfit with a low whistle. She was a slender, dark-haired woman, rather on the tall side and seeming taller in the high-heeled shoes she wore most of the time. No sensible shoes for her. She was wearing ordinary street clothes with a high-necked blouse. This was another of her usual articles of clothing. It concealed the steel collar locked on her neck, and explained why she had not arrived more obviously in bondage as Helen and Janet had done. One warm day, after we had got to know one another, I had asked her why she did not wear a lower neckline: surely that high neck must be making her warm? By way of reply she had opened the top of her blouse and showed her collar to me. The cliché about the relative loudness of actions and words applied here. She was matter-of-fact about it, not at all embarrassed by her 'badge of servitude'. There was a

51

chain attached to her collar which served as a lead or tether depending on what was wanted. Whenever the chain was not in use, it hung down between her breasts where her bra kept it from slapping about. She wrapped the free end around her waist and tied it there with a length of rope.

I had been so struck by her attitude that I had shown her my rings and padlock. We exchanged anecdotes about how and when we had acquired our respective ornaments as we drank tea. We were drawn together by the fact that we both wore the visible signs of our bondage at all times.

Bill broke in to say hello and to ask if I needed any help with the snacks or drinks. I said that I could probably manage, but if he wanted to volunteer Victoria I wouldn't mind. She was agreeable, and we moved off together to the laden table. Soon everyone had a drink and had been pointed in the direction of the snacks with instructions to help themselves. Then I could relax and look around.

The men had gathered around the sofa where Janet still occupied her corner. She had slipped down a bit and needed straightening up. Peter and Bill lifted her and she stretched her legs out to help her stay put. I thought she stretched a bit too ostentatiously merely for balance. It was more of a display, but no one seemed to mind. As they say, if you've got it, flaunt it. She appeared to have recovered fully and was taking an interest in the conversation, though she was herself still gagged. Helen was seated in one of the armchairs while James helped her with her drink.

It occurred to me that Janet might be thirsty after her star performance. I asked Peter if I might get something for her, and maybe take that gag off for a bit. When he told me to go ahead, I unbuckled the straps behind her head and took the hard rubber plug from her mouth. While she worked her tongue about to get the saliva flowing again I asked her what she would like to drink. She asked for a vodka and tonic. I rose to get it for her. When I returned, I sat down next to her to help her drink. It was the least I could do, I thought, after what I had earlier done to her. For her part, Janet showed no resentment toward me.

All around us the party began to come to life as the

others loosened up. Since they all knew one another, there was none of that initial awkwardness strangers feel which prevents the free flow of conversation. But it still takes some time for even the best of friends to get around to paying attention to one another's partners. That is one of the main reasons for having what I call our 'bondage evenings'. We can get better acquainted with our fellow devotees, to phrase it delicately. Or if you prefer, we can get down to some wife and/or husband swapping, but all in the very best of taste and with the utmost civility. I mean that no one made an immediate bee-line for one or another of the bedrooms with someone else's partner in tow. Nor did we just pair off and have it there and then on the carpet, though that sometimes happened to a limited extent. It all depended on who was at a particular gathering. Not everyone has the same bent.

Conversation, which had at first been desultory, became more general, while activities became more particular. Howard had taken over from James and was now holding Helen's drink with one hand. From time to time she took a ladylike sip. His free hand was occupied with Helen's bosom as revealed through the sheer bodystocking. Not to put too fine a point on it, he was feeling her up blatantly. She didn't seem to mind. Or if she did she was a consummate actress, for she never let it show. Plenty of everything else was showing. Such attention as Helen was receiving could lead in only one direction, and I remember thinking fleetingly how difficult it would be to get anything serious done while she was wearing her handcuffs and leg-irons.

We have evolved several stratagems for dealing with this particular problem. The most obvious is to hold a sort of prize draw early on in the evening. Everyone puts the keys to his or her partner into a hat and the punters draw out one key each. That's basically a variation of the exchange of car or house keys so popular at those wicked wife-swapping parties in those awful 60s. This only works well when the sides are evenly matched, or when there is a voyeur or two in the pack who doesn't mind not having a partner for the evening's frolic. Sometimes we just ask urbanely for the keys to someone's husband or wife or girlfriend or lover. All very civilised.

James didn't seem to mind that his wife was being groped publicly. For his part he seemed to have an inordinate interest in Janet, who was seated opposite him. I felt a little flutter of jealousy because he didn't seem interested in me, but there it was. I doubt if he was contemplating a grope. That would not have been very satisfactory to either of them with Janet encased from neck to crotch in her tight leather suit and with her legs bound tightly together. Therefore he must have been thinking about the control box which was lying beside her on the sofa. Janet was still connected up and ready for action. At one point her gaze followed his down to the box, and she shuddered slightly. I don't think the shudder was wholly one of fear.

Victoria meantime had made herself another drink and had come over to sit on the floor at my feet. She rested her head against the outside of my thigh and settled herself comfortably with her shoulder against the sofa. Holding her drink with one hand, with the other she began to play idly with the chain that disappeared up under my skirt. She tugged gently at it from time to time, making me more aware of the small, warm lump of steel between my thighs. As I once more leaned over to give Janet a sip of her drink, I felt Victoria's hand begin to trace my chain up to its secret source. It travelled up my leg from my ankle, over my knee and on up above my stocking-tops until her fingers touched the padlock itself. For a time she toyed with the lock and the rings it held together. Finally she moved on to the real target. She spread my lips and began to rub my clitoris gently in slow circles.

It wasn't so very long before I felt myself becoming warm and wet in the affected area and adjacent regions. Seemingly of their own volition my legs were parting as she continued her soft rubbing and probing. I knew where that would lead, but in the meantime I continued to hold Janet's drink for her and to give her sips whenever she seemed to require refreshment. She was by now talking to James and Bill. They seemed to be talking about her latest performance under my direction. I didn't pay very close attention to what they were saying because I was beginning to pay more and more attention to my own performance under Victoria's knowing hand. She put her empty glass down, and the one hand became two. With one she continued the gentle massage of my, by now swimming, cunt. With the other she alternately caressed the tops of my thighs and slipped around the outside curve of my legs to cup one or the other side of my bottom.

Whenever I shifted my position, Victoria teasingly slid a finger into the crack of my behind and flicked the slowly contracting and relaxing arsehole so conveniently located there. The next time I leaned over to give Janet a drink I knew I was lost. Victoria must have been waiting for something like that because she slid her finger full length up my backside as soon as I shifted my weight to one side. I gasped and jumped and spilled Janet's drink all over her in one smooth coordinated motion. Fortunately there wasn't a lot left in the glass by then, but the ice cubes that ended up in her lap caused her to jump in her turn. She couldn't shift the ice herself, but James quickly came to the rescue. He had probably been waiting for some excuse to give Janet some closer attention. Sometimes men can be surprisingly shy. Once the ice had been disposed of he took his time about removing his hands from her legs, and when he did take them away it was to reach for the control box. Before switching it on once more he replaced Janet's gag.

I didn't catch what happened next because I was soon much too busy on my own account. Someone nearby seemed to be making loud noises. It couldn't have been Janet because she was gagged, and she couldn't have warmed up again so quickly. It might have been Helen, but the last time I noticed her she was sitting somewhat further away from the source of the disturbance. So it must have been me. Isn't logic wonderful?

I remember hands helping me to shift and turning me so that I lay over the arm of the sofa with my head down and my bottom in the air. The hands spread my legs (which didn't need all that much more spreading) and raised my

55

skirt above my waist so that I was bare for all to see. Then the hands continued their slow exploration of the secret crack at the centre of the world. A mouth and tongue joined in the fun. The noises got louder and I was fantasising about being in Janet's place in the electric bodysuit. Need I add that I went over the top several times before I once again began to take an interest in the rest of the party? When I was all done (not to say done in), Victoria helped raise me and sat me down on the sofa while things slowly came back into focus. When things *did* get back to normal I noticed that Janet was still seated on the other end of the sofa. James was holding on to the control box, so she must have been switched on once more. Her eyes were closed and she seemed to be turned inward. I could hear a subdued buzzing coming from her general direction if I listened carefully. The warming-up process was under way then. Helen and Howard were dancing – if you consider standing close together and swaying to the music to be dancing. It looked more like vertical foreplay to me. They were rubbing against one another while Howard's hands cupped her bottom and hers cupped and stroked the member for South Howard. It wasn't much use trying to dance with Helen anyway while she was wearing her short leg-irons. But they were making the best of an awkward situation.

All in all it was turning into a successful evening. Everyone seemed to be having fun and I could relax and enjoy whatever else happened. At the moment the whatever, seemed to be happening to Janet and Victoria. Janet was beginning to squirm about as the vibrators inside her did their work. Her eyes were still closed and it looked to me as if she was keeping herself more closed in than she had been when I was at the controls. Perhaps we had indeed shared a very intimate experience; one which she was not going to share with everyone who happened to switch her on. Soon after Victoria had had her lusty way with me, Bill had attached a lead to her collar and dragged her away in the direction of the spare bedroom. She didn't appear to be offering much resistance. Nor did they look as if they intended to take a nap.

As I sat watching developments Peter came over with a fresh drink for me. I accepted gratefully and we chatted while we drank. When the drinks were done, he asked me gallantly for the next dance. We joined Helen and Howard for a spot of bondage dancing. For those who are into bondage it is another nice way to get turned on. And I did. As we swayed to the music I found that I had recovered from the earlier sensory overload. The circuit breakers had reset. When, sometime later, Peter gently urged me towards the bedroom I didn't make much fuss. He is a gentleman, so I will be a lady and draw a veil over what we did when we got there, lest I shock the overly sensitive.

In deference to them (and they are certainly vociferous if not numerous), I would add that we don't compel anyone to do anything they are opposed to. We like to think of ourselves as the well-known 'consenting adults'. It's amazing how hard it is to find one when you want one. They must be very thin on the ground. There are many feminist groups who would condemn our games as simply another manifestation of the male dominance they see everywhere and in everything. They would regard any woman who submitted to being tied up for sex play as a traitor to the sex, and a wearer of fireproof brassieres into the bargain. I don't deny that submission is a big part of the game for the women I have been describing, but the submission comes after she has chosen to play the game and enhance her sex life.

If I felt compelled to defend my *modus vivendi* I could point out that there are many men who are into bondage. If you don't believe that, take a look at the many offers of 'correction' and 'strict discipline' which you find pasted up in telephone kiosks and Underground stations in various parts of the city. Not to mention the many similar adverts in the 'contact magazines'. These ads are almost invariably placed by female prostitutes and are aimed mainly at men. They don't call it 'the English vice' for nothing.

But I don't often defend my life. It's much easier to keep all this secret from those who might give me a hard time about what I like. I don't waste time trying to convert

others to my views. Nor do I campaign for toleration of
them. The less others know of my private affairs the freer
I am to go my own way unmolested. But that's enough
preaching for now.

3

HOUSEBOUND

Another couple we know, Hilary and Jean, are also into
bondage but not into the public aspect of it. They wouldn't
care to attend a soirée like the one I have described. They
do what they like at home, or on holiday, but always in
private. Not everyone who likes bondage is into swapping
or swinging as it used to be called before the gay transformation of the English language. I wonder what debu-
tantes do now that 'coming out' means something entirely
different from the original usage. Hilary and Jean did let
their hair down a bit with Howard and I after we got to
know them. When they realised that we were into bondage
ourselves they told us the story of their own experience.

Hilary found her way into bondage by a rather risky
route. She was arrested for shoplifting and when they put
the handcuffs on her she found that she liked the idea of
being restrained. But she could very easily have been sent
to prison instead of being sentenced to the house arrest she
in fact got. It went this way.

Hilary and Jean are comfortably off. She didn't need the
things she took. Like many others who go into shoplifting
in an amateur way, she did it for the thrill of getting away
with it. Maybe she was also looking subconsciously for a
way to manoeuvre herself into becoming a prisoner to
someone else. However, I don't pretend to understand all
the reasons why she did it.

Hilary operated in large stores where there is security
staff and often a closed circuit TV system to spot thefts.
Many shoplifters choose this type of store because they

offer a large selection and present a double challenge by their security systems. She was eventually caught and interviewed by the store manager before being released with a warning. This happened three or four times in different stores before she found herself in court. The subsequent embarrassment to herself and Jean put her off theft for a time. She was lucky that time. She got a suspended sentence and she behaved herself for a while. The next time she came before the court, they were obliged to take notice of her previous conviction. This time a custodial sentence was a definite possibility.

But (and here is where the luck came in) the judge observed that such a sentence seemed out of proportion to the offence. He may have meant by this that Hilary was obviously of the upper middle classes whose social position puts them somewhat above the justice meted out to those of lesser status. The fact that Hilary is very easy on the eyes may have had something to do with it as well. The judge pointed out that the prisons were (and are) over-crowded, and that prison terms often lead people to commit other and more serious offences. He cited the deleterious influence of hardened criminals on first-time offenders, and the difficulty of living down a prison sentence, and all the other usual reasons for keeping some people out of prison while putting others inside.

In the end he sentenced her to six months' house arrest. She was ordered to stay at home unless accompanied by her husband. She had to report to the police by telephone, and to reply to random calls from them. All this was intended to keep her at home and out of trouble. Chastened but relieved, Hilary went home to begin serving her sentence.

As she later confided to me, she might have done all that was required of her by the court if she hadn't been caught exactly as she had been by the store staff. She told me that she had tried to run when confronted by the security man. This may or may not have been a panic reaction. The mind does strange things. In any case, she had been caught and taken to an inner office to await the arrival of the police.

The security people apparently thought she might try to escape again, and so they had handcuffed her wrists behind her back. Hilary said that she felt a thrill of sexual excitement as soon as the cuffs were closed about her wrists. This excitement grew as she waited to be taken away.

Like most people, she had never before been restrained in this way, and for her it was an entirely novel and unexpected pleasure to know that she was a prisoner. From then on, she said, she knew that she wanted it to happen again. She can't account for her predilection, any more than your average bondage freak can. Perhaps lengthy analysis might yield some explanation, but the aim of most analysis is to alter one's behaviour. She didn't want to change. When the police arrived she was taken, still in handcuffs, to the station and put into a cell. Jean was called and he came to collect her. She didn't tell him then about the sexual thrill she derived from being handcuffed. There were many other more pressing matters to settle at the time. But she didn't forget the thrill either. Thereafter her course was set.

Hilary went along with the conditions imposed by the court for a month or so. The worst part of it was that she couldn't do anything all day. The time began to hang heavily. And she had made no progress toward realising her new desire. Somehow the time never seemed right to open the matter with Jean. Then one day, she said, she simply left the house and went missing for the next several hours. She did not steal anything. But she had broken the conditions imposed on her by the court. I don't think she was really trying to run away. Where would she go? She had made no real plans for escape. I think she was trying to put into effect her plan to become a real prisoner. When she came back she went up before the same judge, who then modified the terms of her house arrest.

Just now we hear a good deal about the use of house arrest and electronic tagging to keep track of minor offenders. There are plans afoot to make certain people wear an electronic bracelet or anklet which would ensure that they stayed at home or close to it. But the events I am describing took place before electronic tagging was thought of. So Hilary's revised sentence called for her to be physically restrained. For the next six months, the judge ruled, she was to wear a pair of leg-irons supplied by the police and locked on her ankles by a policeman. The keys were to be kept at the village cop shop.

As they lived in a small village, it was possible to make arrangements like this which would not be possible in a larger town or city. The arrangement worked like this: whenever Hilary was to be left at home alone, Jean would drive her to the police station where they would enter by a rear door. Once inside they were taken to one of the interrogation rooms and could have a cup of tea while they waited for the desk sergeant. When he came in they would try to make polite small talk while he was putting the irons on her. She was then driven back home by Jean and entered the house through the door connecting with the garage. She was then effectively confined to the house until Jean got back, for reasons we all know well. When he got back in the evening the procedure was reversed and she would be unlocked until the next morning.

I'm sure you have spotted some of the complications presented by the arrangements, not the least of which was that Jean had to be continually taking her back and forth to the police station. Then there was the matter of visits from friends and neighbours. That could be an embarrassment for everyone. In the end they told their friends and the nearest neighbours about the situation and left it to them to come visiting or not. Some came and some stayed away. Hilary could go out into the back garden but there was always the possibility of an awkward encounter with a neighbour. It was one thing to explain the sentence to the people next door, but quite another to actually see or speak to Hilary as she went about the garden in her leg-irons.

Hilary had to be up and dressed in time for the daily trip to the village before Jean left for work. That meant no long lie-ins. The matter of what to wear was also a problem. If she put on trousers she would be unable to change them once the leg-irons were locked on. The same was true of pants and tights. Gradually she took to wearing skirts and dresses almost exclusively. In the end she went back to stockings and suspenders to solve the problem of the tights.

There is a subtle bit of psychology here, which the judge may (or may not) have been aware of. Your average raging feminist would spot it at once. Hilary was coerced into wearing what they would call sex-exclusive clothing, or what they now insist on calling gender-exclusive. Another example of how language gets twisted in order to placate the vociferous minorities. Gender is a grammatical condition. Sex is a human one. Anyway, they would insist that she was being forced to dress as a stereotypical sex object. The men were treating her as a plaything. And so on. You can sympathise with their viewpoint if you regard sex objects and playthings as absolutely evil. Hilary took a different view. As she wore only dresses or skirts, she said that she became more aware of herself as a woman. And so did Jean. And so did the policemen who saw her daily. The choice of stockings and suspenders had the same effect. And the combination of her dress and her daily bondage had (to say no more) a beneficial effect on her sex life.

In the beginning Hilary and Jean put up with the annoyance of having to visit the police station twice daily. But there inevitably came a time when it was too much trouble to go out in the evening after work, and on that day the situation changed irrevocably. On that evening Jean called the station and explained the problem to the desk sergeant. He pointed out that, as his wife would be wearing her leg-irons all night, they would like to miss out the visit. For the same reason the morning visit would be unnecessary. After consultation (I don't know why the police can never give a straight answer to requests without 'consulting' someone else), the police agreed. And that night for the first time Hilary wore her leg-irons to bed. And they had sex. And she came and came. And Jean confessed to being aroused by her chains. And Hilary confessed her secret desire. And they fell voraciously upon one another yet again. And . . . You get the picture.

The had acknowledged their predilections and there was no going back – nor any reason to. If confession is good for the soul, it may also work wonders for sex sometimes. After that night of what the romantic novels would call 'torrid sex', they were never far from chains or rope. Before that night Hilary had noticed a greater interest in sex on Jean's part. She too found the subject much on her mind. She knew that wearing leg-irons all day was exciting, but she had never been able to pluck up the courage to say so. Now it was done. Who knows what subconscious motives and schemes had led to this denouement? Not me.

But to return to the initial *tableau vivant à deux aux chaines*. They were both agreeably surprised by the encounter. Hilary knew that her leg-irons had greatly heightened her enjoyment, and Jean was strongly drawn to her as she lay on the bed wearing nothing but her heavy irons. It was the classic rape fantasy which underlies a good deal of sex and bondage. Jean was reluctant to leave her the next day to go to work. He said that he had visions of Hilary lying naked on the bed in her chains. When he got home it was a choice of having dinner or having Hilary first. She won.

The next day, a Saturday, they were to go shopping. With Hilary unable to leave the house during the week they had to do it all on weekends. First stop was the police station to have Hilary unlocked. She dressed for town, working a new pair of stockings under her leg-irons with some difficulty. She put on a pair of high heels, which she thought would show off her legs, and they were ready. As she got into the car, Jean asked her if there was any chance they could put off shopping and go back to bed. She flashed a big smile at him and mouthed, 'later'. At the station the desk sergeant was impressed with her too. He seemed a bit flustered as he fitted the key into her irons, and he was having trouble keeping his eyes off her legs. Jean thought he might be reluctant to destroy the effect by taking the leg-irons off her.

Having discovered the erotic effect of Hilary's chains, Jean had resolved to buy a set for her as soon as possible.

But he didn't see any that day. They are not among the things usually available in hardware stores or in the high street. He later found what he wanted by getting the maker's name from Hilary's set. A discreet consultation of the business address directory led him to Hiatt, who have been making prison and police hardware for donkey's years. I mention the name in case anyone wants to deal with them on their own account.

There are others, and Jean tracked them down in the course of following Hilary's fantasies. One thing he noticed in his search was that quite a few sporting goods, fishing and hunting tackle, and novelty shops have a set of handcuffs tucked discreetly into a corner of their window displays. We've noticed it too, and I wonder just how many others have come in off the street to buy a pair after an embarrassed and low-voiced enquiry. But I'm getting ahead of the story. One of the things he *did* buy that day was a coil of nylon linen line. Hilary gave him a secret smile of encouragement when she saw it. He acknowledged it with a grin and a sidelong look at her legs. They were conspirators with a secret in a public place.

They did the rest of the shopping for the coming week and finished the evening with drinks and dinner at a nice restaurant. When they got home, Hilary said gleefully, it was a race to see who could get undressed first. Jean had her take off everything except her stockings and suspenders. He asked her to get out her long kid gloves and put them on. He was packaging her to taste. Nothing loth, she got out of her clothes in record time while Jean cut the rope into convenient lengths. When she was ready she lay down on the bed. Jean tied the cord tightly around her wrists and ankles and spread-eagled her to the four bedposts. When she was satisfactorily helpless he finished undressing himself.

Then he turned his attention to the business in hand. Setting himself strict limits, he began to tease Hilary from toes to tits. As his fingers trailed over her body and his tongue darted into her crevices, she went slowly wild; gasping and tugging at the ropes which held her to the bed.

When he judged she was ready, Jean mounted her. It was sensational, she reported.

Restrained as she was, Hilary could still thrust with her hips, and she did this with a certain degree of abandon. She also expressed her approval with loud and urgent cries and groans which acted as a spur on Jean. Thus a good time was had by all.

When they had done, Jean withdrew and remarked that she should try to be more quiet in future if the neighbours were not to know what they were about. Hilary replied, 'The neighbours be hanged,' or words to that effect. During that weekend they made love much more often than they had in the past. Hilary was always tied up for these occasions in one way or another. Mostly she was spread-eagled on her back because, as countless generations of bondage freaks have discovered, it's the most convenient position. They also discovered that it was more exciting if Hilary was left bound after making love, not knowing when Jean would come back. When he did return, as often as not she had worked herself up and was ready for another gallop round the course. He tried not to disappoint her.

After that idyllic weekend came grim Monday and the return of the weekly routine. In the morning Jean drove Hilary to the cop shop where her leg-irons were locked on. He dropped Hilary off back home and went away to work. Someone has to keep the wolf on the table and the bread from the door. Incidentally, that is one reason why more women than men spend more of their time tied up. The strident feminists I referred to earlier would no doubt say that the preponderance of working men over working women is due to a male-dominated society. They are probably right, but that does not alter the situation. Men mostly work away from home, and most women spend a great deal of their time there. So there is more time for a woman interested in bondage to spend on her hobby. Men who enjoy being tied up usually have to find the odd moment or the weekend. So Hilary clinked about the house during the week, and they made the trips to the police station together.

The next weekend arrived and they used the time to experiment further with their new game. Things went much as they had on the previous occasions, that is to say, swimmingly. As bedtime rolled around on the Saturday evening, Jean suggested that Hilary try sleeping in bondage. She was game, and so it happened that she put on her naughtiest basque and her nicest stockings in lieu of the usual nightie. She looked (as Jean intended) delectable. She completed the job by putting on her long black kid gloves.

When she was done, Jean crossed her wrists and tied them together behind her back. He tied her legs at knees and ankles and gagged her with a pair of her panties which he pushed into her mouth and secured with a sash from her dressing gown. Hilary found that being gagged added another dimension to the bondage experience. Jean carried her into the bedroom and rolled her into bed. He got in beside her after turning out the light. Jean turned Hilary so that she faced away from him and pulled her closer. He reached around from behind her and began casually to play with her in the dark.

Hilary imagined that she was being fondled by an intruder who knew all the secrets of her body. Exciting, she said. She squirmed and made soft moaning sounds behind her gag, trying at the same time to thrust herself against the insistent hands. Jean slid his hand between her bound thighs and found that she was already getting wet. Using his fingers and lips, he continued to arouse Hilary until she was arching and bucking under his hands. Whuffling and whinnying sounds escaped the gag. With a muffled sob and a series of shudders Hilary reached orgasm. Once he knew she had peaked, Jean withdrew his finger from her cunt and held her against him while the shudders subsided and her breathing slowed. When she had quieted, he rolled her over into what he hoped was a comfortable position half on her stomach. He then rolled over himself and went to sleep.

Left to her own devices, Hilary discovered just as quickly as I had that trying to sleep while tied up sounds all right in theory (or fantasy) but is quite difficult in practice. Or if

67

you prefer you could say that reality often falls far short of our fantasy. Getting to sleep was the first problem. Finding a comfortable position when you're tied up is not all that easy. When she did doze off she found that cramped limbs and pins and needles in her hands and feet kept waking her up. She was constantly shifting position.

The third problem was what we both call lurid fantasies – although maybe this is not a big problem unless you're really trying to sleep. She would dream that she was bound and helpless and about to be ravished by a fearsome stranger. Unable to escape, she would nevertheless thrash about and then wake up to discover that she was indeed bound and helpless. And that would make her go hot all over. As she told me later, she and Jean discovered that they would have to limit her all-night bondage sessions if she was to go anywhere the next day. Otherwise she would be worn out from the combination of prolonged excitement and lack of sleep.

On that first night Hilary knew that she would have the next day free. It was a Sunday and so Jean would be home. She wouldn't have to be taken to the police station to have her leg-irons put on, so she decided not to have Jean untie her. This was the first try at a new diversion and she wanted to give it a fair chance. Instead she tried to sleep, or at least doze, and indulge her fantasies. The trouble was that she was in a state of almost continuous sexual arousal which she was in no position to alleviate. Jean awoke from time to time and checked that she was all right. For the most part this consisted in his holding her tightly against him while he caressed her breasts, belly and legs. When she was thoroughly aroused he would slide a finger into her cunt or up her backside, which drove her wild. She would strain against the ropes that held her and thrash about until he brought her to orgasm. Jean apparently took the position that she was all right as long as she could come. When she had done so, he would release her and go back to sleep. Once he caught her in a doze and she woke up on the brink of what seemed like her hundredth orgasm. Had she not been gagged, her screams would have been heard streets away, or so she averred.

When Jean got up to make the morning coffee, he untied Hilary. He found her asleep when he came back with the coffee and the morning papers. She slept until just after midday and when she awoke, so she told us, she was a fully fledged bondage freak. When she got up she went looking for Jean. She wore the outfit she had slept in and added only a pair of high heels before parading before him. He said that he had an erection almost as soon as Hilary came out to join him. After all, he had been in bed all night with a bound female who kept having orgasms while all he did was sleep. They spent a large amount of time helping him get rid of the obtrusive presence. 'Trouble was,' he said ironically, 'it kept coming back.'

They went to bed early that night after all the athletics. Jean had an early appointment the next day, and that meant a correspondingly early trip to the police station. In the morning Hilary got dressed, choosing stockings and suspenders and leaving her pants off. By then she had learned the consequences of mixing pants and tights with leg-irons. At the police station they entered by the usual side door, leaving the car close by in the station yard. The part that Hilary disliked most was the walk from car to door (or vice versa) with her ankles chained. She always had Jean drive the car up close to the door where she would wait until he signalled that the coast was clear. He would open the door and she would dive in.

She did not want passersby to see the attractive, well-dressed woman emerge from the police station in leg-irons and be driven away in a private car. And therein lay the deterrence factor the judge had intended when he imposed the conditions on her. It worked. It was bad enough having to have the desk sergeant lock and unlock her. It was somewhat easier when a WPC was available, but still embarrassing. Once at home, of course, Hilary enjoyed her role as prisoner. It was just the public bit she could do without. But there was no help for it at first.

They arrived early at the police station and were shown into a room just inside the door. Presently the duty officer came in, dangling 'her' leg-irons. When he had locked them around her ankles, Hilary nodded briefly. It didn't seem to be the kind of situation that called for a formal 'thank you'. She walked carefully to the door, where Jean was waiting with the car. She dived in. Often on the drive home Hilary wondered what she would do if the car broke down. Die of embarrassment, she supposed. But nothing happened. At home, the door between the house and garage made the exit easy. Hilary went inside the house and locked the door; Jean drove off to his appointment.

She went about the house collecting the washing, making the bed and putting away the rope with which she had been tied that weekend. That brought a pleasant glow to the otherwise routine housework. She decided that it would not be too long before they did it again. By keeping busy she made the morning pass agreeably enough. In the afternoon she called the police station to ask if she could skip the visit that evening and just continue to wear her leg-irons until further notice, that is until she had to go out. After the usual consultation they said yes, but they might want to send someone round in a day or so to check that she was still secured unless she came in sooner.

When Jean came home that evening she told him of the new arrangement. He was satisfied as long as she was. It saved him a trip that evening and meant not having to start quite so early the next morning. All that evening Hilary jingled and clinked about the house, getting dinner, clearing up afterwards and looking, she hoped, provocative. She was half-expecting a good screw that evening, but Jean said no. He suggested that they wait and let him spring it on her when she was not expecting it. Hilary said that she would always be expecting it while she was wearing her chains.

The next two days passed more or less as the first had done. Hilary became accustomed to walking about the house and doing her work while wearing her leg-irons. It was either that or sit idly all day. She discovered that the leg-irons chafed through her stockings after a day or so. She had to change them in order to avoid chafing her ankles. On the third day the police phoned to say that they

70

would be sending someone round to check on her, and would two o'clock be convenient? Yes, it would.

As the time approached, Hilary found herself standing near the window watching for her visitor. It wouldn't do to open the door to just anybody who rang, she thought with a little shiver. Promptly, at the appointed time, a uniformed WPC turned into the drive and walked up to the door. Since Hilary had spotted her, she opened the door as soon as the bell went. The WPC seemed embarrassed by the situation. That makes two of us, Hilary thought. The somewhat stilted conversation went something like this:

WPC: Good afternoon. Mrs Lebrun? (reddening slightly)
Hilary: Yes. Good afternoon.
WPC: I've come to check your compliance with the court order of 17th Feb . . .
Hilary: (interrupting) My leg-irons, you mean?
WPC: Well . . . yes.
Hilary: (showing her ankles and wondering just how many women they expected to answer the door in leg-irons) All correct?
WPC: (even more flustered) Well, I have to check the locks for security. May I come in?
Hilary: (standing aside) All right. But don't you think your hardware is any good?
WPC: This will only take a moment.
Hilary: (closing the door) What do you want me to do?
WPC: If you'd care to sit down for a moment . . .? Thank you. (stooping and reaching for Hilary's left ankle) I'll just see that this is still locked (giving a tug to the locking bar) That's OK. Now for the other. (reaching for Hilary's right leg) All correct. I'll see myself out. Thank you. Goodbye.
Hilary: Goodbye.

That was the ritual they evolved whenever it was necessary for someone to come round to check on Hilary. After

71

a few visits the embarrassment began to lessen on both sides. It finally got to the point where the WPC could ask Hilary if she was comfortable. That seemed an odd question to ask. Hilary had to wear the leg-irons, comfortable or not. But on reflection she concluded that it was just the constable's attempt to ease the tension.

There were occasional variations in the routine down at the police station. For instance, Jean took Hilary down one morning to be locked up only to learn that 'her' leg-irons were not available. They had been used for 'other purposes' which the police were typically unwilling to discuss even though it wasn't hard to guess what had happened. In the meantime, she was told, she could have a pair of handcuffs. The police were apologetic but there was nothing else for it unless she wanted to be taken into custody for the day. Quite naturally Hilary elected to wear the handcuffs. She held out her wrists and the cuffs were locked on.

Jean took her home and she began to make other discoveries. There are certain things you can't do while wearing handcuffs. Changing a blouse is one of them. Going to the loo was a bit difficult. The first time Howard left me in handcuffs he locked my wrists behind my back before going out. He said he'd be gone for an hour or so. Almost as soon as the door closed behind him I felt myself bursting for a pee. Of course I didn't know well enough then to go to the toilet before he left.

That first time I had no idea what I might have to do for myself or how to manage things when I couldn't use my hands. To complicate things, Howard didn't come home in an hour. Nor yet in two or three, as it turned out. I held it in as long as I could, but in the end I had to do something. The trip to the bathroom was accomplished well enough, but the trouble began soon afterwards. In the ensuing tussle I managed to wet my skirt and tights, and then had to wait until he got back before I could do anything about it. In Hilary's case she could feed herself and do most household tasks, albeit slowly and sometimes awkwardly. On the plus side, she found the handcuffs made her as randy as the leg-irons.

72

On another occasion (and for the same reasons) she was offered a choice between handcuffs or a pair of modern ratchet-type leg-irons. Hilary said that for a moment she was tempted to take both, but that would have given the whole game away. She chose the leg-irons. They were put on by the same sergeant who on an earlier occasion had seemed to enjoy locking the irons on the ankles of this striking woman. She got an additional fillip as he tightened the adjustable irons on her ankles. They were rather tighter than her usual ones. Maybe tighter than was strictly necessary, thought Hilary, but she said nothing. The sergeant double-locked the irons, explaining that now they could neither be removed nor tightened further without the key.

Once again Jean took her home and left her there. The tight steel bands on her ankles reminded Hilary all that day of her status. She said that she was steaming by the time Jean got home. She suggested, if that is not too weak a word, that they skip the usual trip down to the police station and adjourn directly to bed. Not surprisingly, Jean was agreeable. There ensued another evening of torrid sex, as Hilary put it later. Every variation seemed to please and arouse her. The cliché about variety and life comes to mind. She decided that evening to explore any other variations they could think up 'lest one good custom should corrupt the world', though I'm afraid that Tennyson might argue about the use of 'good' in this context. After they met us we were able to make several other suggestions.

I got to meet Hilary and Jean through Howard. He had met Jean in the course of his business: they had progressed to the lunch and drinks at the pub stage. These things take one of several fairly predictable courses, either they never develop beyond the pub lunch stage, or they lead on to an exchange of visits at home. Of course the whole thing could just peter out, but Jean and Howard liked one another well enough not to allow that to happen. In order for such acquaintances to develop beyond the first stages it is necessary for the respective partners to meet one another. That could create an awkward problem due to Hilary's house arrest. We didn't know about that when Howard invited them over for a meal *chez nous*. Jean therefore had to explain the situation to Howard, and Howard told me about it when he got home that evening.

I am always glad to make the acquaintance of another bondage freak, so I voted for a meeting. As I always say, there's variety, if not safety, in numbers. One should never pass up the opportunity to learn something new. We decided to make the first visit so that Hilary would feel easier on her home ground. We also timed it so Jean was at home so that Hilary would not be embarrassed by having to wear her leg-irons before strangers. Howard suggested that Jean explain to Hilary that I was already a card-carrying member of the International Union of Sex Freaks, B & D Branch. In that way we could dispel any awkwardness that might arise when we discussed Hilary's house arrest. We met on that basis, and the acquaintance progressed to the point where I felt free to visit her during the day when she was in leg-irons. The obvious advantage to her was occasional company plus the convenience of having someone who could pop out to the shops if anything was needed.

The first visit, by arrangement, Howard again drove me to Hilary's house and left me off there. We had decided that things would be easier for her if I showed up these first times in my leg-irons – what I call my 'public chains'. Accordingly Howard dropped me close to their garage door and I scuttled inside without being seen. Hilary still seemed to be embarrassed, but I was determined not to let that continue. I suggested that a cup of the universal English social solvent and panacea would be nice, and she got busy with the tea things. By the time we were seated at the table with cups in hand the initial awkwardness had largely passed away.

Naturally enough the conversation turned to the subject of sex and bondage. I told her a bit about my own experiences, and she admitted that she was beginning to feel much easier about her own situation. In the course of this exchange I learned about the visits from the police. In fact the WPC was due that same afternoon. It was my turn to feel apprehension. Hilary in leg-irons would be normal, but how to explain a visitor similarly encumbered? We had decided that I should disappear until the WPC was gone. My moment of awkwardness made Hilary feel less diffident. From then on we got along quite well. There's not much point in listing all the things we talked about. Everyone spends countless days doing exactly the same thing with visiting friends. This tale is about the extraordinary things we bondage freaks get up to; our everyday life is as boring as everyone else's.

In addition to the usual girl-talk we talked about sources of bondage gear. She was just beginning to explore her preferences and might find the information useful in thinking up new ideas. I was able to put her onto several sources and suppliers of what are so quaintly called 'restraints'. The currency of that circumlocution says a great deal about the status of B & D, as we groupies call our thing. No firm selling handcuffs, gags or chains ever comes out and says that their stuff is for tying people up. It's always 'police hardware', 'restraint items' or, even more obscurely, 'Houdiniana'. This latter would appeal to escapologists. 'Collectors' are invited to send for illustrated catalogues. 'Collectors', never 'users' or bondage fans.

Leather and rubber gear is usually called 'fashion clothing'. Some of the firms are quite imaginative. One of the makers of leather straps and straitjackets and the like, promises to 'give a new meaning to the term "housebound"'. A maker of whips and riding crops invites potential customers to come join their friends in a paddling pool. It's all very coy and sometimes confusing to those who don't understand the language. If you're not careful you might miss something, or get the wrong sorts of things through the mail.

During the early afternoon the WPC came to check on Hilary. I retreated upstairs until she had gone. She seemed to be taking a long time about doing the simple thing Hilary had described. When I saw her leave, I went back down and discovered that they had had a cup of tea. So the relations between them had eased. Hilary told me that at first she had felt like a prize cow on display with people pawing at her legs and testing the locks on her leg-irons. Now, she said, she was beginning to feel more at ease. I told her that during our bondage evenings there was a fair amount of the same sort of inspection, but it rarely stopped with just testing locks and knots. That may have been what put her off attending our gatherings. That was a bit disappointing but not surprising.

Hilary and I shared an interest in bondage, but just because someone enjoys sex more while tied up doesn't necessarily mean that she will feel easy about baring her soul (or body) in front of others who share the same interest. Even after we had spent some time together that day Hilary was still reticent about letting down her guard before a relative stranger. In fact it took several visits to make her feel easy with me.

The reticence to parade oneself is one of the reasons that social commentators have called bondage 'the last taboo'. They point out that gays and lesbians have parades, gay rights groups and street presence. On the other hand you rarely see bondage freaks parading the streets in handcuffs lobbying for greater freedom. Their reaction is more likely to be the same as Hilary's and mine. We keep out of public view, Hilary more so than me. We don't want any more rights or attention. On the whole we prefer to be left alone to get on with it.

I sometimes wonder just how large a group is represented by the gays and lesbians who go in for public demonstrations. Probably the majority of them would just like to be let alone to pursue their pleasures. But of course that is not always possible even in this best of all possible worlds. I know that there is an economic basis for some of the demonstrations we see. There is a long tradition of sacking, without appeal, those whose sexual preference make them a threat to 'national security'. There are very few people who can get along without their jobs. Of course these people are more of a threat to those who like Mrs Grundy find any talk about sex terrifying. I don't think there will be any sudden or dramatic change in this attitude no matter how many people take to the streets. Like most changes, it will come too gradually to be noticed. I will close this lecture by noting that not everyone wants to be 'allowed' to do as they like. They just get on with it.

4

TURNABOUT

Someone who just gets on with her life is Harriet Jones. We call her 'our Miss Jones'. If you're lucky, you might meet someone like her one day yourself. She follows two professions. By day she is a nurse/receptionist in a doctor's surgery where she appears quite ordinary and unexceptional. But by night (and on weekends and holidays and in any other free time) she whips into the nearest torture chamber and transforms herself into that most dreaded and sought-after creature, the dominatrix. We bondage freaks are as ambivalent about our desires as the next lot. There are many women, mostly prostitutes, who advertise a sideline in what the trade calls bondage, domination and humiliation. I imagine you have seen their adverts in magazines and even some newspapers (not to mention scrawled in phone boxes with a number to call beside them).

The dominatrix in leather harness and stiletto heels is a popular figure among fantasy writers, and many of the women who advertise their services try to fit this mould. Perhaps some of them do fit; and perhaps their clients are happy with what they get. Good luck to them, and to anyone who can find what they want in this crazy world. But most of these women I regard as amateurs in the sense that they do not take much pride or pleasure in their work. Whether or not they take money for what they do is not important, except maybe to them. I don't condemn them for that. Everyone has to live somehow. Our Miss Jones is paid for her services as well, though she also does favours for those she knows and likes. The difference lies in her attitude.

She likes what she does and is always looking for new ways to please her clients and friends. She takes pride in a job well done. Quite often a woman offering bondage and domination services adopts a name she thinks fits the job. There are quite a few Miss Steeles about, but have you ever heard of a Mrs Steele? The very type seems to preclude marriage!

Not our girl. She is plain Harriet Jones. She looks quite ordinary too. I don't mean that she is ugly or homely. Just that she is not the blonde Valkyrie type so often associated with the domination trade. Harriet is not the svelte and severe mistress with the whip in her hand and cowering slaves at her feet. She is rather the shorter, chunkier, tweedy type in sensible shoes and brown stockings. The archetypal thirtyish headmistress or matron whose solidity is put into everything she does, whether she is riding a horse or wielding her riding crop over a client. Whatever steel she has lies in her voice.

Harriet is the type who rides horses and fills out a pair of jodhpurs tightly. She usually wears boots when riding either a horse or a client. By insisting on her own ordinariness she compels others to do what she says as a matter of course – not to be questioned. No one would look twice at her in the street, or question her errand as she goes to the doors of those she visits. She is discreet to the point of reticence, but most people do as she asks at once. Harriet has a live-in lover named Tom who is naturally of a submissive nature. He too does what she asks. She can be formidable when she wants to. As someone once remarked about the recent Prime Minister, she has a whim of steel.

On those occasions when she takes her own pleasure she is likely to be found hanging from her wrists in a barn or stable while someone like herself lashes her about the bottom and over and between her sturdy thighs. Even then she is restrained in her demeanour (as well as in the usual sense too). She doesn't scream, limiting herself to a polite squeal as she comes. When she is on the receiving end she submits as completely as she forces others to submit to her. She calls it playing up school.

I met our Miss Jones a few weeks after the bondage evening I described earlier. Before she went home, I let Janet know that I wanted a chance to try out her electric bodysuit when it was convenient – meaning as soon as possible, but I was too polite to say that. She understood me clearly enough. Janet may have decided there and then to include Harriet in her plans for the event. When Janet brought her bodysuit a few days later for me to try, she told me that she was looking forward to our encounter. She hoped that I would enjoy it as much as she had done when I was in control of her. I was pretty sure I would.

Over coffee I examined the suit while Janet pointed out its less obvious features. There was an underwired bra arrangement inside. From the semi-circle of heavy wire, electrodes spread over the fabric inside the cups. I noticed that they were concentrated in the nipple area. There was a similar network of electrodes over the stomach, abdomen and buttock areas of the suit. The two vibrators were simply inserted in the appropriate holes and held in place by the tightly fitting crotch of the suit. The trailing wires from all these were gathered together and led up to the socket which emerged from the neck opening. The whole thing generally resembled a sleeveless leotard. It fitted closely everywhere except at the back above the waist. In that area there was a pouch where the arms were crossed in the small of the back.

Janet showed me how to get into the suit, and helped me to insert the two plugs where they would do the most good. She crossed my arms behind my back and closed the heavy zipper over them. Finally she buckled the matching leather belt tightly around my waist. When she was done I knew how an armless person must feel. With my arms inside the suit I could make no use of them. When I tried to walk I almost lost my balance. I realised that I could neither open a door nor take a drink, and the toilet was competely out of the question. Had my legs been tied as Janet's had been on the night I put her through her paces, I would have had no control over any part of my body. I would only be able to bend at the waist and knees, or move my head. I would have been quite unable to stand unless someone stood me up and helped me to balance.

The plan called for me to be delivered to Janet the next day after Howard had secured me inside the bodysuit. As she unzipped me and helped me get out of the suit, she said that she was looking forward to the meeting. She said that I could add an extra dimension to my experience by telling Howard how to secure me for delivery. I would become the instrument by which I was rendered helpless. There was no animosity on Janet's part. Indeed she professed to have enjoyed our last encounter. But then she was accustomed to it, and this was my first experience with bodysuits. I was developing the familiar feeling of anticipation and mild dread which gives an extra *frisson* to erotic bondage. After more coffee and a chat she took her leave, promising me a real treat the next day.

I was still in a state of excited apprehension when Howard got home. He was amused. I had a hard time getting to sleep that night; I thought it would help if we had sex, but Howard said that I had better save my strength for the next day. I was up with the lark in the morning, still feeling jittery. Since it was a Saturday, there was no need for a horribly early start, so my anticipatory jitters were prolonged. Howard enjoys stringing these things out. It was mid-morning before he told me to get ready. I went straight to the toilet. Be sure to do the same when you know you're in for a long session – unless you're fond of your own piss and shit. Some people are.

Howard laid out the things I was to wear. There wasn't a great deal of it. There was a pair of heavy support tights which Howard sometimes likes me to wear, a skirt and a pair of high heels. And the leather suit of course. I put the tights on first. Howard helped me to insert the two vibrators before I pulled the tights fully up. Then he assisted me to get into the body suit: first my legs through the openings, then the crotch pulled up tight holding the two plugs inside me. I could have managed that part myself, but I had to have help for the next stage. Howard doesn't mind helping me when I am going to be tied up. He helped me

81

to ease my tits into the cups and made sure there was good contact with the wiring. He gathered all the wires and led them up through the neck opening for later connection to the control box. Then he crossed my arms in the small of my back and zipped the suit over them. As I am slightly bigger than Janet in some places, I found myself tightly confined by her suit. When he buckled the wide belt around my waist I was helpless inside the leather sheath.

The next step was the skirt. I stepped into it while Howard held it for me. He buttoned and zipped it before helping me to get into my shoes. He had chosen a pair of stiletto heels with ankle straps. He eased my feet into them and buckled the straps. There is something very sensuous about helping a woman with her shoes. Indeed there are even some very queer people who make a fetish of it. But they are utterly beyond the pale.

A glance in the mirror revealed a striking picture. A woman without arms stood in the centre of the room, teetering slightly on a pair of very high heels. As I watched, a man approached her holding a pair of leg-irons. Stooping, he locked them onto her. I woke from my reverie as the steel bands closed around my ankles. Howard stood before me ready to deliver me to Janet. I imagined her waiting impatiently for her victim to arrive.

Howard draped a coat over my shoulders, cape-fashion. He did up the top two or three buttons to conceal my strait-jacket from the casual observer, and we were ready to go. He led me out to the garage and held the car door open for me. When I was seated he buckled my seat-belt and then went around to get in the other side. After backing the car out into the street he went back to close the garage doors. There was no one about, which was just as well. I wouldn't bear close inspection. I settled myself in the seat as well as I could to wait for him. Howard had left the motor running so it could warm up, and I began to imagine what I would do if someone were to appear from nowhere (which is where intruders come from in romantic novels), jump into the car and drive off with me a helpless captive beside him. I could neither undo my seat-belt nor open the door. I would be completely at the mercy of this sinister stranger who would . . . Well, there was the familiar abduction and rape fantasy again. It goes with the bondage mentality. Harmless enough, and almost always exciting.

Howard came back and we drove off. I found myself chattering inanely about what he planned to do during the day, and what we would do afterwards. In other words, everything but the matter in hand. That's what the shrinks call avoidance behaviour. Howard drove unconcernedly through the quiet lanes while all the time Janet loomed ever larger in my mind.

They lived out in the country on what had once been a farm. There was a good deal of land still with the house, some of it still under cultivation on lease, and some of it – the bit nearer to the house – given over to woodland. That was just as well for those who like to do some of their bondage outdoors. There was very little chance of being seen as we drove up, or of being heard if I later screamed under Janet's ministrations. They had a barn which was used as a combination stable and garage which was set some distance from the house.

We pulled up to the front door. Howard got out and helped me out of the car and up the front steps. He rang the bell and I stood there beside him feeling as unobtrusive as the regimental band and pipes and drums of the Scots Guards. Janet seemed to be taking forever to answer the door. When she finally came she let us in with a wide grin. She took my coat off for me and invited me to sit on the sofa. I felt myself clenching tightly around the dildoes inside me. My stomach felt hollow too. Nevertheless I went over to the sofa and dropped down onto it. I landed slightly off balance, teetered a moment, and then fell over sideways. Planting my heels, I managed to lever myself into a more or less comfortable position. As I squirmed, I could feel the plugs working in and out. I lost some of my anxiety as I began to feel warm in the crotch.

Meanwhile Howard, Janet and Peter were pouring drinks and making small talk. Peter offered me my usual vodka and lemonade, and held the glass for me while I sipped at it. He and Howard had arranged to be elsewhere for the day and would soon be off. Janet was wearing her riding gear: jodhpurs, boots and close fitting jacket. Her riding crop was lying on the coffee table before me, as was the control box for my bodysuit. I considered the juxtaposition for a moment. An accident? I didn't think so. When I looked up again the men were taking their leave and Howard was handing the keys to my leg-irons over to Janet. She stuffed them casually into her pocket. Janet saw the men to the door and came back to me. 'Comfortable?' she asked.

'As comfortable as the circumstances permit,' I replied. I was surprised to hear my voice shaking slightly. Apprehension? Anticipation? Both, as usual.

'We can't have that,' she retorted cheerfully. 'You're here for a spot of discomfort. Come on. Up with you and we'll go out to the barn and put you over a few jumps.' She helped me to my feet and pointed me towards the door while she paused to pick up her riding crop and the control box.

I walked over to the door and stood waiting for Janet to open it. She remarked that I was all hers for the day: 'We'll soon see what you're made of.'

Opening the door, she gave me a crack across the backs of my thighs to get me moving. I yipped in surprise and almost fell over. When I recovered my balance I moved outside. 'Keep on to the barn,' said Janet as she paused to shut the door behind us. I went, walking carefully on the uneven ground and hoping fervently that no one was around to see this little cavalcade. Janet seemed not to care. She caught up with me shortly.

'It's going to be a fine day,' she remarked, cutting again at my thighs with her riding crop. I managed to confine my remarks to a hiss of pain or a short yip. This seemed to please Janet. The leg-irons made walking difficult, as they were designed to do. The sharp heels of my shoes kept sinking into the soft earth. Janet seemed to think I should be trotting. At any rate she was encouraging me to keep up my best pace.

'Come on! The sooner we get you to the barn the sooner the fun can begin.' She was switching me about the thighs and bottom as she said this.

When we reached the barn I waited once again for Janet to open the door for me. She tugged the heavy door open and motioned me to precede her inside. The barn was about equally divided between horses and cars. The horses had the rear of the building, and there was a loft given over to hay storage and the usual miscellany of nondescript things that accumulate despite the best intentions. It was a warm day and Janet left the door open. There were several large windows in the barn so there was no need to turn on the electric lighting. She herded me toward the rear, or horsy, end of the barn where there was a pile of hay and a tack room near the stalls.

Janet directed me to a wooden bench where I sat down. She went into the tack room to fetch some rope (which seemed to be in goodly supply – very handy if you happen to be a bondage freak). There was thin cord like grocer's twine, thicker stuff like linen line, and even thicker and hairier manila which would make for a prickly time. Janet selected some of the nylon linen line from a bin containing short pieces cut into handy lengths.

Returning to the bench where I sat, Janet dropped the rope to the floor and fished the keys from her pocket. She stooped to remove my leg-irons. When they were off she hung them on a nail and proceeded to tie me as she had been tied on the night of her own ordeal at our place. 'Turn about is fair play,' she remarked. 'And it's so much more fun when your legs are tied.' I didn't reply, but I could feel my heart beginning to thud in that old familiar way. She tied my ankles first, quite tightly. The cords dug into my flesh. In a similar way she tied my knees and thighs together.

When she had finished I was utterly helpless. I could use neither arms nor legs. This latter thought must have occurred belatedly to Janet, because she looked annoyed when she realised that she would have to move her now thoroughly immobilised charge further back into the barn by the pile of hay. The problem seemed to perplex her momentarily. However, she brightened when her glance fell on a wheelbarrow apparently used for gardening and other, less pleasant, jobs. She wheeled it over and positioned it behind me with the handles facing away from me. She came around in front and lifted my ankles. I went over backwards and landed in the barrow with a thump that took my breath away. With my bound legs hanging over the front, Janet wheeled me over to the pile of hay in the corner. Tipping up the handles, she very nearly set me on my feet. If my legs had been free I would probably have ended up standing. As it was, I teetered and was just beginning to go over when a hand in the middle of my back decided things for me. I landed face down in the hay.

'There now. All right?' asked Janet.

'Clearly a rhetorical question,' I replied, my face buried in the hay. I managed to turn over by dint of much squirming, which made me aware once again of the two plugs deep inside me. Lying now on my back in the hay, I watched Janet as she returned the barrow to its place amongst the gardening things. When she returned to me she was carrying the control box. I lay and watched helplessly as she connected the box to the socket which emerged from the neck of my bodysuit.

'Now you can consider yourself to be well-connected,' said Janet as she finished. 'Soon you'll be feeling more lively,' she said cheerfully. She seemed to be enjoying herself hugely. 'Don't go away. I'll be back after I've had a ride. It would be a shame to waste such a lovely day.'

I was amazed. I had been expecting to be put through my paces as soon as Janet had finished securing me. Now it appeared that there was to be a further, indefinite waiting period while she went galloping about across the fields. I was to be left bound in this barn where just anybody might wander in and find me. As if she were reading my mind, Janet remarked that I needn't worry about visitors in her absence. We were far enough from other houses, she said. She picked up the control box and did something I couldn't see. I tensed, expecting to be jolted by a surge of

86

electricity across my private parts (to use the polite term), but nothing happened. Janet finished her adjustments and hung the box on a nail out of my reach. She turned away from me and went to get her horse from its stall.

As she saddled the horse she kept up her conversation with me. 'You'll be all right while I'm away. I've set the timer to begin warming you up at odd times until I get back and we can really begin. In the meantime this will give you a little foretaste of what to expect. There's no need to gag you. No one will hear you if you scream your head off. In fact you may find that screaming is some relief. Enjoy yourself. Oh, – I almost forgot,' she fetched another length of rope with which she tethered me to a post by my ankles. 'We can't have you squirming over and trying to kick the wires loose or interfering with the timer.'

On that rather ominous note she left me. I listened as the retreating hooves faded away, and then went on listening for any other sounds that might indicate I was not alone. In the silence I fancied that I could hear the thumping of my heart. The barn smelled of hay and horses. All rural and tidy and quiet. It was I who was out of place here. I glanced over at the control box hanging on the nail far out of my reach. Even if I had not been tethered I probably could not have reached it. I could only wait for the timer to switch me on. I tensed, waiting for the shock I knew must come. Nothing was happening. Unbroken silence.

Was that a footstep? My hearing seemed to be unnaturally acute. Or maybe my imagination was running away with me. I have said that an active imagination is a help in playing bondage games, but there is a price to pay for such a faculty. Other unidentifiable noises came from time to time – scuttlings and chitterings. Were there mice in the barn? In the straw with me? I could feel the panic rising. This is nonsense, I admonished myself. I had to do something. But I couldn't do anything. I began to struggle against my bonds, squirming and thrashing about in the hay as I tried to get free. Fruitlessly, it turned out. My arms were immobilised inside the bodysuit; the zipper was outside the suit, out of reach behind my back. And Janet had tied my legs much too well. There was no give in the cords that held me.

I could not even sit up. With my arms pinioned inside the suit I couldn't use them for support. When I tried to sit up, the hay under my bottom simply yielded. Even though my stomach muscles could have lifted my upper body, I couldn't get any leverage. I rolled over onto my side and sawed at the rope which tethered my ankles to the post. Jerking and pulling at it got me nowhere. I flung myself about as far as my bonds permitted. In the process I got sweaty and bits of hay got stuck in my hair and on my face. Some bits got on my tights and between my legs and began to itch. The two dildoes were sliding and working inside me. I don't know how long I kept up the futile exercises, but when I finally paused I was quite sweaty and out of breath. And just as helpless. None of that 'with a single bound the hero was free' stuff you get in comic books.

Nor was there any muscular hero around to free the helpless captive and hold her quivering body against his broad chest while she gasped out her gratitude. What there was (when I began to take notice of my surroundings again) was a solid-looking woman in a tweedy suit and dark brown tights. But at first I didn't see any of this. I heard a strange voice. I was lying on my side in a sweaty heap and the voice which came from behind me made me jump in surprise. So much for Janet's 'no visitors' reassurance.

'And what have we here?' I heard. 'It looks to me as if you're all tied up.'

This was so blindingly obvious as to call for no comment on my part. A hand reached out and tested the cords which bound my legs together. The hand was joined by another. Together they turned me onto my face in the hay while the stranger inspected the zipper of my bodysuit. What shook me was that the voice and the hands were not Janet's. She was still off on her ride. I jerked about like a landed fish and managed to turn my head so that I could see the strange woman.

'Lie still', she said amiably, 'or I shall have to whip you.'

I stopped and the hands grasped me by the shoulders and turned me over onto my back. I found myself looking into the pleasant face of the woman who had suddenly appeared at my side. She looked me up and down and gave an approving nod. I didn't know if her approval was directed at my behaviour, my utter helplessness, or both. She carried a riding crop like Janet's, so I knew that her threat to beat me had not been idle. Recovering quickly, I asked, 'Who are you?' Very original.

'I'll ask the questions here,' she said decisively. 'First, what are you doing lying here all tied up?'

My first impulse was to retort, 'Why, I'm just lying here all tied up. Isn't that what one does on bright Saturday mornings?' But a glance at her riding crop caused me to change my mind. I gave her instead an edited version of the story so far. I told her that Janet had left me like this while she went off for a ride. The why of it was a bit more difficult to explain. I could hardly say that I was there for punishment when I had allowed myself to be bound and wired for pleasure (although a certain amount of pain was necessarily allied with it). Nor had I done anything to Janet which deserved punishment. Nor did I add that I was looking forward to the experience with a mixture of emotions. In those bizarre circumstances it did not strike me as odd that my interlocutor failed to press me for further details. Nor did she ask my name. She acted as if she came across people lying bound every day – which was I learned later indeed the case. And most often it was she who had tied them up.

No prizes for guessing who the stranger was, although I didn't know her at the time. Later I was properly (or maybe that should be improperly) introduced to Harriet – 'our Miss Jones' as Janet called her. She was often sought out by people who wanted 'discipline' or 'correction' for themselves or others. She was skilled in the infliction of pain with erotic overtones. No mere sadist or torturer, our Harriet. More about her other work later. Let us return to our muttons. Just then she had other business. With me. She noted the socket and the wires that connected me to the control box with a critical eye. 'All wired up, aren't we?' she observed brightly.

This was turning into a day for rhetorical questions. However, her next act was anything but rhetorical. She switched the power on and flicked the control which sent a shock through my tits and nipples. 'A eeeee!' I said, rather loudly. Screamed, in fact. Seeing my reaction, she immediately switched off, but 'accidentally touched the switch connected to my belly and bottom. 'Aaarrggghhh!' I remarked, rearing and bucking in the hay. No repetition, you'll observe. Original expressions of dismay, every one. Was this what Janet had felt but been prevented from expressing by her gag? That gag must have been very effective.

In case anyone is wondering how I can remember all this so clearly. The short answer is, I can't. But it was being videotaped by none other than my friend Janet. I saw the tape later and formed the impressions I am now describing to you. At the time I was too busy to take notes. My memory kept dropping off line, as the computer types express it. I can remember the sensations of mixed pain and pleasure which combined to drive me wild, but not the details of action and dialogue. These were all faithfully recorded on the tape. The video camera is to the present generation of amateur performers what the Polaroid camera was to the last. Janet had ridden off a short way and then returned leading the horse silently over the grass. She had met Harriet by arrangement, briefed her and then gone to get the video equipment going. That was the private joke Janet had seemed to be enjoying when she left me in the barn.

'You really *are* sensitive,' Harriet observed, switching off the current. 'That was only a very mild shock. I'll have to make the next one a bit stronger. Build you up gradually and that sort of thing.' All this was said in a cheerful, remorseless voice as her fingers made further adjustments to the control box. I tensed, expecting another jolt, but felt instead a gentle vibration begin in my rectum and vagina as she activated the two vibrators. I could hear the gentle buzzing from my crotch as I had heard it on the night of Janet's performance. Harriet came over and laid a hand on the smooth, tight leather between my legs to check that the dildoes were working properly. Satisfied, she hung the box back on its nail and sat down opposite me to see what I would do.

I didn't do much of anything at first. The effect of vibrators is gradual, so I had time to observe my warder. She was seated rather primly on the bench opposite with her knees together. Her skirt fell away sufficiently to reveal a pair of sturdy thighs which matched her ankles and calves. A chunky, solid frame with wide hips and bottom. Solid bosom. Not fat. Pretty but on the heavy side. As I found out later, her character and her appearance were well matched. Others saw her in much the same way.

In the meantime she was also observing me closely. Conversation seemed superfluous, so we were silent. When we became better acquainted later we found conversation quite easy, but I didn't know how to react to her then. She seemed to know well enough what I was doing there. The silence stretched out between us until I thought of Janet's return. What would she do when she discovered this visitor who, by her attitude, plainly intended to stay for some time? I summoned my wits and asked this apparently resolute woman if she hadn't better switch me off and leave me as she had found me before Janet got back.

Miss Jones replied that she would 'deal with' Janet when she returned. I was not to worry. You will have noticed that I didn't ask her to untie me. Strange as it may seem to others, that idea had not occurred to me. I had put myself willingly into this situation. The protocol under which we bondage freaks operate calls for us to stay tied up until the active partner sees fit to change things. The one who is tied up can of course thrash about and beg to be untied, but unless there is actual distress these noises are treated as part of the ambience. On her side, Harriet had given no sign that she intended to let me loose. If she were going to free me, she would have done so at once. She had not. By then, of course, I was deeply into the idea of my

91

own helplessness – a true bondage fanatic. As I've said, being left bound and helpless is a deeply-rooted fantasy. There's a whole cottage industry serving the needs of us types.

But to return to the matter in hand: Miss Jones continued to observe me as I gradually got warmer and wetter between the legs. I could feel my heart beginning to accelerate. My breathing was becoming more ragged by the moment. On the sound-track of the tape I watched later I heard my little groans and whimpers – wordless acknowledgement of my growing arousal. I also saw that I was beginning to writhe slowly and to draw up my knees from time to time, trying apparently to curl up around the twin vibrators which were driving me inexorably to orgasm. My hips began to rise and fall as I squirmed in the hay, making the dildoes work inside me. It was a repetition of what I had done earlier when Howard had tied me up in our vacation cottage. The driving force then had been the itching powder inside my corselet. Now it was a few volts of the Central Electricity Generating Board's best in a rather more intimate place.

At some point on the rising graph of my ecstatic arousal I ceased watching Miss Jones and began to concentrate exclusively on what I may call inner reality. Bad mistake. She must have been waiting for that to happen, because she shot me down in full cry. First I was shocked by a short jolt across the tits, followed in quick succession by a much longer one across the belly and bottom. The former brought me out of my reverie. The latter convulsed me. I began to fling myself from side to side and to roll over in the hay. Watching the tape later, I was reminded sharply of Janet's spasmodic heavings. It felt as if my belly and bottom were being ·stung simultaneously by hundreds of wasps.

The sound-track preserved my remarks, chiefly long drawn out screams, quite loud, interrupted by a gasp of indrawn breath and followed by more screams. It was all very shrill and piercing and heart-rending, but Harriet was remorseless. When it seemed as if I couldn't bear any more, she showed me that I was mistaken. She switched on the current to my tits. It felt as if they were hot and being jabbed by hundreds of pins. My body arched and jerked. I drew myself into a tight ball and flung myself out straight again, all taut and quivering. I bucked and writhed and rolled over and over in the hay, pursued by those tongues of fire.

When I regained my composure, I was covered in sweat and bits of hay. There was even some in my mouth and nose. I was almost as wet as if I had been hosed down. Later, but not too much later, I discovered that sweat was a good conductor of electricity. If I had spoken I'm sure I would have been hoarse. Why do we go through all this when it would be so much easier to be straight and conventional?

Harriet was still there. The box was hanging on its nail and she was walking around the barn examining its layout. And of course I was still bound as helplessly as Janet had left me. At the end of one of her turns, Harriet noticed that my eyes were open. She interrupted her examination and came back to where I lay. 'Back with us again, are you?' she asked. There seemed no adequate reply to the question, so I said nothing. 'I won't ask you how you enjoyed that last bit. It's a bit too early to have formed any lasting impressions. After it's all over you can think about it and let me know. For now we'll just continue as we've begun.' She walked over to where the control box hung on the nail.

'Nnnaaaoooooohhhhhh!' I croaked.

'Yes!' she insisted. 'However, I think I'll gag you before we begin again. I'm not worried that your screams will attract someone to investigate. It's just that too much screaming can be hard on your throat and vocal cords, and too loud for my ears. What can we use? You aren't wearing pants by any chance, are you? No, of course you wouldn't be. No need for them under your bodysuit. And I couldn't get at them anyway. Still, we can always use mine.' Harriet lifted her skirt to her waist and slid her dainty red panties down her sturdy legs. She stepped carefully out of them. Looking around the barn, she spotted one of Janet's bandannas lying near the stalls. She brought it back to where I lay and said, 'Open wide, please,' in her matter-of-fact voice.

I found myself doing as she asked unprotestingly. Harriet wadded up her pants and stuffed them into my mouth. She pulled the bandanna between my teeth and rolled me over onto my stomach. Lifting my hair out of the way, she knotted the scarf tightly behind my head before rolling me over once more onto my back. In my mouth I could now detect essence of Miss Jones mingled with essence of horse from Janet's scarf. I was gagged, but not as effectively as Janet had been. Although I could not scream, I could still whimper and squeal. Janet had been reduced to groans and a kind of nasal whinny. Harriet, however, was satisfied. She marched over to the control box and switched on the vibrators. 'Enjoy yourself,' she ordered as she walked away. 'I'm going for a walk. Back soon.'

'Mmmmmff,' I retorted through my gag. Then I was left to my own (and Janet's) devices. My own devices were limited to jerking at my tether and flexing my legs. By squirming and heaving I managed to roll over onto my stomach. With my face pressed into the hay I closed my eyes and tried to rest from my earlier sweaty exercise. But the vibrators were buzzing away inside me, and I could feel myself getting warm and slippery between the legs. I squirmed a bit more, experimentally, and could feel my two plugs moving about. My nipples must have become erect. They were feeling sensitive as I twisted about in my leather suit. My tits felt swollen. I rolled about looking for something hard enough to press myself against in the pile of hay. When I thrust with my hips I could feel the warmth spreading through my belly.

I have to rely on the tape once again for the details of my performance. I do remember that I rode the crest of a truly magnificent orgasm. When you forget that sort of thing, it's time to retire and write romantic novels. I was making a considerable row which the gag muffled down to soft moans. The movements became wilder each time as I peaked, which I must have done several times. I remember wondering fleetingly if Janet's orgasms, like mine, had been heightened by the preceding ordeal and the threat of the one to come. But there was not much time for coherent thought. It was all action. When I was done, I was nearly as sweaty as before. Since I was well beyond the glowing stage, I must conclude that I was no lady. Definitely horse class.

No sooner had I finished than Harriet reappeared. Was that just good timing, I wondered, or had she been watching me as I went through the motions? No matter. With what I now thought of as her usual brisk efficiency she switched the vibrators off and gave me a jolt across the bottom which brought me back to reality with a jerk. Where I was sweaty and dishevelled, she was cool and determined.

'Good! I see that I have your attention again,' she said. 'Now we can continue with the business in hand, or should that be in the hay?' Without further ado she began to manipulate the various switches. Not long thereafter – instantaneously, in fact – I was dancing to her tune as the electricity shocked my already tormented body. Belly and bottom, tits and then bottom again, and round and round. Stifled gasps, and jerks and heaves. I was alternately contracted into a tight ball, and then my legs would shoot out straight and quivering. I rolled wildly as I tried to escape the stabbing fire that was attacking my sensitive parts so remorselessly.

As I heaved and jerked I broke out once more in a sweat which conducted some of the electricity to the parts not directly connected to the wires. The sweat trickled between my pumping thighs and it felt as if the electrodes at my bottom had extended down my legs. I thrashed and strained against the rope and leather that held me. Vainly I tried to separate my legs and break that contact. Janet's knots held. I was flinging myself about as if trying to squirm out of the suit which imprisoned me. Just as Janet had done. They say that history repeats itself. I was once more gasping for breath and trying to scream, but only a high-pitched whining got past my gag. In the pauses between shocks I sometimes saw Harriet watching me and nodding approvingly. She might have been a fitness fanatic determined to bring others up to her high standards. Once I remember wondering if she was aroused by what she was doing to me, but I had no time to pursue or confirm the idea. I left that project for the indefinite future.

The torment stopped as abruptly as it had begun. I was limp and breathless. I tried to say, 'No more!' What came out was 'Nnnnmmm' or words to that effect. I don't think Harriet paid any attention. She rarely does. From her manner she seemed intent on wringing me dry, and so far she hadn't done badly. I had no idea how long I had been stretched out on the bed of these painful pleasures (if you don't mind the oxymoron). It could have been hours. Harriet let me lay for an indeterminate time before she jerked me back to attention with a sharp jolt across the tits. I thought that might be the prelude to another shocking experience, but nothing more happened. Through the fog in my mind I gradually became aware that the vibrators had been switched on again. The shock was merely Harriet's quaint way of telling me that it was fun time once more.

Initially I didn't think I had any more fun left in me, but I was wrong. I often am. It wasn't terribly long before I felt myself getting heated up again. The process took a bit longer than normal, for reasons you can guess, but eventually I was climbing the familiar peak once more. The noises I was hearing were my own little low sounds of contentment. My hips were working up and down and the muscles inside my vagina and rectum were clenching rhythmically around the plugs inside me.

Abruptly, though, as I reached for the prize, the current lashed my belly and bottom and brought me thrashing back to earth. But the shock was not repeated, nor were the dildoes switched off. They brought me slowly to the brink of orgasm, and again Harriet shot me down before I could fall over the edge. The pain and the pleasure were being wound skilfully together so that I had a hard time telling which was which. Janet must have felt something like this when she found herself in my hands. I believe that the interweaving of the two opposite sensations is the essence of the bondage experience. It's not for everybody, but those who enjoy it swear by it.

Once again Harriet let the dildoes do their thing. This time, though, she let me continue well past the point of no return. I was peripherally aware of her hands on the control box and was half expecting the next shock. When it didn't come, I thought Harriet had misjudged. I was soon in the throes of a truly remarkable come. The old waves of pleasure were spreading from my two entrances and washing me away. I arched my body again and again, thrusting with my hips and rolling from side to side in the hay. And the waves broke over me. And I came, and came, and came. Shattering. I guess that's what they mean by a roll in the hay.

Did I say that Harriet had misjudged my reaction? She hadn't. She had allowed me to go over the top, well past the point of conscious control. On the way down, while I was still moaning and thrashing, she hit me from an entirely unexpected direction. The vibrators had been modified so that they could shock. And how they could shock. When she switched modes it felt as if the wasps' nest I mentioned earlier had got inside me. I snapped into a tight ball and whinnied through my gag. Then, mercifully as in all good romances, the bound and helpless heroine fainted away.

When I woke up I became aware of eight legs standing close to me. There were two brown, two white, three black and one black-and-white. They resolved themselves into Harriet (two brown), Janet (two white), and the horse. Harriet was saying to Janet, 'You've come just in time. I'll need some help with your friend here. She needs a wash. If you'll help me carry her outside, we can put her in the horse trough.'

Janet, helpful as ever, suggested the wheelbarrow she'd used earlier. Harriet nodded and Janet went for the barrow. Together they lifted me into it. Harriet disconnected the control box and untied my tether, while Janet went to open the doors at the rear of the barn. With a low grunt Harriet lifted the handles and trundled me outside to the horse trough. Fortunately it was full of clean water. Janet removed my shoes and the two of them lifted me from the barrow. I thought they were going to untie my legs and take the bodysuit off me. Wrong again. It was getting to be a habit. They set me on the side of the trough and pushed me over backwards into the water.

The water wasn't all that cold, but it closed decisively over my head before I could raise any objections. Bound as I was, I thought I'd drown, but Harriet grasped my hair as I came up and guided me to the side of the tough where I could lean. The water only came up to my breasts as I sat on the bottom. With my legs stretched out I could brace my feet against the opposite side and so prevent myself from slipping under. As she headed back towards the barn, Harriet said over her shoulder, 'You have a nice wash and we'll soon be back to fetch you. I'll just be giving Janet a hand with the horse.'

So I sat in a horse trough bound and gagged in the late afternoon sunlight, soaking away the traces of my recent ordeal while reconsidering its pleasurable aspects.

I judged that I must have been in the barn for four or five hours. It was getting on for sunset. There was no one in sight and the birds were singing away in the woods behind the house. They sky was that deep blue you sometimes get towards autumn. Just the sort of day to be outdoors. I noticed a camper van drawn up to the front door of the house and surmised that it must belong to Harriet. The no-nonsense style of the woman fitted the solid, outdoorsy look of the vehicle. I could imagine her driving off at the weekends to camp in rugged places, setting up her tent in the woods or at the seashore. She'd be up with the lark (or the gull, as the case may be), tramping along on her sturdy legs, breathing in the cool air which generations of English people have regarded, though with no clear evidence, as a sovereign remedy for whatever ails you.

The air hereabouts was getting cool as the sun sank. I was beginning to wonder how long I'd have to soak before anyone came to fetch me. Even if I managed to get out unaided, which would have been difficult, I could only roll onto the ground and lie there in the dirt. Not a pleasant thought in the barnyard. However, It wasn't too long after these thoughts that Janet and Harriet reappeared in the door and came towards me. Janet was dangling my leg-irons from the same hand that held her riding crop. She looked pleased with herself and gave me a mischievous grin as she came up.

'Sorry I couldn't attend to you myself, but I understand that our Miss Jones handled you quite well. I've got it all down on videotape with sound so you can enjoy the spectacle at your leisure. I had originally intended to set up the camera and do you myself, but that would have given me a shot only from one fixed angle. Quite artificial. And you might have moved out of shot. You were moving quite a bit, you'll recall. Then I thought of enlisting Harriet's help to put you through your paces while I ran the photography end of it. She's much better at it than I am. You might even think of her as a professional, while I am but an amateur – a gifted one, but an amateur nonetheless. I hope you had a good time.'

All things considered, I *had* enjoyed the experience. I would have said so but for the gag. Harriet perceived the difficulty and moved over to untie the water-soaked bandanna. I pushed her wadded-up pants out of my mouth with my tongue and they landed with a plop in the water. She retrieved them, rinsed them out thoroughly and wrung them dry. She did not, however, put them back on. She remarked that she and I had become well acquainted during the hours we had been together, and that while the conversation had been rather one-sided we had nevertheless achieved a certain *rapport*. 'Haven't we, dear?' she asked.

I replied that I was glad to make her formal acquaintance. To Janet I said, 'Do you do this often? You and the bodysuit, I mean.' I was thinking that it could be an exhausting experience if done too frequently.

'Often enough to keep my hand in,' Janet replied. 'But it's only one scenario, as they say in show biz. From what

I saw and heard in the barn you seemed to be having a good time. Did you really like it?'

I said that it had been enjoyable if a bit wearing – a hint that I thought it was time for them to untie me. We have a certain etiquette about these things. Once you've allowed yourself to be tied up you're not supposed to ask to be let loose except in cases of genuine distress. It's your partner's decision to untie you or not. Of course you can shout and scream for release when being beaten or otherwise undergoing 'discipline' or 'correction' – to use the jargon. In fact the victim's pleas add a certain spice to the performance. Nevertheless, Janet either took my hint or had already decided that it was time to move on to other things. She opened the tap at the bottom of the trough and the water began to drain away. When the level had sunk below my legs, she and Harriet lifted me out and sat me on the side of the trough.

Janet knelt beside me and picked at the water-soaked knots. When she finally got the ropes off I felt a rush of blood to my feet and legs. She put my shoes on for me and buckled the ankle straps. I could barely feel her touch. I had been bound tightly for several hours and was feeling the exquisite tingling of returning circulation. Janet asked me if I could stand up.

'Of course she can,' Harriet interjected. She dealt me a hearty crack across the tops of my thighs with her riding crop. It made a wet smacking sound on my wet tights and left a red weal in its wake. I jumped hastily to my feet and would have fallen if Janet had not caught me. My legs had been out of action for a long time and didn't want to support me.

'Come on,' Harriet continued, as much to Janet as to me. 'Let's get her into the house and find some towels. She gave me another flick across the thighs to get me moving. I jumped again and let out a yip. I also started off for the house. Janet and Harriet fell in behind me, driving me on with more stinging cuts from their crops. I think we got to the door in record time. That was just as well, as it was getting distinctly cooler as the sun set. Not the time to be outside in a soaking wet leather suit and a pair of tights.

Once inside Janet laid my leg-irons on the sideboard and led me through into the bathroom. She unbuckled the waist belt and unzipped the bodysuit. When she had helped me to shed the suit, she took off my tights and pulled the plugs from my openings. Plup! Plop!

Like my legs, my arms had been bound for some considerable time, and I had to wait a few minutes before I could make any use of them. Janet asked me to rinse out the suit after I had showered. Before leaving me, Janet gave me a bathrobe to put on. I suddenly realised that I had no clothes to wear. I had arrived in tights, shoes and body suit. The skirt and coat I had worn were all I had to put on. Howard usually sees to this sort of thing, but this time he hadn't. And I had forgotten.

I took a shower and washed my hair. Having rinsed off the bodysuit, I hung it on the towel rail and dried myself off with the towel. Then I put on Janet's bathrobe and went to find her. I intended to ask her if she had anything I could wear. I found her and Harriet in the sitting room having a drink. She offered me one and I sat down, suddenly tired. Janet and Harriet included me in the conversation, in the course of which I learned most of the things I have already recounted about 'our Miss Jones'. Janet had known her for three or four years and had mentioned her in conversation, but she had never gone into great detail about what Harriet did. Now I was to be let in on the secret.

5

CHEZ HARRIET

I have already said that our Miss Jones – Harriet as I will have to call her henceforth – worked as a nurse/receptionist at a doctor's surgery. She also keeps what the tabloids would call a bawdy house, but one with a difference. She is the village disciplinarian and her place is kept for the local and visiting bondage devotees. There her clients can be kept in any sort of confinement they desire. Harriet thought of herself as a head jailer or prison governor rather than as a madam. The afternoon had constituted my formal introduction to her. Thereafter I could be admitted to her house whenever mutually convenient.

Harriet expressed her pleasure at making my acquaintance and added that I would be coming along with her that same evening for a short stay. This was a complete surprise to me, but I gathered that Janet (and Howard too) knew all about the plan. It was clear from her manner that Harriet expected me to do as I was told. I found myself agreeing (she is hard to disagree with) and thinking that my other plans for that evening would have to be altered to accommodate this turn of events. It never occurred to me to object, which says as much about my state of mind as it does for Harriet's manner.

To Janet she said, 'You'll be coming along as well. You can keep one another company.' Janet was caught off guard. Clearly she had not been expecting Harriet's announcement. She started to demur, but Harriet carried on as if what she had said was the most natural and reasonable thing in the world. 'If you'll both take off your clothes

I'll just pop outside and get the van ready, you know, warm the engine and open the doors so you can jump in without catching cold.' Janet opened her mouth to protest again, but Harriet was already moving to the door. She found herself talking to a retreating back.

When she had gone, Janet and I looked at one another. Janet shrugged resignedly and said, 'That's Harriet.'

The remark didn't call for a reply. I took off Janet's bathrobe and laid it on the nearest chair. From outside there came the sound of the van's engine starting up. Janet finished undressing and we stood about in the nude waiting for Harriet to come back. I must admit that my heart was beginning its old familiar hammering as the excitement of the unknown got to me again.

Presently Harriet came back inside. 'Splendid,' she said when she saw that we had done as she asked. 'There's just this,' she added, giving each of us a pair of handcuffs. They were of the modern ratchet type but looked as if they had been well used. 'If you'll both put these on we can go. Hands behind your backs, please.'

Janet and I took the proffered handcuffs from Harriet and obediently locked them on our wrists. Harriet stepped behind me to inspect my work. 'I think these should be a bit tighter,' she observed, closing my handcuffs two or three notches more. They were now snug around my wrists. 'I'll just double-lock them for you,' she said. Harriet turned to inspect Janet. 'Very good,' she said approvingly. 'I don't think I could have done a better job myself.' She double-locked Janet's cuffs as well and turned to lead us outside.

As she turned, her glance fell on my leg-irons lying on the sideboard. Harriet asked Janet what she had done with the keys. Janet told her and she retrieved them from the pocket of the jodhpurs. Stooping, she locked one of the irons on Janet's left ankle and motioned for me to come stand beside her. She locked the other iron on my right ankle and pocketed the key. 'All ready, then. Outside,' said Harriet tersely.

Janet and I moved in lock step through the door. The

103

van was drawn up close to the door with the motor running. With some difficulty we climbed into the vehicle through the sliding door in the side. Harriet closed and locked it behind us when she saw us seated. There were curtains on the windows so that we were screened from casual observers. Harriet went round and got into the driving seat and we drove off into the night.

I thought that Harriet would live out in the country for the sake of privacy, but it turned out that she lived in Chelsea. There were some nervous moments as we overtook other cars or were overtaken, but as far as we could tell no one spared more than a passing glance for the ordinary-looking van or its two captive passengers. It was just in my overheated imagination that the van had turned into a glass carriage with floodlit interior. We drove for something like three hours before reaching the suburbs. Unable to use our hands, Janet and I were tumbled about a bit but managed not to fall to the floor. It was a bit draughty in the back seat – not altogether the ideal conditions for nude motoring.

Other cars, pedestrians, traffic lights and frequent halts became more common. That too was a bit nerve-racking. It's not every day that you come across two nude women in handcuffs being driven through the streets. Janet probably felt as conspicuous as I did, but Harriet took no notice. Nor did anyone else.

Eventually we wound our way on down to the river and to the converted warehouse where Harriet lived. We drove into a walled courtyard through open gates and I saw *Schloss* Harriet for the first time. It was an ordinary terraced house on two floors. There was a basement as well. After closing the outer gates, Harriet checked for neighbours before opening the door for us to get out. As she led us across the courtyard to the basement entrance, I saw that it would be hard for anyone to see what went on in the yard without trying hard. Nevertheless, I was glad she was being cautious.

Harriet led us down a half-flight of steps and fumbled for the key. We felt very exposed standing around in the altogether. Harriet dropped the key-ring with a loud clash and I jumped a foot. Now, did she drop the keys on purpose to put us on edge? She seemed to take three weeks longer than forever to pick them up and find the right key. Finally she fitted her key into the lock. The door looked unusually stout and had no glass panels whatever. We stepped inside and she closed and locked it behind us before turning on the lights. I was grateful to be under cover once more. We were at the rear end of the basement which ran clear through to the front of the house. Harriet had turned the whole area into a bondage freak's dream home. To the left of the door we had come through was a raised stage or dais which occupied one corner of the room. Down the same side of the room there was a long run of cupboards which, I found out later, were filled with the tools of Harriet's trade – everything necessary to realise her clients' fantasies. The main part of the room was open, with several posts to support the ceiling. The beams were exposed, and Harriet had installed hooks here and there for convenience in suspending people from. There were ring-bolts in the wooden floor which served as anchor points for the clients. The walls were of brick and were also furnished with ring-bolts at various points. As Harriet led the way inside I saw that there were two rooms at the far end with doors that looked suspiciously like those seen on police cells. They were in fact cells, each with a bed, a toilet and a washbasin – better than the average prison but still quite secure. A short hall or passage led between the cells with a flight of stairs leading upward to the rest of the house as I later learned.

You could call the place a torture chamber, but that would be an overstatement. It was actually the place Harriet used for servicing her clients. She did not inflict extreme or excruciating pain unless that were demanded beforehand. Most of the work consisted in the skilful administering of calculated pain for the purpose of heightening sexual pleasure. Indeed she had done that to me just that afternoon at Janet's place. There was a rack against one wall, but I saw no tongs or pincers. Nor were there any branding irons or smoking braziers. That would have been against the fire regulations in any case. In the glass-fronted storage cupboards were handcuffs and strait-jackets, manacles and chains of all sorts, leather straps and what looked like miles of rope. There were gags and hoods, canvas and leather sacks to envelop the entire body, a selection of whips and riding crops. In short, there was almost anything needed to render one helpless.

London house prices being what they are, all this was done on a much smaller scale than you see in self-respecting castles and fantasy tales. Still, the equipment was remarkably complete. It was clear that Harriet (or someone) had spent a good deal of time, thought and money in assembling this collection. She had either a wealthy backer or an understanding bank manager. Harriet even had the necessary equipment for erotic piercing, and often used her nursing skills in the practice of this minor art. The cellar was a room for special people run by a specialist.

Harriet let us look around for a bit before she turned to Janet and said, 'You'll both be here for the rest of the weekend unless someone comes to collect you earlier. You won't need any clothes because you won't be going anywhere. If you get cold there are plenty of blankets in your cell.' She stooped to remove the leg-irons that connected Janet and me and then motioned both of us toward one of the cells at the far end of the space. 'You can keep each other company for an hour or so while I freshen up. Afterwards we'll have some fun.'

We entered the small room and Harriet closed the door behind us. There was the sound of a bolt shooting home. Harriet looked in at us through the narrow barred opening in the door before she slid the panel shut decisively. We heard the sound of retreating footsteps, the closing of a door, and we were left alone in our prison.

'No telling when she'll be back,' Janet remarked. 'I wish she had taken the handcuffs off. Race you to the loo? There isn't much else to do for a while,' she continued.

'You first,' I replied. 'I'm not in a hurry.'

Janet managed to do her business well enough. We had

both had plenty of practice. I dried her off with a bit of tissue. Janet gave a hiss as I brushed her crotch.

'Are you sensitive there?' I asked innocently.

'After watching you writhing about the barn all afternoon, of course I am. There's only so much satisfaction to be had in watching. One wants to take part as well.'

'I thought you'd enjoyed making the video well enough,' I continued as I finished drying her.

'Of course I did. Why do you think I'm so steamed up now?' Janet gasped as I touched her once again.

'I must have hit the spot again. Sorry,' I said, 'or did you want me to try again?'

'Yes, but we'd better not. Harriet has something in mind for us, and I think we should wait to see what it is. We may be in for a long session. Better if we sit down and I finish telling you about our Miss Jones.'

So we sat on the narrow cot and Janet filled me in on the subject of Harriet Jones, dominatrix extraordinaire. After seeing her in action and then seeing her base of operations, I guessed that Harriet was a true devotee of the art of erotic bondage, the genuine article amidst many imitations. The perfunctory service offered by most of those who advertise themselves as 'stringent disciplinarians' should get them into trouble with the Trading Standards Office, but standards are falling everywhere.

The recital was interrupted by the arrival of the lady herself. There was the sound of footsteps, then the bolt was drawn and Harriet opened the door. 'Enjoying yourselves?' she asked brightly as she shooed us out into the main basement. 'It's time for the main event. We'll begin with you, Janet.' To me she added, 'You can watch her going through her paces and rest up a bit. She watched you this afternoon. But what shall I do with you in the meantime? Something simple. The simple things are usually the best. Ah, yes! Come over here.'

Harriet led me over to one of the posts that supported the floor above. She placed me with my back to it and unlocked one of my cuffs. It didn't require great intelligence to guess what she intended to do. I backed up to the

107

post and brought my hands together behind me. Harriet replaced the cuff and double-locked it once more, leaving me chained to the pillar. 'Thank you, dear. You *do* understand,' she said to me. 'You'll have a good view from there.'

She went to collect Janet. Taking her by the elbow, Harriet led her towards the raised portion of the floor that resembled a small stage. Janet, it appeared, was about to perform for us. On the stage was an exercise bicycle, but not the ordinary type. For one thing, I noticed that there were two strategically placed holes in the saddle. Janet must have guessed their purposes as soon as I did, because she gave a little gasp and shiver which were not wholly due to fear. There were also some rather suspicious-looking loops or eyes on the handlebars and saddle which would do nicely for fastening one to the bicycle.

Harriet was explaining it to Janet. 'This is something new since you were here last. One has to keep moving ahead. To stand still is to be bored. And boring. You enjoyed your friend's performance this afternoon, and you must be all ready for something nice yourself. This is just the thing for you. You're already dressed for the part too. You can do your own impression of Lady Godiva. Unfortunately for the people, you won't be riding through the streets of Coventry. You have magnificent boobs and you'd be a welcome sight on horseback in any town. I'd like to see them bobbing about myself, and so would lots of other people. I'm sure your friend would, wouldn't you dear?' She turned to me but did not wait for my reply. Another of her rhetorical questions.

'Anyway,' she continued, to Janet, 'you can show them off to us as you ride by on bicycle back. Now if you'll just mount the saddle . . . So. That's good.' Janet awkwardly got aboard.

I had never boarded a bicycle in handcuffs, but I guessed it wouldn't be too much longer before my turn came. I didn't suppose I'd be any more graceful than Janet was. Once she was seated, Harriet proceeded to tie her to the bicycle.

'Can't have you falling off, can we!' she asked of no one in particular. 'Put your feet on the pedals, Janet.' When she had done so, Harriet tied a length of rope to each of her ankles and looped it around the pedals so that Janet's feet were held firmly down. With her feet secured, Harriet removed Janet's handcuffs. Once Harriet has tied someone up, she makes it a rule never to allow him or her to be free from some sort of restraint until the end of the session. Harriet had Janet grasp the handlebars so that her wrists could be secured to them. When her hands were tied, Janet was powerless to free herself.

But Harriet was not done yet. She went next to her storage cupboard and fetched the two inevitable plugs for Janet's two openings. I remembered the type well from my afternoon in the electric body suit. Janet knew what came next. Without being told, she stood up on the pedals while Harriet screwed the vaginal and anal plugs into the appropriate holes in the seat. She applied a light coating of lubricant to them and guided Janet down to a two-point landing. She seated Janet firmly onto the plugs, a movement accompanied by a faint sigh of pleasure from her as she was penetrated fore and aft. But of course Harriet wasn't quite satisfied. She is somewhat of a perfectionist. She had Janet stand once more while she made final adjustments, her tongue caught between her teeth as she concentrated on the task. Harriet applied some more lubricant to the plugs and once more eased Janet down onto them. A faint groan from Janet signified her satisfaction with the seating arrangements. Finally Harriet used more rope to tie Janet to the bicycle seat, looping it around her waist and thighs and around under the seat. When she was done, Janet could only wiggle a bit on the seat as she pedalled the exercise bike – which she would be forced to do, and rather energetically at that, soon enough.

Janet squirmed slightly on her perch as she seated herself more comfortably. Her breath caught once or twice as she clenched herself around the plugs. Harriet meanwhile was oblivious to all this. She was busy with matters electrical.

'Good bondage these days almost requires one to be an

109

electrical engineer,' she observed to the room in general, as she connected wires to the bases of Janet's twin plugs. 'One doesn't want to get this part of it wrong. That would spoil the effect, wouldn't it?'

I thought the effect wouldn't be the only thing spoiled by a mistake of that sort, but it seemed tactless to point it out. Besides, I could see by the lack of hesitation that Harriet knew what she was about. She usually did.

Harriet led the wires clear to one side and then paused as if a new thought had struck her. 'I've forgotten about those lovely tits of yours, dear. I'll have to do something about them. And aren't your nipples tight with the thought of that?' Indeed they were. I was getting a bit tight in the old erectile tissue areas as well as I watched Janet being readied for her performance. Harriet had probably been thinking about the effect on me of watching helplessly as Janet was prepared. For my part, the effect was heightened by wondering what was in store for me. The familiar excitement of not knowing was coming over me.

Meanwhile Harriet had gone to her treasure trove and found a leather brassiere. As she passed me, she paused to show me the inside of the cups. They were covered with a light silvery mesh in order to spread the current more evenly over the wearer's tits. She carried her find over to Janet and connected two more wires to the cups' terminals. Ordinarily Harriet thinks of everything, but it looked as if she had done things out of turn when she tried to fit the bra onto Janet. With her wrists tied to the handlebars it was impossible to get Janet's arms through the shoulder straps. There was a momentary pause while Harriet considered the problem, then with a small frown she undid the adjustment on the straps completely. It was then an easy matter to stuff Janet into the bra and do up the shoulder straps again.

As she was connecting the wires to the control circuit, Harriet explained the ground rules to Janet. 'I suppose you know in general what is going on, dear, but here are a few of the finer points. Those plugs inside you are electric vibrators. They are the carrot, and will give you a nice ride if you do things right. But of course they, and the bra you're wearing, can also be the stick. They will shock your – er – sensitive areas if you fail to keep up the pace. This,' she explained, holding up a small plastic box, 'is a reverse current relay, or a voltage regulator to the untutored. We might also describe it as a Janet regulator, for that is what it will do. Now, we plug the wires in so, and so, and the first part of the hookup is done. Let's see. Switch off? Yes. Now comes the battery. An ordinary twelve-volt automobile battery of the sort that can be depended upon to go flat on the first morning you really need it. But it isn't flat now, I assure you. There is a coil in the circuit to – uh – exaggerate the effect. Nothing lethal,' Harriet said as she saw the look of alarm on Janet's face. 'Just a little sting in the right places.'

Harriet connected the wires to the battery, and Janet tensed as if expecting the 'stick' to be applied. But not a bit of it. Harriet was not yet ready. 'There's a dynamo on the rear wheel of your bicycle which I'm afraid you can't see from where you're sitting. No, no need to twist round, Janet. You can take my word for it. It is the ordinary kind, the type used to power the lights on a bicycle as the wheels turn it. I will now connect the dynamo to the Janet regulator, and the circuit is complete, as the electricians would say. I need only switch on to set things – you, in this case – in motion. Here are the final rules, dear. I'll set the regulator for a nice easy pace, say ten miles per hour to begin with. We don't want you to work yourself into a lather right away. Maybe later. Just a nice even pace and a light sweat for now.

'What you have to do is keep going. There's a speedometer on the handlebars so you can check your speed. So long as you go at a steady ten miles per hour nothing will happen. The dynamo will be charging the battery and the current will flow only in that direction. If you go faster, the regulator is set to give you a nice buzz where it will do you the most good. The faster you go, the stronger the buzz, and you know what that leads to. That's the carrot to keep you going. But if you go slower than the set speed, you will

111

get a sharp reminder through your plugs and the bra you're wearing. All clear?'

Janet nodded. Harriet set the regulator down on the floor, surreptitiously flicking the switch 'on' and then 'off' for a second. Janet jerked upright and yipped in surprise. 'Sorry, dear,' Harriet said insincerely, 'just testing. Everything seems to be in order. If you'll just start pedalling, I'll turn this on when you get up to speed.'

Obediently, Janet began to pedal. When the speedometer registered ten miles per hour, Harriet switched on. Janet tensed up as if expecting another shock to her 'relevant areas'. But nothing happened. To put it another way, everything was going as Harriet had planned, and she looked pleased with her handiwork. Heartened, Janet began to pedal a little faster, and was doubtless rewarded by the promised 'buzz' because her attention seemed to turn more inward as she held the pace. Soon enough other signs of her pleasure began to appear: the light sweat (due partly to her exertions); the heaving of her breasts; the wriggling of her bottom on the seat; the little gasps as her breath quickened.

Not all of this was due to the vibrators or even to the mere fact of penetration. Even the most unliberated of women must know by now that orgasm is not brought about primarily by the presence of a male organ (or reasonable facsimile thereof) in the vagina. It is more a matter of foreplay and ambience. If a woman's pet fantasies are being catered for, she is much more likely to be satisfied with her sexual experiences. In the case of people like myself and the others I have been speaking of, those favourite fantasies have to do with bondage, helplessness, and the need to obey someone else. When these are combined with pain or the threat of it, sex becomes magic for the bondage freak. Unless you're a complete masochist (and some of us are), the pain is not the most important factor. Masochists transmute pain into sexual pleasure and revel in subservience. Most of the rest of us regard pain and subservience as an extra *frisson* and not as ends in themselves. I'm not condemning masochists when I say

112

this. As the joke has it, some of my best friends are masochists. And some of them are sadistic to a greater or lesser extent. We all have elements of both in our own make-up. It takes all kinds. Also it's mainly a matter of degree. We all have to find out what we like and then enjoy that as best we can.

But to return to Janet. She was pedalling faster and beginning to show signs of increasing excitement if one were to judge by her abstracted gaze and heavy breathing. Little sighs of pleasure escaped her from time to time. And every so often Harriet would step in and help her by sliding a hand between Janet's legs and rubbing her relevant areas. Janet showed her appreciation by squirming and clenching her bottom on the bicycle seat. I have no doubt that she would have been hammering up and down on that same seat if she had not been tied so firmly down to it. Since she is a true bondage freak, Janet was using her lack of freedom to drive herself to the brink – and over.

It wasn't too long before Janet was gasping and panting like a foundered horse (if you'll pardon the inelegant simile), but her legs kept going. She had her head down as she beavered away at the pedals. The little sobs and moans were coming faster now as she approached the finish line. As Harriet had remarked, Janet was not exactly working herself into a lather, but there was definitely a sheen of perspiration on her body as she drove herself to the brink of ecstasy, I would have said, if that phrase had not been appropriated by the genteel romantic novels. Let's say instead that she was single-mindedly intent on making herself come as soon (and as often) as she could manage it.

Janet's eyes, which earlier had been open but fixed on nothing in particular, were now shut tight as if she were intent on nothing but her inner sensations, which must have been truly sensational. Her back was straight and her head was thrown back, displaying the lovely tense arch of her throat. She was whimpering steadily, the sounds forced out of her by a kind of inner pressure. The whimpers were punctuated now and again by a gasp of indrawn breath and by a loud 'Haah!' as she released it. The 'Haah's!' were soon coming thickly too. I wondered where she was getting the breath for the physical exertions as well as the vocal fireworks. She was clearly inspired.

From my vantage point I was enjoying the spectacle too. I could feel myself becoming warmer, wetter and looser in the belly and between the legs. With my hands handcuffed safely out of the way there was no relief save what I could get by clenching my thighs together. I did so energetically. But this was Janet's show, and it was soon evident that her time had come. She grasped the handlebars so tightly her knuckles went white. She lowered her head and seemed now to be huddled about her centre from which the waves of pleasure were emanating. 'Hah! Haaah! Heeaaah!' she cried, the sounds rising in pitch and volume. All very expressive and accompanied by some quite prolonged shudders as if waves were washing over her straining body. Her climax was not a single sharp peak. It seemed to be rather a series of peaks and troughs, and she went on coming for some time if the shudders and noises were any indication. Through it all Janet continued to pedal. Apparently she retained enough attention to remember that her own efforts were producing her bliss. With what seemed a superhuman effort she produced a finishing burst of speed which had her straining at the ropes which held her and squirming on the seat. And then she began to come down from the heights, moving slower and slower as she fought to catch her breath.

The pedalling slowed too, and that was unfortunate. I could see what was coming next, but Janet had apparently forgotten the stick. It was applied suddenly. She jerked upright as if stung, as indeed she had been. All her muscles sprang into relief. She let go of the handlebars and tried to pull her wrists free of the ropes. Her legs were straining to push her off the seat and the ropes were cutting into her thighs.

'Yiiiiieeee!' she said. Also 'Aiieeee!' and 'Naaooohhh!' But it was no use arguing with the laws of electricity. That's show biz for you: one minute you're at the top and the next you're looking for an escape.

Harriet was at her side, telling her to pedal to relieve herself. 'Ten miles per hour, dear. Remember? Keep going. You don't want to let a little thing like this stop you. Go on!' Harriet encouraged Janet exactly as if she were urging on a horse about to fall over. Janet, however, was in another world, one in which Harriet's exhortations went unheeded. 'Damn!' said Harriet as she realised that her advice was falling on deaf ears. But true to form, she reacted decisively, striding over and turning off the current at the regulator.

The effect on Janet was immediate and dramatic. She went limp as a wet string and she slumped down onto the seat, head hanging between her outstretched arms as she gasped for breath. 'Silly cow!' remarked Harriet. 'I told you what would happen if you stopped pedalling. Now you've caused all this bother.'

'Bother' seemed the wrong word to describe Janet's electrification. It was too weak entirely, if it was anything like what I had gone through yesterday, no, that very same afternoon. It was still the evening of the same day that Howard had zipped me into the electric body suit and delivered me to Janet's place. Time flies when you're having fun.

Harriet fetched a towel and dried the sweat from Janet's body. She made no move to untie her. Janet looked beseechingly at the inexorable Miss Jones and whimpered, 'No more. Please!'

'Of course there's more,' Harriet replied briskly. 'You just don't know what you can do. You can go for hours yet if you try. No more nonsense from you. No, not another word.' She said this last when Janet made as if to remonstrate further. Harriet continued, 'I think we need to make a tiny modification to the arrangements before we put you back on autopilot. I'll set the box so that you'll have five minutes' rest from the time you stop pedalling until the current is applied. You'll have time to come down from whatever cloud you're on. But remember,' she admonished Janet sharply, 'five minutes. By then you had better be making ten miles per hour if you want to avoid another dose of what you just got.'

Janet's mouth started to shape a 'please', but Harriet wasn't having any. 'Not another word or I'll be forced to gag you. Then you'll have even more trouble breathing.'

So Janet calmed down and Harriet finished towelling her off. This done, she went to the regulator and made an adjustment. With her hand hovering over the switch, Harriet again addressed Janet: 'Ready? Begin.'

Janet began to pedal with some alacrity, and Harriet switched on. Apparently all was well. Even though Janet tensed as if about to be struck, she was not convulsed. On she went. Or was driven, if you prefer.

Harriet made a final inspection of the arrangements, which I thought were devilishly clever. With Janet on autopilot, all she had to do was check that everything went according to plan. Harriet seemed always to have a plan before she acted. She only gave the appearance of having to think things out. Satisfied, Harriet could now turn her attention to other matters – me, in this case. I had thought that I would be a spectator, but it didn't look that way any more. Harriet strode purposefully towards me, her heels clicking on the floor.

Our Miss Jones had arranged a surprise for Janet and me, although she didn't know that she was going to be included in it. She had arranged for three of her friends to 'burst in' on us at a critical moment and pretend to be intruders who of course would then take advantage (as my grandmother would have phrased it) of three helpless women. In short, they would help us act out the classic rape fantasy which many women toy with but never realise. It occurred to me later that Harriet had either given them a door key or had admitted them herself whilst Janet and I were locked in the cell. I had heard no sounds of forced entry (of the usual kind, I mean, not the kind you're thinking of; that came later). The first warning I had was when they threw open the door that led to the living quarters and strode into the basement.

The men were dressed in ski trousers and black wool jumpers. They wore ski masks and looked altogether menacing. Harriet turned as the door opened and I let out a yip of alarm. Then they were upon us, as they say in the adventure stories. Or rather they were upon Harriet. Janet and I were already helpless. Two of them grabbed her while the third looked around for something to tie her with. As it turned out he hadn't far to look. There was no shortage of rope lying around for the taking in Harriet's basement 'studio'. The third man gathered some of it up and came back towards Harriet, who was (I now know) pretending to struggle in the grip of his two companions. Janet had by now become aware of what was happening and had stopped pedalling in surprise and alarm. She soon turned her attention to thoughts of escape while the 'intruders' were busy with Harriet. Pulling at the ropes which bound her to her trusty steed did no good whatever. One who has been tied up by Harriet rarely escapes. She had studied the art too well.

It appeared that she was about to become a victim of that same art as practised by the three men. Apparently they too had studied the art of human bondage. The two men holding Harriet forced her arms together in front of her and held them while the third man tied her wrists together. When he was done, he searched the ceiling for something to tie her to. This being Harriet's 'studio', there was no lack of points of attachment, some with pulleys for lifting her victim off the floor. It was to one of these that they dragged Harriet, still 'struggling' against her captors. The one who had tied Harriet's hands pulled down the rope dangling from the pulley and tied one end of it around her wrists. By pulling on the other end of the rope, he hoisted her arms above her head and let the other two step back. With another sharp pull he hoisted her a bit higher so that she was standing on tiptoe and her bound wrists were stretched high over her head. By now Harriet was looking alarmed herself. Apparently this was not part of the script. One of the 'intruders' brought a roll of tape to gag her with. Harriet began to protest and jerk at the ropes that held her. The protests were quickly cut short by the gag, and Harriet could only thrash about like a landed fish. This didn't do her much good because her feet were too far off the floor to give her the necessary traction.

117

With Harriet secured, there was time for other matters. Janet and me, for instance. But once again I was saved by the bell, as it were. Janet had been trying with singular lack of success to free herself. She had used up her five minutes and was still vainly struggling when the timer tinkled its warning. A moment later Janet jerked upright and let out a shrill 'Yiiieeeeee!' This time, however, she remembered Harriet's admonition and began to pedal madly. At the specified ten miles per hour the current cut off and her tense muscles relaxed. Janet's task was laid out before her. She had no great interest in the rest of the proceedings. One of the 'intruders' went over to examine her, taking in the wires and the control box on the way. He seemed to understand the set-up and spent only a short time in his inspection. Indeed he paid most attention to Janet herself. She made a most attractive sight as she worked away at the pedals. She was once more covered with a light sheen of perspiration and the movable bits were jiggling appealingly. He turned away and left her to get on with it.

'This is it,' I thought. 'How do I relax and enjoy it?' But the concern was premature. All three men seemed to be more interested in Harriet, who was strung up like a side of beef. The one coming towards me only came to check that I was secured too. Satisfied, he joined the others standing around Harriet. So far none of them had said a word, which made them seem all the more menacing. It looked as if all this had been planned beforehand, as indeed it had been. But that came out later. They had to secure Harriet to make it look good to Janet and me. She was privy to that part of it, and not at all averse to playing the victim on occasion. But I think the gag had surprised her. The undivided attention she was getting from the three 'intruders' seemed to unsettle her. She looked questioningly at them, but they remained silent. The knowing grins on their faces served to unsettle Harriet even more, as they did me. Screaming was pointless, as Harriet had assured us that her place was soundproofed. Harriet had to be gagged lest she blurt out the truth and ruin the arrangement. They wanted to keep Janet and me thinking that they were simply passing burglars and rapists. Their sense of fun had led them to make Harriet their third 'victim' without letting her know.

Had she not been gagged, I feel sure that Harriet would have remonstrated with her captors, she being what she is. However, her comments were limited to the odd 'grunt' as they proceeded to strip her. Her skirt was no problem. One of them unbuttoned and unzipped it and let it fall to the floor at her feet. Her blouse gave them a moment's pause. They could not get the sleeves off her arms without untying her. One of them produced a pocket knife with which he cut the sleeves lengthwise and ripped the material from her. He cut her bra away next and stepped back to get a better view of her. There were nods of approval from the others. I had never seen Harriet undressed, and now I too got a good look. Her ample tits stuck out with only the slightest droop. I had the impression that she had trained them that way by requiring them to stand at attention for an hour each day! The large nipples were a dark rosy brown and were swelling before our eyes as she shook herself and pulled at the ropes that held her. Her tits bobbed about as she struggled, but only a little. They had left her wearing only her stockings and suspenders. Her sturdy legs looked rather appealing as she tried to pull herself free. She was stocky and solid rather than fat, with legs and tits to match. Her waist was thick and was balanced by a rather large bottom that looked as if it was just made for the whip. Judging by what happened to it soon afterwards, the three men must have thought the same.

Still without saying anything, the men took their clothes off. They kept their masks on. Well, I thought, if one's rape fantasy is going to be realised, it might as well be with well-hung rapists. Two of them were erect and the third was hardening as they eyed Harriet's struggles. Illogically, I was beginning to feel a bit neglected. Janet was on autopilot and seemingly beginning another climax over on her bicycle. At least she was pedalling faster than I remembered and was beginning to look preoccupied with internal matters. I was the only one not being catered for, which shows you how the mind can shut out almost anything when sex is in the air. I was being ignored by three men who could well be maniacs for all I knew.

One of the masked men took position behind Harriet. He reached around her straining body and fondled her breasts, cupping them and stroking the nipples, which obligingly became fully erect under his hands. They were crinkly with her excitement. Harriet had jumped when he first touched her, but after a few minutes he had her calmed and she relaxed against him as he continued to stroke her. The indignant squawks which had been muffled by her gag died away as her body changed gear and became softer. It wasn't long thereafter that Harriet was purring like a cat. Her head came back until it rested on his shoulder and her eyes were closed. There was a soft half-smile on her face.

She was taken completely by surprise when the lash wielded by another of the masked men landed with a loud crack just below her navel. The man with the whip had probably not used his full strength, but the blow was loud and firm. Harriet came out of her reverie with a jerk, rearing away from the man holding her and letting out a loud grunt of pain. There was a comic expression of dismay on her face, which was divided into an 'above' and a 'below' by the tape sealing her mouth. However the one holding her did not let her escape. He continued to caress her breasts and nipples, while the one who had struck her bent down and kissed the weals he had raised. At first he too had to hold her tightly to prevent her from writhing away, but as his lips strayed southward into her pubic hair she grew more tractable. When his tongue found her crack the scene went into reverse. Instead of recoiling in pain and surprise Harriet began to push herself toward him. Between them they soon had her purring again. Just goes to show you what a little pain followed by a lot of gentle pleasure can do for a body!

The one holding her from behind began to nuzzle Harriet's neck and shoulders with his lips. She was sighing with pleasure when his hands left her breasts and began to stroke her ribs and belly. Her eyes were once more closing when the third man stepped close and landed two sharp stinging blows from his lash across her heavy tits and stiff nipples. Once again Harriet came abruptly back to reality, but the one holding her quickly covered her affronted tits with his hands and began to stroke them, drawing his hands from base to nipples as though extracting from her.

Harriet couldn't resist the gentle pressure on her stinging tits or the searching mouth that was exploring what the Victorians used to call her nether regions. The pain was being soothed away, but by then she must have grasped the pattern of their attentions. She probably guessed that there was more pain coming soon, but in the meantime she gave herself up to the pleasure licking through her taut body.

As I've said, Harriet never does anything by halves. She was enjoying fully the position she had got herself into, even though it was now beyond her control. There is probably a lesson somewhere in that, but Harriet was not interested in lessons. She was giving all her attention to the job in hand. The third man stood by watching his companions as they stroked and nuzzled her into surrender. He was as hard as any man I have ever seen. Harriet's feet, which had earlier been scrabbling at the floor, became still. Her thighs loosened and parted to let the man in front have free access to her cunt. He buried his head between her sturdy thighs and his tongue must have been very busy indeed if Harriet's purring was any indication.

The third man was watching and waiting for the proper moment to intervene. Suddenly he swung his lash across Harriet's flat stomach. She sucked in a breath with a loud hiss of pain and surprise. But this time it was not merely one blow. He continued to lash her cringing belly as she sucked it in, in an attempt to escape the stinging blows. The man at work on her tits chose that moment to transfer his attentions to her bottom. The moment her tits were uncovered, they began to attract a good deal of attention from the man with the lash. It landed again and again across her straining breasts and stiff nipples while the other two men busied themselves with her back and front entrances. Harriet was being driven into a fine distraction by the contrasting sensations from top and bottom. Her eyes were wide open and her head was thrown back exactly at Janet's had been when the electricity had shocked her earlier. And she was trying to make the same sounds Janet had made, though her gag prevented that. She did manage a loud mewing sound which could have been pleasure or pain or both. And then it was all change again.

The man behind Harriet stood up and thrust himself into her. She stiffened in surprise when he penetrated her but relaxed almost immediately. I couldn't see which entrance he used, but I guess it was the Khyber Pass because his companion was occupying her from the front. That was the signal for him to stand aside for a rest. The one inside Harriet began to stroke and knead her breasts once more, and the one with the lash transferred his attention to her belly and the fronts of her thighs. Harriet apparently welcomed the invasion wholeheartedly because her audible comments began to sound more like a purring than a mewing. Her fingers clawed the air above her head as she pulled at her bound wrists.

For his part, the one lashing her seemed to have softened his blows and would only occasionally land one hard enough to raise a weal in her flesh. Whenever he struck at her lower belly or at the vee of her thighs Harriet thrust forward as though seeking the lash. Or she might have been trying to escape from the penetration, but I doubt that. The man inside her was thrusting strongly and deeply while he kneaded Harriet's nipples between thumbs and forefingers. Once again her head had fallen back onto his shoulder and he was using his tongue and lips to nuzzle and lick her neck and ears. He and his companion were driving Harriet wild. I was witnessing a rare sight indeed: our Miss Jones losing control of the situation and of herself simultaneously. By now Harriet was clearly out of control and was writhing in the throes of her orgasm. She was shuddering and moaning and thrusting with her hips, meeting the lash on one thrust and the cock inside her on the counter-thrust.

The muscles in her thighs and calves stood out in bas-relief as her legs strove both to support her and to thrust her forward and back. In her excitement she occasionally lost her footing and then her full weight came onto her bound wrists. Harriet merely grunted and struggled to get her feet under her once again. That done, she continued to writhe and moan as her spasms took her in quick succession. While Harriet was leaping about, the man inside her was also pumping faster and faster. The excitement was clearly not all on Harriet's part. He grasped her tits so hard she gasped, and then jerked as he shot himself into her in spurts. She must have reached one more of her many peaks about then, because they both seemed to go sort of limp. He remained behind Harriet for a few minutes supporting her. Then he withdrew slowly. Harriet hung limp in her bonds, oblivious of the strain on her wrists and arms. Clearly she had had a good time.

While our Miss Jones had taken centre stage, Janet had been beavering away on her exercise bicycle. She had little choice in the matter in any case. Since she had used up her five minutes' grace earlier on, she had to keep going to avoid getting another jolt from the Janet regulator. The goings-on with Harriet must have excited our Janet too. When I switched my attention back to her she was pedalling her way to another orgasm, silently and determinedly. She must have been inspired by Harriet's bravura performance. The masked man who had been nuzzling Harriet's front entrance shifted his attention to her. He walked over to Janet and began to fondle her breasts in the leather brassiere. That didn't do too much for either of them: the leather was too stiff and unyielding, so he took a few moments working out how to get it off. In the end he merely reversed the steps Harriet had taken in stuffing her into it. Having freed her breasts, he resumed fondling them.

Janet seemed to appreciate his efforts. She pedalled harder as he stroked her nipples into erection. Her pleasure was being effectively doubled – she was getting stimulation both from her plugs and his hands. When he bent to kiss her nipples she seemed ready to faint. But she didn't. Instead she was working herself into the lather Harriet had warned her about earlier, but she didn't seem to mind at all. Sweat was running down her ribs and she was making small gasping sounds as she dragged air in and let it out again in a low, ragged groan. Important as orgasm is, it does seem unfortunate that we are so often inarticulate when in its throes. The onset of Janet's own climax was signalled by a series of 'gasps' as the wave took her – I could have said, to a place she'd never been before, but that's not true. She had been there before. We all have. But it's nice to go back.

When she was spent Janet went limp all over, but the relentless laws of electricity ensure that she didn't stay that way. She snapped erect, straining at her ropes and scream-ing in a way guaranteed to damage one's ears. The man working over her tits took pity on her and leaped to switch her off. Janet slumped forward with her head between her outstretched arms. She was gasping for breath and shud-dering from the after effects of the climax and the electric shock that came hard on its heels. Pausing to satisfy him-self that Janet would recover, the man who had switched her off glanced at his companions and nodded in my direc-tion. The time for watching had come to an end. I felt my stomach tighten in – what? Fear? Well, a little. But also in anticipation, the mark of the true bondage freak.

The tallest of the three came straight over to me and looked behind me to see how my hands were secured. When he had seen, he said simply, 'One of you get a key. There must be one somewhere. Try her skirt pocket.' He nodded towards the pile of clothes on the floor at Harriet's feet. These were the first words any of them had spoken. I thought that his voice was not that menacing. Rather pleasant. More reassuring than the silence in which they had hitherto conducted their business. One of the others went over to where Harriet still hung by her wrists. He rummaged in her skirt pockets and presently came up with the key to my handcuffs. He passed it to his companion to unlock me.

'Wait a minute,' said the third man. He stepped closer

to me and ran his hand between my legs. Naturally he came across my rings. This made him grunt in surprise and stoop for a closer look. 'She's pierced,' he announced to the others. 'And,' he continued running his finger inside my cunt lips, 'wet. I think she's been enjoying our performance.' To me he said, 'Whose rings are these?'

'Mine,' I replied. I didn't think there was time to go into my history as a bondage freak for him.

'No,' he continued, 'I meant, who had you pierced?'

'I did,' I replied. 'It was a birthday gift. For my boyfriend,' I added.

'Well, if you're that way inclined, you've come to the right people.'

I reflected that it was more a matter of the right people coming to me. He stepped back and his companion reached behind me and unlocked one of my handcuffs. It was a relief to be able to move my arms and get some of the stiffness out of them. With the handcuffs dangling from one wrist I stretched and worked my arms. My exercises were cut short when two of them took my elbows and propelled me gently but insistently toward another of the posts supporting the ceiling. The third man had laid a foam rubber pad nearby. There was little doubt about their intentions. I found myself getting that pleasant tight feeling in my belly that usually means sex is in the offing.

He gestured for me to lie down on the pad. There seemed no other course to take even if I wanted to – not that I did. I had been nicely warmed by watching Janet and Harriet being put through their paces and I was about ready for my own ordeal by sex. I lay down on the pad on my back. The one who had brought the pad pulled my arms above my head and around the post. Then he replaced my handcuffs and I was once more a prisoner, my hands locked together around the post. But they were not yet finished with me. Gathering more of the ubiquitous rope, they tied a length to each of my ankles and pulled my legs apart. They tied the ends to two of the ring bolts that were scattered about the floor, obviously placed there just for that purpose. That left me lying helplessly on my back with my legs spread. Exactly right for what I knew was coming next. I was wetting myself once again.

Two of the men took position kneeling on either side of me. One began fondling my breasts as he had done with Harriet. He must be the tit man, I thought irrelevantly as he carried on. The other set to work between my outstretched legs with his mouth and hands. It didn't take too much labour to make me begin panting and heaving. When I was thoroughly aroused, the third man (the one who had been lashing Harriet, I think) nodded to the other two to stand aside. When they did, he mounted me in one swift glide and I gave myself up to the waves of pleasure that came to carry me away. To put it more vulgarly, I came almost as soon as he penetrated me, and I don't think I stopped until he had finished himself. The last thing I noticed clearly was that his helpers had taken themselves off in the general direction of Janet and Harriet. I was much too preoccupied to watch what they were doing to my two sisters in bondage.

What was happening to me then – to all three of us – was almost as good as my rape fantasies. The thing about fantasies is that they *are* fantasies. The can't be lived out. That's why they are both so pleasurable and so unsatisfactory. Reality can be so intractable at times. But this was as close to my fantasy as I could get short of going out and trying to find the friendly neighbourhood rapist, a course of action fraught with all sorts of dangers; though I know of one woman who takes those risks fairly often in pursuit of her own fantasies. I'll get to her in good time. Since these men were strangers to me (although not to Harriet), I could realise my fantasy of being found in bondage by an intruder who then had sex with me. At the same time there was no real danger of the violence that acccompanies or follows real rapes. Harriet had taken some trouble to arrange that evening's event.

I lost track of time as the masked man rogered me thoroughly. I dimly heard some small shrieks of ecstasy, mine, but they weren't important. Janet said later that from where she sat I seemed to be enjoying myself immensely. I didn't exactly pass out, but I certainly tuned out everything else. The world had shrunk to a bound woman being had by a masked man.

Some indeterminate time later I surfaced and began to take an interest in other things. I don't know how much time that took. Long enough in any case for there to have been some changes in Harriet's and Janet's situations. I was still tied as they had left me. My masked rider of the plains was nowhere to be seen. Or maybe he was, but I couldn't tell because of the mask. There were only two of them in the room when I came back to the world. Janet was no longer seated on her bicycle. She had been untied while I was being so thoroughly seen to and had been placed in a position similar to mine. From where I lay I could see that the men had not bothered to find any handcuffs for her. They had merely brought her hands around a post and tied them with rope. Her legs were spread and tied like mine. She was on 'hold' while the two men attended to our Miss Jones.

Harriet, still wearing her stockings and suspenders and high heels, was now standing more solidly on the floor. She was still strung up by the wrists but they had lowered her so that more of her weight was on her feet. Despite what they say in bondage fantasy books, it is not a good idea to suspend a person by the wrists for long periods of time. Both gravity and the person's weight combine to cut off circulation in the hands and arms. Serious injury could result if the blood were not allowed to flow again soon. They were being careful about that. But they were not through with her. She was still gagged, and they were getting her ready for some further frolics. They had tied her ankles to opposite ends of a broomstick so that her legs were spread as mine were, although she was standing and I was lying on my back. She looked statuesque standing there helplessly and with her sturdy legs spread apart. Her heavy breasts and her belly still wore the red stripes from her earlier lashing. She was worrying at her gag and making grunting noises, to which her captors paid not the slightest attention.

127

As I watched, one of the men carried a wooden bench over to where Harriet stood. He placed it between her straddled legs. It was obvious that our Miss Jones was going to get another screwing. Whether she was looking forward to it or not I couldn't say. The two men attending her took up station in front of and behind her and were engaged in what amounts to foreplay when your lady-in-waiting is tied up and can't assist – or resist!

The one in front was lying on his back on the bench between Harriet's outstretched legs. He was using his lips and tongue on her exposed crotch. The one behind began to fondle her breasts. This was the kind of foreplay that Harriet liked best if one were to judge by her reaction. She obviously didn't resent what was being done to her, though from time to time she appeared to be trying to speak despite her gag. Maybe she only wanted to say something like, 'Don't stop'. In any case, they didn't. It wasn't too long before they had Harriet warmed through and beginning to look for relief. She was swaying backwards and forwards and making little thrusting movements with her hips.

The one working on Harriet's breasts and belly paused and went over to untie the rope that held her suspended. He lowered her until his companion on the bench between her widespread thighs could grasp her hips and guide her home onto his erection. When she was fully impaled, Harriet was left sitting astride the one who was having her. She gave a tiny sigh of gratification as she settled herself. Her legs were bent at the knees, which were just clear of the floor. Her wrists were still tied together above her head, as the one lowering her tied the rope off again as soon as he was firmly in the saddle. Harriet set about using her arms to pull herself up and down on the shaft inside her. She was making contented sounds, which slowly turned to frantic squeals as the second man took up where he had left off on her heaving tits.

I don't think Harriet had recovered fully from her earlier session because she seemed to be taking a good deal of time to work herself up. She was moving about energetically and working up a sweat. There were dark patches on her stockings where the perspiration had soaked through. Other rivulets of sweat trickled down her ribs, over her stomach and down between her straining thighs. As her excitement mounted Harriet began to twist her head from side to side; an involuntary and unconscious sign of her approaching climax. She was losing control again and could not resist what was being done to her. Once again her bound hands clawed at the air and inarticulate cries came muffled through the tape sealing her mouth. She was shuddering when she finally lost herself in her orgasm. The masked man between her legs grasped her by the hips and rammed her down onto his cock as they finished.

Afterwards the tension left Harriet's body and she hung limply from her bound wrists. The man who had been working on her tits stooped to untie her ankles and help her stand up. He loosened the rope that held her hands over her head. While her erstwhile sexual partner cleared away the bench, the one who had helped Harriet to stand up took the tail of rope on her wrists up between her legs and tied it around her waist. Harriet was left with her wrists bound together at her belly and the rope running tightly up her central valley. Altogether a groovy thing, you might say. Together the two of them laid Harriet on the floor and tied her ankles and knees tightly with more rope from her store. There they left her to recover her breath and whatever else might have been recoverable.

As they finished with Harriet, the third man came back into the basement from the stairs leading to the living quarters. No one remarked on his return or said anything about where he might have gone. He called across to the other two, 'There's coffee upstairs if you feel like taking a break. Or a drink or two if you prefer. And maybe our guests need a break as well. They've been hard at it for some time. We need to talk about what comes next.'

'Next?' I thought. Sex is great fun but it takes a great deal out of one. I had been at it in one way or another since mid-morning and could use some rest. I guessed that Janet and Harriet needed some recovery time as well. That 'next' suggested that there was more to come. The three men went upstairs and we were left on our own. I called across to Janet, 'Are you all right?' She said yes, and asked me the same question. I was all right too. There was no way to check on Harriet because she was gagged, but I could see that she was lying quietly and assumed she was resting. Her eyes were closed. That seemed like a good idea to me. I wasn't going anywhere, and the sleep might do me some good. If this had been real life, I would probably have been worrying about what the 'intruders' would do to us. But we had been in their power for some time and no harm had come to us. Indeed it was the perfect rape fantasy, with the promise of more to come. I slept.

I woke some time later. Something had awakened me, but I didn't know what. I glanced across at Janet. She seemed to have nodded off as well. The noise came again, this time definitely from Harriet's direction. She was still tied and gagged as our captors had left her, but she was far from asleep. When first I looked her way, I thought Harriet was struggling against the ropes that held her. She was lying on her side facing in my direction and tugging at the rope that ran from her bound wrists and between her legs, right straight through the centre of things. She was red faced and sweaty as she struggled on the floor. She wasn't making any progress in freeing herself, but it soon became apparent that she was working herself up to orgasm by sawing at the rope that passed over her clitoris. Her bound hands were busy in the same area. She may have begun by trying to get free, but she had an entirely different objective now.

I don't think Harriet was paying any attention to us or to her surroundings. Though she seemed to be staring right at me, I doubt if she saw me. As I watched she drew her legs up and bent at the waist until she resembled a ball as nearly as a human can do so. I knew from my own experience that the effect of this was to tighten the rope running between her legs and cause it to rub on a highly sensitive spot. This in turn had a very agreeable effect upon our Miss Jones. Even I felt a little tingle in the relevant area as Harriet worked herself up to the moment of truth. The

130

ropes at ankles and knees were biting into her flesh as she tensed her leg muscles. Harriet squirmed and jerked on the floor and got even redder in the face. Muffled sounds of what I took to be pleasure trickled past the gag. Finally, with a long drawn out moan she rolled over onto her back and her bound legs went out straight and rigid. Her hips thrust up and down as she came – and came – and came. It must have been highly satisfactory if the jerks and the sound effects were any indication.

Janet was watching Harriet's performance from her own coign of vantage. She must have been woken up by the same noises that I had heard. If she could have applauded, I am sure she would have done. But to return to our tableau. *Tableau vivant* is a better phrase, if you like French, but it didn't remain static for very long. I wondered what the three 'intruders' were doing upstairs. I imagined them sitting around a table littered with empty beer bottles and planning what they would do to us next. I was beginning to fantasise like mad again. But when the three men returned to deal with us it was only to get us ready to travel.

They began with Harriet, since she was the more readily portable of us three. Since she wasn't tied to anything it was only necesary to blindfold her. They did this by placing a leather bag over her head and pulling the drawstrings tight around her neck. Two of the men lifted her by ankles and shoulders and carried her upstairs into the living quarters. They were gone for about five minutes as far as I could tell. While they were away the one who had remained behind came over to me and began to untie my legs. He unlocked my handcuffs and helped me to stand up. I stretched my cramped arms and legs gratefully and he watched the show as I moved about. It's always nice for a gal to know that she is admired. We are *such* egotists.

As I was stretching the other two returned Harrietless. I imagined her lying in the dark upstairs, bound and gagged in her own bed and waiting for whatever or whoever came to her. Shivery, but nice-shivery.

But there wasn't any time for those fantasies. It was time for me. The two who had borne Harriet into the outer darkness came over to me, rope dangling from their hands. One of them pulled my hands behind my back and held me while his companion tied them together. They sat me down on a bench and tied my legs at the ankles, knees and thighs. Next came the gag; more of the tape they had used on Harriet. They left me sitting while they untied Janet from her post and allowed her to stretch a bit. Then they tied her as they had done me.

Since we were being entertained at Harriet's place, all the gear was ready at hand – part of the furniture! I don't want to give the impression that all the bondage gear fell from the skies or appeared out of thin air as it was needed. On the contrary, these things have to be collected, either bought or made at home. A really ambitious collection such as Harriet's cost a fair bit. Most of it had been bought by her 'clients' and left with her for whenever they returned. One of the reasons Harriet is called in for bondage games is the size and variety of her collection. Of course there is also the purpose-built cellar as well. But chiefly it is her inventiveness and enthusiasm that make her so sought-after. Enthusiasm goes a long way. You don't need all the elaborate equipment every day. But sometimes it is nice to have whatever you need.

Janet was tied and gagged next and two of the men went out the back way. There was the faint sound of a car engine starting up outside. I guessed it was Harriet's van being brought up to fetch us. We two seemed to be packaged for transport. All the loose bits securely tied up out of the way. The man who had remained with us fetched two more hoods of the type used earlier on Harriet. These went on over Janet's and my heads and we waited in darkness for the next development. There was the sound of returning footsteps and I was lifted like a bag of grain by two men and carried out to the van. I felt a rough carpet over steel as they laid me down on the floor. Then they went away. When they came back there was a slight bump as another body – Janet, I supposed – was laid next to me. Then I heard the sound of doors closing. The engine started and we drove off nakedly into the city.

132

Here was another chance to relive my fantasy of being driven through the streets while helplessly tied and gagged. But in truth I had been up and at it for a long time, and even the most ardent bondage groupie must have rest. Byron's 'So We'll Go No More A-Roving' might be the best way to describe my state at that time. I fear I dozed as we bumped our way out of town and towards an unknown destination. I woke up when the van stopped and the doors were opened, letting in a blast of cool night air. Or it could have been cool morning air. I had no idea of the time as I hadn't seen a clock since leaving Janet's place. Hands lifted me again, exactly like a parcel being delivered. I recollected my first idea of mailing myself to Howard. It might have gone like this. The same hands carried me into a house, or at any rate into some sort of building. They laid me on a sofa. I could feel the cushions beneath me. They arranged me (artistically, I hoped) on my side. And then they went away.

I was once more alone in an unknown place. I tugged a bit in an experimental way at the ropes that held me but got nowhere. It's only in thriller movies that the villains tie their victims so loosely or so sloppily that they can wriggle free as soon as they are left alone. I settled in to await developments. And dozed again. It *had* been a long day. I woke when another pair of hands began to loosen the drawstring of my hood. The light dazzled me when Howard – for it was indeed my knight errant – took the blindfold away. He pulled the tape away from my mouth and asked me if I had enjoyed the adventure while he untied me. Sometimes Howard asks rhetorical questions too. When I was free, I stood up and stretched before making a beeline for the loo. I noticed from the window that it was now full daylight outside. So I had been tied up for at least twenty-four hours. I thought briefly of Harriet and Janet. I guessed that Janet was going to be delivered home as I had been. But how long would Harriet have to wait for release, and what would happen to her between now and then? It shouldn't have mattered to her. The last time I had seen her she seemed to be enjoying the affair. When I

133

emerged, I found that Howard had turned down the bed-clothes for me. That was thoughtful of him. And so I went to bed.

6

WEDDING

Howard and I decided not to get formally married. Living together suited us well enough and so there seemed no compelling reason to change an arrangement that was working out satisfactorily. Some of our friends and fellow bondage freaks are married and some are not, about the same mix you'd expect to find in 'straight' society. However, almost every group has rites of passage, if only as an excuse to hold a party. Therefore we held a private do when we decided to live together on a permanent basis. We both gave up our separate flats for a larger place more suited to the needs of two people such as ourselves. Howard continued his work and was the main provider. Logical enough when you consider that there were certain days when I was unable to work – reasons left as an exercise for the class. I worked freelance from home whenever something came up needing my particular talents.

After we had decided to become what the gossip colomnists call an 'item' we announced the decision to our friends. They took the matter from there and decided to throw a 'wedding' party for us. Being what we are, it could hardly be a public ceremony. They made most of the arrangements. It was to be held at *Schloss* Harriet, the only place both large and private enough for the purpose. On the eve of the 'wedding' I went with Helen, Janet, Harriet and Victoria for the traditional hen party. Howard went with his friends on the stag night. The evening was mainly a pub-crawl but no one wanted to drink very much because of the party set for the next day. My friends had also planned a surprise for me and they wanted me to be sober enough to appreciate the gag – if you'll pardon the pun!

Among themselves they had arranged what you might call a bond-a-gram, a clever variation on the more mundane kiss-a-gram. Instead of hiring someone to accost me in public with a kiss and a grope they had arranged to leave me tied up at the end of the evening, in case I changed my mind and tried to escape, they said later. We bondage types are nothing if not inventive. I had intended to have a relatively quiet evening myself in view of the morrow's revels. I expected that there would be a good deal of public bondage, with me getting most of it, as it was going to be my day.

We visited the usual places, the locals of all those in our group. There was the usual talk and laughter, and I endured the usual jokes about shy virgins and wedding nights. It didn't matter that none of us were virgins and few were shy. Fittingly for one on the eve of her 'wedding' my rings were padlocked together. The familiar warm lump of steel hung between my thighs. Howard had taken the key with him, remarking that the knight was now going off to the wars and his lady was safely locked up.

The talk and laughter of friends together made the evening pass enjoyably. We bondage freaks don't get *all* of our fun from sex and bondage. At closing time we all said our goodnights and went our separate ways. There were several more parting jokes about nervous brides and missing bridegrooms. It was a warm May evening and we were fairly close to Helen's place. She invited me over for a coffee, remarking that I could call a cab from her house. We walked the short distance through the emptying streets to her front door. She let us into a silent house. James was apparently still out with Howard & Co.

Helen hung our coats in the entrance hall and led the way into a spacious sitting room whose wide Georgian windows faced the street. She closed the light green drapes after switching on the table lamps and wall sconces. Helen indicated a comfortable-looking couch that faced the open fireplace across a low coffee table.

'Make yourself at home while I go through and make the coffee. There's the remote control for the telly if you want to watch it. Shan't be a tick,' she said as she went through into the kitchen.

A ginger tom appeared silently on cat's feet and studied me calmly with that self-possession common to cats. It approached and condescended to be stroked, arching its back in the feline way I have always envied. Apparently satisfied with my credentials, it trotted into the kitchen after Helen. 'Mrroww,' it said, the catty equivalent of 'I'm hungry, thirsty and neglected. Attend to me at once or have your cat-lover's card revoked.' Taciturn animals, cats. They get a lot of mileage out of very few words. From the low noises that followed I gathered that Helen was opening a tin of cat food and brewing our coffee. Contented-cat noises emerged from the kitchen. Soon after that I heard the back door open and then shut and guessed that Thomas Cattus had been put out to do what cats do when unobserved.

Helen emerged shortly thereafter bearing the coffee things. She set them down on the coffee table and poured for both of us. We kicked off our shoes and made ourselves comfortable. The conversation turned naturally to the preparations for the next day. We had arranged for me to come over early the next morning to get dressed and make final preparations for the 'wedding'. I had bought a pale blue knitted dress which, I thought, would flatter my figure and please Howard as well. Like most men, Howard prefers his woman in clingy, that is, revealing clothes, and I was dressing for us both. I had chosen a pair of high-heeled shoes in a matching colour. I was going to wear white stockings, suspenders and bra – all in keeping with my well-known virginal modesty. Howard thinks that the success of a woman's outfit is measured by how much it makes men want to tear it off her. There's something to be said for that view.

By the time we had finished the second cup of coffee I was feeling tired. I asked Helen if I could use the loo before I phoned for a taxi. 'Time for all decent people to be home in bed,' I remarked.

Helen invited me to stay there for the night if I liked. She offered me the use of the guest room. I was thinking of having to get up early in order to pick up my outfit and then get back to her place to get dressed. I said no, thanks, and she offered to call a cab for me while I went to the bathroom. When I got back she was just putting the phone down. I stifled a yawn and sat down again to wait for it.

'They'll be along in about half an hour,' Helen said. 'You can have a little lie down on the couch if you're tired. I'll put the coffee things away and I'll wake you when the cab arrives in case you nod off.'

She got up and started to collect the cups. I made a move to help but she said not to bother. She went into the kitchen with the debris and I put my feet up on the sofa. I heard the back door go once again, and presently the cat reappeared. He came to me asking to be stroked again. I obliged because I like cats and always feel vaguely flattered when they come up to me. Helen came back and we talked about cats. I said I was thinking of getting one after the 'wedding'. Hers jumped up onto my lap and curled up for a nap. There's something contagious about a cat sleeping on your lap. Makes you want to fall asleep in sympathy. Helen encouraged this tendency by putting her feet up. We fell silent and I drowsed. The cat slept as soundly as cats ever do.

I mention all this to show you what lengths we sometimes go to in order to set up a bondage situation. Helen was manoeuvring her victim – me – into a position from which there was no immediate escape. She must have put something in my coffee to knock me out. I must say she carried it off very well. She never gave a hint of what she was up to. We chatted normally. None of that brittle, too-bright chatter of someone nervously trying to distract attention from a plot. You mustn't misunderstand me about Helen. There was no reason for her to be devious. If she had told me that she wanted to tie me up that evening, I would probably have gone along with her if only out of politeness (leaving aside any pleasure I would derive from the event – I can be terribly selfless when I have no alter-

138

native). But then the element of surprise would have been lost. Looking back now, I still say she did a good job. And I enjoyed the scenario she manoeuvred me into.

When I woke up I was bound and gagged in what I assumed was Helen's guest bedroom. As in all good fantasies, my clothes had vanished. Helen (or someone) had spread-eagled me on my back, my arms and legs were outstretched and I was tied to the bedposts. Surprise, as they say, was complete, or as complete as it could be for someone who continually put herself in the way of being tied up. Being what I am, and in the company I keep, I am never far from rope. That's why I so often find myself tangled up in it. It was still dark outside and I had no idea how long I had been out. There were no clocks in the room, or none that I could see at any rate. I had no idea either of how long Helen planned to leave me. An indeterminate time now lay before me.

The rest of the house was quiet. Everyone else was asleep or on silent routine, as they say in the submarine service. There was virtually no traffic about at that hour, and the neighbourhood was still save for the occasional cat noises that go on while the rest of the world sleeps. Though I was almost sure I couldn't get free, I nevertheless felt impelled to try. Every fictional heroine who finds herself tied hand and foot must struggle to free herself. It's *de rigueur*. Besides, it was just possible that Helen (or whoever had tied me up) had made a slip. Several minutes of pulling and jerking at my ropes produced no result. Breathless, I subsided. I had been securely tied and snugly tucked into bed. I had done my duty by trying, and now there was nothing else to do but wait for rescue.

I was on the verge of drowsing off again when the door opened with a creak that sounded as loud as a shot to my startled ears. I raised my head with a jerk and said, 'Mmmmmff!'

'Mmeoowrf,' replied the cat, and jumped lightly onto the bed. Relief made me go limp all over. I was not going to be raped by a brutal intruder. The cat rubbed himself on my face and hair, surprised and pleased that I didn't push him away. Then he curled up on my stomach and began making soft cat noises. There seemed nothing else to do but follow his example, so I went back to sleep. Not all at once, nor without some pleasurable fantasising. I slept fitfully at first. Every time I woke up the cat was still there. And I was still tied and gagged. But finally I slept.

And eventually I was awakened by noises in my room. Helen was drawing back the curtains. Light flooded into the room and fell across the bed where I lay. It was a bright morning with a deep blue sky. The birds were well into their morning routine. Helen turned to me and said, 'Oh, are you still here? I rather thought you'd be able to free yourself with a single bound and make good your escape. You must be well tied indeed. I wonder who could have done it. Still, I'm glad you could stay the night because Howard has asked me to prepare you specially for the "wedding". If you can force yourself to stay in bed a bit longer I'll see about some breakfast for you.'

'Mmmff,' I said, but Helen was already heading for the door. The cat, faithless as all cats are, jumped to the floor and followed her out of the room, tail in the air. That's the gratitude I got for warming him all night. I lay back and thought of English bacon. The bright morning promised a good day for the do.

The light coming through the window reflected on the blues and greens of the wallpaper, carpet and drapes, giving the room the serene aspect of an undersea grotto. My clothes had not vanished after all, I saw. They were folded neatly on an armchair near the door. There was a vase of fresh flowers on the bureau. A restful room, I thought.

I was drowsy again when I heard the doorbell go. This was followed by the sound of the front door opening, cheery 'hellos' and 'good mornings' and the sound of footsteps downstairs. I recognised the voices of Janet and Harriet. Evidently they were here to help Helen get me ready. They moved around downstairs and I began to salivate at the aroma of fresh coffee and eggs. Presently Helen came back upstairs with the others. She bore with her a laden tray which she set down on the bureau.

140

Harriet greeted me with a brisk, 'Good morning. Did you sleep well?'

'Mmmmff,' I replied. Monosyllabic, me!

'Oh, good. We want you rested up for the big day. It looks like being a long one.' All this was delivered in her usual cheery, not-paying-any-mind manner. 'You'll have to get moving if you're to be ready for the main event.' She began to hum *Get Me to the Church on Time* as her glance darted about the room, taking in the bed and me tied to it quite casually. She turned to the others. 'We'll have to untie her if I'm to work on her properly. You can finish dressing her here but I'll have to have her downstairs first in order to do her top half. I think the kitchen would be best.' She can be a bit like every recruit's worst nightmare of a sergeant-major when she's giving orders.

Helen began untying my left wrist and ankle. Harriet did the same for my right side. She removed my gag as well. When I was free I made a bee-line for the bathroom. I felt more myself after a pee and a quick splash. After spending most of the night with a gag in my mouth, I needed a toothbrush and a rinse too. I managed the rinse. When I got back to the bedroom Janet was making up the bed. Helen invited me to help myself to breakfast. The coffee and juice, bacon and eggs and toast all looked good to me. As Harriet had observed, it might be a long day. No telling when I'd get anything else to eat.

Between mouthfuls I asked, 'Has anyone brought my clothes along? I had planned to bring them myself, but I was otherwise occupied.' Here I darted a glance at Helen, who smiled innocently back at me.

'Not to worry,' said Janet. Dangling my keys, she added, 'We broke into your place last night and got what we wanted.'

I wondered if what she wanted was what I had planned to wear. If so, it was nowhere in sight. But I said nothing and continued with my breakfast.

Harriet was pacing about the room impatiently. She had assumed her let's-get-on-with-it manner. When her glance fell on me, my heart began to thud with the familiar anticipation mixed with dread. Suddenly I was having trouble getting the food past the lump in my throat. In those bizarre circumstances in which I often find myself, it is not hard to figure out who is the victim and who is the dominant one. A rough guide is the relative amount of clothes being worn by the people involved. The one dressed mainly in goose-bumps is almost always on the receiving end. Unless one or more of the others took off their clothes, I was going to be the centre-piece. But then this was *my* 'wedding' day.

Harriet lost patience while I continued to eat. She informed everyone that she was going downstairs and that they should 'bring her along when she's finished'.

In due course 'she' finished and we all went downstairs to the kitchen, where Harriet had laid out her things. They all looked suspiciously like surgical instruments. I've already said she's a nurse. No prizes for guessing who was to be the patient. It was a bit like those fairy tales in which to think of some fearsome thing is to bring it upon oneself. Unfortunately the same process doesn't work for the desirable things.

Harriet beckoned me over to the chair set ready beside the kitchen table. From her hand dangled some rope. I sat down and she brought my hands around behind the chair back. She crossed my wrists and tied them tightly. With the trailing end of the rope she pulled my hands down and tied it off to a rung near the floor. Next she fell to work on my elbows, tying each one to the upright chair back.

Helen meanwhile was working on my legs. She bent my knees and spread my legs so that she could tie my ankles to the back legs of the chair. She tied a piece of rope to my left thigh and pulled it around under the seat of the chair. She pulled it tight and tied the free end to my right thigh.

Harriet produced a key which (surprise! surprise!) fitted my little padlock. Reaching between my outspread legs, she unlocked me and laid the lock and key on the table. It looked as if she and Howard shared possession of me.

Helen tied a length of rope around my waist and pulled me upright against the chair back. Then she wormed another piece under my bottom and up the central valley. One end of this was tied to the ropes around my waist in front. She took the other end up behind me and tied it off. My bottom was pulled back against the chair and I was effectively wearing a saddle strap. Squirming might produce some interesting results. I squirmed a bit.

'Not now,' said Harriet. 'There'll be time enough for that later.' Cupping my breasts, she began to tease and harden my nipples. 'We have business with these now,' she said.

If this is business, I thought, I wonder what pleasure is like.

'Helen, please come around here and take over. She is being absolutely disgraceful, and I have some more preparations to make,' said Harriet.

Obediently, Helen came over and took me in hand as Harriet returned to her things. She picked up a syringe which she filled carefully from an ampoule. Nurse Jones in action, I thought, as she laid the syringe aside and pulled on a pair of surgical gloves. Helen meanwhile continued her pleasant manipulation, pausing every now and again to kiss my hardening nipples and to breathe warmly on them.

I was glad she had the breath to spare. Mine was getting short.

Glancing over at Helen's handiwork, our Miss Jones gave a satisfied nod. 'She's coming along nicely. I think you can tie her off now.'

Helen produced two short lengths of rope which she tied tightly around the base of each of my now swollen breasts. Said breasts got even tighter.

More business, I urged silently, more business! I was sawing away at the rope running up my central groove. If I had had more freedom of movement I would have been flinging myself about as things hotted up. I lunged and the chair slid on the floor. I gasped, 'Ohhhh! Yesssss!' Not deathless prose, but to the point. Helen gave me a friendly wink and continued her work.

Helen's cat, attracted by the row, came to see what was causing it. 'Mrrroww,' it said, enigmatically. I remember

143

thinking that if this were one of those pornographic novels, or if the cat were simply better trained, he would come over and use that rough, raspy tongue where it would do the most good. However, he did nothing except watch until Janet gave him some cat treats. Then he lost all interest in the proceedings. Cats are so fickle.

'Ohh, Helen! Don't stopppp! Mo ... mmmff!' Harriet cut me off in full cry with a wide strip of surgical tape. In order to make doubly sure, she applied two more across my mouth. Things got quieter but no less intense.

'Absolutely disgraceful,' said Harriet. 'I don't know how I'm supposed to carry out a professional service while you're giving way to your baser instincts. And you're no better, Helen! Imagine helping her like that. You should both be ashamed of yourselves. What will the neighbors think of all this noise? Good job I was here to exert some degree of decorum and control,' she concluded with a smile.

I suppose somebody had to be in control. I wasn't, and I didn't mind. Even if I didn't know where I was going, the ride was fun. The reports reaching headquarters from my outlying areas all spoke of riotous behaviour and lovely warm waves sweeping in from all sides to carry me away. I surrendered without protest, as I usually do in these circumstances. When the ride was over and the last shudder had subsided, Harriet motioned Helen aside. It was back to business.

Harriet tested my ropes to be sure I was still securely tied to the chair. She tightened things up here and there and finally pronounced herself satisfied. The moment had arrived. To make a long story short, I was going to be 'erotically pierced', as we initiates call it. No, not that way. Besides, I had already been erotically pierced there – my rings, you know. Today the target was my nipples. Hence the earlier preparations which had got out of hand.

Harriet took me in hand once more. The feel of the skintight latex on my skin-tight breasts was disturbing. I caught my breath as she handled me.

'None of that now,' said Harriet reprovingly. 'You've

had your fun. Time to pay the bill. I'm just going to give you a local anaesthetic like the ones dentists use. Be sure to tell me when you go numb,' Harriet said in her bright, what-fun voice. It may have been fun for her. It takes all kinds. She held my left tit firmly in her gloved hand and made a quick firm jab in the nipple area. I jerked reflexively but she held on and pressed the plunger of the syringe. She repeated the performance on the other side and laid the needle aside. We settled down to wait.

While we waited, Harriet told me that the piercing would be on the scale of an ear-piercing. There wouldn't be an extended healing period such as I had endured with my rings, which are much thicker. The pins she planned to put through my nipples would be like those used on ear rings. She remarked that the work on my rings was very professional. 'I'd ask you who did it but I know your lips are sealed,' she remarked as she jabbed a pin into my tit. I jerked and whuffed. 'Not ready yet, I see. Well, we have time enough.'

I sat and watched the patterns of light shifting and changing on the kitchen floor. When you are tied up and can do nothing, you have time to notice such things. And sounds. You can hear sounds you ignore when you're going about your usual business. I could feel a growing numbness in my tits. They were beginning to feel as if they belonged to someone else. Harriet was laying out a series of fine surgical steel pins. They were T-shaped, the cross bar about three-quarters of an inch wide and the long pieces about twice that. No point in delaying any longer, I thought. Best get on with it. I 'mmmmffed,' and nodded tit-wards.

'Ah. Ready, are we?' asked Harriet in her best bedside manner. She selected one of the pins from her tray and made several experimental jabs around my nipples. I saw the indentations in the skin but felt no pain. She flicked each nipple with a gloved finger. I heard the thwack and saw my breasts bounce in turn but I felt nothing.

'We're ready,' Harriet agreed. She swabbed my nipples with antiseptic. Lying on the table was a pair of gold

145

thimble-like objects with a flattened base or shield surrounding the opening where the finger tip would go in. It didn't take a genius to see that the nipple would go into the hollow section and that the flattened shield would more or less cover the areola. Harriet picked up one of the pair and described some of the less obvious features of these shields I was to wear. She showed me two small opposed holes in the hollow part. 'The pins you see there go through one hole, through the nipple, and out the other side. Inside the thimble-like bit there are two rows of tiny prickers that will remind you that you're wearing these shields every time your nipples erect. Which will probably be quite often unless you mend your wanton ways.

'I could have knocked you out with a general anaesthetic for this job, but then you might be groggy for a long time afterwards. You'll need your wits about you today. Besides, I wanted you to be awake and aware of the full horror of what was being done to your tender, helpless body. You may recoil in horror whenever you're ready.

'Don't you want to? Well, then, maybe you'll enjoy the experience. There's no telling what you kinky bondage types will go for. I don't know where you get your ideas. It's all too much for us poor nurses. Why can't you be like those jolly gays? You know what they want from the start. Or those nice transvestites. Give them a corset and a pair of stockings and they'll amuse themselves for hours and cause no trouble whatsoever. But people like you have to be tied up and waited on. Leave you alone for a few hours and you'll wet yourselves and the bed. More work, and I'm run off my feet already.'

Harriet sometimes suffered these lapses into the irrelevant and the inane. I was tied to a kitchen chair about to have my nipples pierced, and she was yattering about now much work it all was. Or was it so irrelevant? While she was talking I had lost myself in what she was saying. My apprehension had largely washed away in the tide of the everyday.

When she began work on my right breast I was relaxed. I felt no pain as she pierced the nipple near its base. There were only a few drops of blood. She withdrew the needle and dabbed some more antiseptic around before fitting the gold cap to the nipple. When it was in place she lined the holes up with the one she had made in me. Choosing one of the T-shaped pins, she pushed it through the holes and my nipple was transfixed. Harriet leaned closer to inspect her work. Satisfied, she repeated the process on my left breast. I could feel nothing. My breasts still belonged to someone else.

Harriet cleaned me again with an antiseptic swab and gave me a final inspection before turning to gather up her equipment. Methodically she sterilised her instruments and put them into their case. When that was done she picked up a mirror and held it before me so that I could see my new ornaments.

I thought they looked all right. Quite fetching, in fact. It looked as if I could take the shields off whenever I wished simply by withdrawing the pins. Miss Jones had thought of that.

As if reading my thoughts, she said, 'Those pins are barbed. You can't see it now but you can look later. The only way to get them out is to snip off the barbed ends with a pair of cutters which I will give to Howard later on to-day. As long as they are in place you'll feel no pain. But if you try to pull the pins out you'll only hurt yourself. You've been a good patient, dear. No screams or shudders. I'll leave you for a while until the anaesthetic wears off and then we'll get you dressed for the "wedding". I'll send the others in to enjoy the view before we cover it up.'

She went out toward the sitting room and I was left alone with my newly-pierced and shielded tits. I wondered how Howard would get at my nipples. And how I would like it when both my tits and my cunt were locked away from me. I suspected that I would like it a lot. That's why Howard calls me his kinky broad. Helen and Janet and James came to view my new acquisitions and to make the appropriate admiring noises. At first I felt like a prize cow on display, but that passed when I realised that they genuinely liked my new bits. Everyone likes to be admired. Of

147

course only those with our curious bent would regard with approval erotic piercing which the piercee can't remove.

I can think offhand of at least two groups of women who would regard me as (at least) unhealthy and perverse. On the one hand, the strident feminists would consider me a hopeless case, enslaved to the male sex and wallowing in the degrading life of a sex object. These are the ones who appear to regard men as an obstacle to be overcome in the forced march towards a brave new unisex world.

If a woman mixes her sex with bondage and the odd whipping, she is utterly beyond the pale except as an object of pity or (most patronisingly) a victim to be rescued and set upon the true path. It would never occur to the dyed-in-the-wool feminist that I and others like me do as we do freely and with pleasure in mind. If nothing else, we are consenting adults, though the front line of feminists would regard us as madwomen.

I don't like to sermonise, but it is important to point out that there is a legitimate and wholly acceptable pattern of behaviour somewhere between the two extremes of bra-burning and the battered wife syndrome. I occupy a piece of that middle ground. I do what I do freely and with my eyes open (except when Howard blindfolds me), and, unless he ties and gags me, I go where I please and say what I like. The fact that I like sex and bondage is what the feminists find incomprehensible or totally abhorrent.

On the other hand, there is the sex-is-dirty brigade. Their number is legion, despite the sexual revolution of the sixties. Most of them regard sex as a repulsive and regrettable necessity if the race is to survive. If organised religion is dead as some people claim, its legacy certainly lives on in this persistent set of beliefs. The range of opinion runs from the lie-back-and-think-of-England group to the keep-your-lustful-hands-off-me-you-filthy-beast crowd. Indeed, now that I think of it, feminism may be a sublimation of this latter view. I'll have to give the idea some more thought.

But whether I'm right or not, the problems created by the sex-is-sinful brigade remain. They pass their silly views along to their children and the virus spreads. I won't try to change their attitudes. They are entitled to live their lives as they see fit. I don't for a moment think they would adopt a similar attitude to me. Anyone (especially a woman) who genuinely enjoys sex is an embarrassment to them.

The smug and deplorable missionary spirit which lives on even in our 'enlightened' times would force them to 'save' me from myself. I don't need salvation. I feel quite blessed as I am now. The only defence that works (and it works equally well against both groups) is to keep a low profile and avoid being noticed. In this way you may be allowed to live as you like insofar as anyone can do that. And of course you need to choose your closest friends quite carefully. You can never tell which guise the thought police will adopt. Best keep it dark. Too good for the common people.

After I had been duly admired and complimented on my new ornaments, the others went their several ways to get ready for the do. I was left alone once more, but not solitary. Noises off, as they say in the theatre, told me of comings and goings. Bird-songs from the garden; the shifting pattern of light and shade as the trees swayed; street noises. All that told of a world going about its business while I was sidelined.

As the anaesthetic wore off, I gradually began to regain sensation in my tits. At first they tingled a bit. Then they began to feel heavy, as well they might. The ropes tied around them kept them hard and engorged. I looked down at my new caps and was struck once again by their clever design. Like little Amazon's shields with a large boss in the centre. My tits seemed more finished somehow. I wondered how they would appear under my clothes. There would be more than just the hint of nipple that has become so common since brassieres have lost their armour plating. I would look positively aggressive. But anyone who copped a feel would be in for a surprise.

Helen came to make coffee for the others and to check on me. Harriet returned briefly to gather up her equipment. I sat on in my bonds, and my enforced silence, as a houseful of people carried on around me. In the midst of all this activity I alone was immobile. The still centre. I didn't have any decisions to make, and nothing to do. I had no responsibilities. Various people were doing things for me and to me, but I remained passive. A wonderful sense of release stole over me. I drowsed in a self-absorbed reverie.

I came back with a start when Tom, Harriet's other quarter, came in to untie me. He freed my legs, and I stretched the cramped muscles while he worked on the rest of the ropes. He left the ropes around my tits, and my hands were still tied behind my back when he took my arm to help me stand up. He steered me into the hall and up the stairs. We went into the bathroom. I sat on the toilet while he prepared the shower for me. When I was done he wiped me dry and helped me into the shower stall. There was a cap to keep my hair dry. He adjusted the water temperature and began to wash me. If he paid special attention to my erogenous zones, I didn't mind. I was beginning to feel like one large erogenous zone by then anyway. When he was done he dried me carefully and led me back to the bedroom where I had awakened that same morning.

The three women were waiting for me and took charge as soon as I had been delivered. As Tom turned to go I noticed a bulge in his trousers. He was either well-armed or just glad to see me.

He had barely gone out the door when Harriet took charge. She directed me to sit on the dressing table bench in front of the large mirror. I sat. 'We're going to do your face and hair. Don't make a fuss,' she said. She pulled off the surgical tape across my mouth. I didn't make a fuss.

Janet did my lips and eyes. Bold strokes for a bold girl, she said. Helen brushed my hair until it shone, then she arranged it so that it hung down my back. Passive still, I relaxed under their hands, watching my transformation in the mirror. When they were done, Harriet resumed her role of quality control inspector. She peered at me from several angles before pronouncing herself satisfied: 'That will do. Untie her.'

The ropes on my wrists and breasts has soaked up water in the shower and had swelled up. While they worked on the water-soaked knots I glanced around the room for signs of my dress. On the bed lay a red and black basque and a pair of shiny black stockings. There was no sign of my dress. I should have expected a change in plans from the moment I woke up tied to Helen's bed. In addition to the stockings and basque there was a pair of knee-length boots in black leather and a pair of elbow-length gloves, also in black leather. There were no pants in evidence. Not much for a 'bride', I thought, but I said nothing.

Harriet broke the silence abruptly. 'Time to get dressed,' she said. 'Chop, chop! Time's passing and you've been sitting about long enough. Time you did something useful. The others are waiting for you. Let's get you into your basque.'

She picked up the garment and held it for me to admire. It was of red satin with black lace trim. There were hooks up the front and laces up the back. I saw that the cups had been altered to allow my newly-pierced nipples to poke out through the holes. This morning's operation was obviously not a last-minute plan. Harriet put the basque on me and fastened the hooks, then moved around behind me to do up the laces. The result was a pronounced hourglass figure and a corresponding shortness of breath as my waist and rib-cage were compressed. She adjusted the cups so that my gold shields protruded and my tits were pushed up and out. Served up on a plate, is the usual expression.

Janet handed me the black stockings and I sat on the bed to put them on. At that point I found that I couldn't bend very well in my tight corset. Seeing the difficulty, Janet took the stockings back and put them on me herself. They were extra long, it seemed to me, reaching almost up to the crotch. I stood up and Janet straightened the seams and clipped the suspenders to the stocking-tops. Next came the boots – high stiletto heels and laces up the front. When Helen had laced them for me my legs from ankles to knees felt pleasantly confined. Finally came the long kid gloves.

Helen added a whiff of perfume to the sides of my neck,

151

the insides of my wrists and the backs of my knees. When I looked in the mirror, a tart stared back at me. I was pleased with the overall effect. It was a vast improvement over the rather more staid outfit I had planned to wear. I believe that most women would like to dress as a tart once in a while, if only to prove they can pull it off. And I'm certain that most men like women to dress provocatively on occasion. Only with me it's more than an occasional thing.

James appeared at the door bearing a tray with coffee things. He whistled when he saw me and complimented me on my outfit. 'You'll be a knockout this afternoon,' he said.

It occurred to me then that I would be travelling to Harriet's place. Surely there would be something else for me to wear on the trip. Wouldn't there? They could use Harriet's van for the journey. I could travel unseen inside it. Small tingles of excitement in my tits. And elsewhere.

It seems odd to me that even after the 'sexual revolution' of the sixties we still have no satisfactory words for what we have to call our 'private parts'. There are only the Latinate, medical terms – too remote and academic – and the old four-letter words. These usually sound abrupt or offensive or dismissive. Lawrence had the same problem when he came to describe the physical aspects of the liaison between the lady and the gamekeeper. The business of John Thomas and Lady Jane is too coy. This is one of the better efforts from a practising novelist, and it is still unsatisfactory.

These thoughts were all swept aside as Harriet set down her coffee cup and stood up. She opened her handbag and extracted a half dozen tie wraps. Those are the tough plastic straps the electricians use to tidy up their bundles of wires. The bondage community – and indeed the police as well – have adapted them to their own peculiar needs. Their chief virtue is that they can be used to immobilise someone very quickly. Once pulled tight around wrists or ankles, they cannot be removed. They have to be cut off, but as they are so cheap it doesn't matter.

152

Harriet passed a tie wrap through each of my rings. She brought the straps around my thighs and secured each one. A quick tug on the ends of the straps brought them up snug and Harriet cut off the excess with a pair of nippers. Instead of being locked together, my rings were now held apart. A bit of symbolism there, I thought. A lot of bondage gear is symbolic.

Janet and Helen left to finish their own preparations. Harriet stayed behind to finish me. She produced a sturdy leather waist belt which she buckled on me. The tight corset had nipped my waist in, and so there was no chance of the belt slipping off. There were 'D' rings sewn to it at the sides and back. The tongue of the buckle had a loop in the end which fitted through the elongated holes in the end of the belt. When buckled it could be locked with a padlock. Harriet used my padlock for this purpose.

'I'll return the key to Howard when we see him later on,' she said as she dropped the key into her handbag. She reached into the wardrobe and came out with a knee-length leather coat. 'There's just this,' she continued. 'Slip the coat on and you'll be ready to go.'

I remembered a newspaper story about a girl who went to meet her boyfriend at the station dressed in nothing but a long coat. Now I was about to do the same thing. The girl met him every day while they were courting. In time they got married, and then everything changed. She no longer went to meet him, nor did she dress provocatively. Marriage had set in. I hope to avoid a similar unfortunate change, so I continue to experiment with our sexual practices.

Even though the day was warm, I put the coat on. It sometimes cools off unexpectedly, and I didn't have much on underneath. Harriet tied a length of rope to each of my wrists and directed me to put my hands into the coat pockets. When I did so, I found that there was a hole in the bottom of each pocket. Harriet led the ropes through these holes and down inside the coat. She tied the ropes together and took the ends up between my legs. When she pulled the ropes tight, my hands were jammed down into

153

the pockets. She tied the ends to the ring at the back of my belt. I couldn't pull my hands out of the pockets, and pulling at the ropes only caused them to dig into my crotch. The knot ended up sawing at a rather sensitive spot. Harriet had arranged things so that I could amuse myself by pulling on the ropes if I dared to do so in public.

Harriet buttoned the coat for me. I saw that it would fall open at the bottom when I sat down. I would be showing quite a bit of leg. More gilding for the lily, I thought. I was dressed provocatively and bound securely, but no one could tell that by looking at me. I could walk down any street and I would look just like any other woman with her hands buried in her coat pockets. So long as I didn't have to use my hands, there was no way to tell that I couldn't. The cool smooth leather lay heavily on my newly-pierced nipples. Even under the coat I could see the outline of my gold shields.

Helen came into the room to see how I was getting on. Harriet said that she was finished and wanted to go back to her place to see that everything was going smoothly. Helen accepted custody of me and Harriet went out with a cheery, 'See you later.'

'Excited?' Helen asked me.

I was. That was the object of the exercise, wasn't it?

'Come along downstairs and we'll wait for the others,' Helen said. 'You can have a cup of coffee or something before we go.' Taking my arm, she led me out of the room and across the landing to the stairway. She steadied me as we went down. I had made enough trips up and down stairs while bound so that I knew the importance of going slowly. At the bottom Helen released my arm and led the way to the kitchen.

I sat in the same chair I had occupied earlier. Harriet's things were all gone and the table cloth had been changed. There was no sign in that cheerful room that unspeakable things had been done to me that very morning. The sun slanted in at a different angle and the birds were silent. I began to appreciate the quiet of this end of town. We chatted much as two women might after coming in from shopping. Helen bustled about making coffee for us.

154

The talk turned naturally enough to the day's event. Helen asked me what new plans we had made. I replied that we had made none, since we were only going to move into a larger place. I planned to go on working at home whenever something came up. Children were not on the menu.

We don't have children because we don't feel the compulsion as strongly as others – indeed most others – do. That may be only a nicer way of saying that, from the usual point of view, we were too selfishly intent on our own pleasures to take the time to rear children. I am not convinced that having children is the main reason for living. In self defence I could cite the usual economic and environmental reasons against having one or more extra terrestrials. Over-population is not one of the problems we are contributing to. But mainly I would say that what we do or don't do is entirely our own affair.

Some of our friends are married. Mostly they are the ones with children. They usually go to the home of a childless couple for a bondage *soirée*. In their case the usual reasons for the not-before-the-children custom is reinforced by the nature of what they don't want to do before the children. It wouldn't take much to alert the innumerable Mrs Grundys, and the outcry, even if only local, would be most embarrassing. If a child knew of the bondage aspect of his parents' relationship it wouldn't be too long before it got out. One of those school sessions along the lines of 'what does *your* mummy do all day?' would elicit the startling news that she wore handcuffs about the house. Or that when daddy got home he would tie mum up and she would sit at his feet while he fed her. Or that later he would put his hands all over her and mummy would go all funny. You get the picture. To coin a cliché, truth made naked is almost always an embarrassment.

I was a bit jittery because I knew I would be the star attraction later on. The talk distracted me and helped me to relax. Presently Janet came down and it was time to go. She put a black beret on me and pinned it in place. If it slipped I wouldn't be able to retrieve it. The result, she said, was a certain air of *gaminerie* which she found fetching. 'And no bride is complete without a hat,' she declared. We went out together, the 'bride' and her attendants.

I had expected us to go in a car or perhaps in Harriet's van. They had decided on public transport – a bus. There was some talk about not wasting such a good day shut up in a car. I pointed out that we would be just as shut up in a bus. Janet said that we should support public transport: use it or lose it, she said. The whole argument was specious. Neither of them was particularly keen on public transport or nature. I suspected that this choice was intended to give an extra *frisson* to the trip. Travelling in public while undetectably bound is a frequent fantasy amongst bondage freaks. There aren't so many opportunities to fulfil one's fantasies that such opportunities could be wasted. It is the counterpart of the urge to have sex in public places which others enjoy whenever they can. There is always the fear of detection to keep one alert.

They set off in the direction of the bus stop, walking briskly and talking (I thought) much too brightly and hectically for ordinary people. They were sure to attract attention. In my state of incipient paranoia almost anything seemed to call attention to us, to me, really. But then they *were* ordinary, for today at least. I was the one who was tied up under my coat. I had to follow them and trust them and luck to get us to our destination. I was careful not to stumble. As always there was a queue at the bus stop, which we duly joined. It was all so ordinary that I felt impelled to do something. What would happen, I wondered, if I suddenly announced in a loud voice to all these ordinary people that I was practically naked under my coat; that I was being taken, bound, to a sex orgy? Why do we always qualify 'orgy' by 'sex'? Isn't there any other kind of orgy?

I could imagine their blank, uneasy stares if this strange woman, who looked like a tart or, worse still, a foreigner, were to speak to them, to ask for their help. I would be breaking the national rule against speaking to strangers in any case. How much more uneasy and alarmed would they be if I shouted that I was tied up and jerked at my hands to show them it was true. They would move away ever so slightly. I doubted if any of them would do anything. The desire to be let alone and to avoid the *outré* at all costs is too deeply ingrained. in all of us. Of course I said nothing. But I often wonder about the effects of such a 'coming out' as the gays phrase it.

After what seemed like ages the bus came and we all got aboard. Helen was close behind to catch me if I stumbled. Luckily there was a seat near the door which we reached before the bus started to move. Helen sat beside me to wedge me in and Janet took the seat across from us. The coat rode up my thighs and fell open as I sat. I was showing a lot of leg and looking even more the tart, but there was nothing I could do about that. It would have been even more conspicuous if Helen had tried to help. In my state of heightened self-awareness I felt that any movement would give the game away.

With a sudden flush I wondered what would happen if one of the passengers saw the rope running between my legs, or glimpsed the tie wraps around my upper thighs. It seemed as if everyone on the bus was staring at me, although I don't suppose that much could be seen. And if someone were to notice anything the propensity to let people alone would no doubt prevent anyone from making a fuss. At most someone, greatly daring, might ask if I was all right. And if I answered yes, as I would have done, they would let the matter drop, only too glad to be let off the hook. The conductor came for the fares. Helen paid for all three of us and he went his way, giving no sign he had seen anything out of the ordinary. Beneath the nagging worry about being discovered was a secret thrill at having a sexual experience in public. Make no mistake: being dressed and tied as I was is a sexual experience.

Despite my misgivings we reached our stop without incident. We got off and walked the short distance to Harriet's place. It was the obvious choice for a gathering such as ours because it is both large and private. Additionally there was the secluded rear entrance that would shield our comings and goings from all but the most persistent of snoops. And of course there was her cellar with the collection of bondage equipment in case anybody got a sudden urge. Harriet met us at the door with a smile.

Everyone was waiting to greet me as I was led in by my attendants. There was a burst of applause for me and my outfit as I made my entrance. No one had wanted to upstage me on my big day, so I was the only one nearly naked. The others, both men and women, were in party dress. Several of the women wore leg-irons, much as others would wear jewellery. I was relieved to learn that I was not the only one in bondage. It was to be my day, but they helped me feel easier. The others drifted up from time to time to say hello and to compliment me on my outfit. A receiving line would have been much too formal.

Howard was waiting for me as I entered. He had been discouraged from seeing me earlier – all very proper and traditional – so as not to spoil the surprise. Helen unbuttoned my coat and untied my hands. When she took the coat away there was a renewed burst of applause for my tart's outfit. Howard's smile made all the effort worthwhile. He led me by the hand to the raised stage which occupied a corner of Harriet's basement. We stepped up onto it and he held up his hands for silence.

'I won't make a long speech,' he said. There were cheers. 'But I want to thank all of you for coming. We both wanted you to witness the beginning of our unwedded bliss.' Small groans and ironic laughter from the assembly. 'And I know you'll all enjoy the party,' he continued when silence fell. 'There's only the ceremonial bit left, so I'll ask the best man to give me the box he's been guarding – if he hasn't lost it.'

Tom, the junior partner in the Harriet and Tom duo, went to one of the storage cupboards that occupied one wall of the room. He brought a small wooden box to Howard. Tom opened the box and picked up a plain iron collar which he handed to Howard. Howard stepped around behind me. I bent my head forward and he fitted the collar around my neck. It locked in place with a distinct click. There was applause from the assembled multitudes, but there was more to come.

Still inside the box, where only we could see them, were my handcuffs and leg-irons. I guessed that Howard planned to put them on me and complete the ceremony. There was no script for this part of the performance, so I ad libbed. I took the manacles from the box and held them up for the others to see. Then I sat down on a chair and locked the leg-irons around my ankles, liking the cool hard clasp of the steel through my boots. I stood up and locked one of the cuffs on my right wrist. In full view of them all I turned so that I faced Howard with my back to the room. As they watched, I placed my hands behind my back and locked the other cuff around my free wrist.

I had voluntarily made myself helpless – put myself in Howard's power if you like. My actions said more clearly than words ever could that I now belonged to him. It was a free choice, as my earlier choice of the rings and padlock had been free. As my more recent piercing had been. The important thing to remember is that I was following my own wishes. I was not surrendering myself body and soul forever and ever to Howard. He had taken possession of my body but I expected to enjoy my new status. And so I have. So have we both so far, but there are no guarantees for the future. We were taking the same chances that everyone else does.. No one could say how long we would last. Nevertheless Howard's expression of pleased surprise told me that I had made the right gesture.

He helped me step down from the stage and we crossed to join the others. We were at once the centre of a knot of well-wishers and admirers. It wasn't easy to concentrate on small talk. My mind kept straying to other things: my outfit; my chains; my newly pierced nipples jutting out for all to see. Now and then I allowed myself to dwell on what was to come later when Howard had me to himself. I wasn't nervous any more, as a bride is supposed to be on her wedding day. Rather I was having little flutters of anticipation in the stomach, and elsewhere.

My conversation was studded with blank pauses. The

others no doubt noticed but did not remark on these lapses. I saw several tolerant or knowing smiles on the faces of people around the room. I suspect that I was the subject of several conversations. Even if my ears weren't burning other parts of me were beginning to smoulder. My nipples were erecting on a schedule of their own. I was made aware again and again of the little prickers inside my gold shields. Little gasps of surprise and pleasure interrupted the flow of my conversation.

Being unable to eat or drink unaided meant that I didn't get much of either. From time to time some one or other of the guests would notice my plight and would hold a glass for me or offer a sandwich. But I felt constrained not to ask. It was the old thing about not wanting to be a bother nor appear to be a glutton. The guests milled about in that sort of Brownian motion which occurs at parties. They paused to talk or to inspect one or other of the items of bondage gear in Harriet's arsenal. They ate and drank and moved on. I was glad the do looked like being successful even though I could do nothing personally to influence things.

At one point Howard called for silence while he proposed a toast to the future. That was nebulous enough to allow everyone to drink to it. Janet held a glass for me. When we had all drunk there came the first dance of the 'bride' and 'groom'. Naturally enough we didn't have a live band. Instead there was recorded music. Howard came over to me and with mock courtesy asked, 'Would madame care to dance?' Without waiting for an answer he led me to the centre of the floor. As the music resumed he put his arms around my waist and held my hands as they rested behind my back. We danced slowly, being careful not to step on the chain between my ankles.

He held me tightly against him and my nipples erected again as we rubbed together – not wholly by accident. Further south I could feel something hard being pressed against me. As we danced alone on the floor I was certain that everyone was staring at us. But that was the object of the exercise. When the others came to join us I felt less like

160

a prize cow on display. That was just as well because all that friction was making me warm and wet between the legs. My nipples were by now fully erect and straining against the shields. Those devilishly clever prickers were making themselves felt. Likewise the pins which transfixed my nipples. My breath was getting short and my chest tight. Doubtless that was part of the plan.

The dance ended before I did. I can't be sure if Howard had planned it that way, but I ended up panting just short of the goal. He must have been aware of my state, but he led me over to talk to Bill and Victoria as if nothing was happening. If I was having trouble concentrating on small talk before, you can imagine how much more I had after that vertical love-making on the dance floor. I managed to be coherent, but my usually sparkling repartee must have left a lot to be desired. Bill finally noticed my agitation and took me in hand with a simple, 'Shall we dance?'

It was the last dance all over again, only this time I didn't need a slow arousal. I was still fairly high up the slopes of that particular mountain from Howard's earlier efforts. Well past base camp, as Bill could plainly see. We began as I had with Howard. Bill put his arms around my waist and held my hands. As we danced his hands gradually slipped downward until he was cupping and stroking the lower slopes of my bottom that were exposed by the cut away basque. I buried my face in his shoulder to hide my flushed face and to stifle any noises I might make. Those moving hands were driving me wild. I knew I was going to explode if he continued. He did, and so did I. My legs felt as if they were going to collapse. Warm ripples spread from the centre of things and became waves that threatened to sweep me away. A not unfamiliar state with me, I can hear you thinking. But I have always said that sex is sport *numero uno* for me.

Bill held me tightly against him with his hands on my bottom. I ground my hips and breasts against him and kept my face buried in his shoulder to keep the noise level down. I had the fleeting thought that it would have been kinder to have gagged me before taking me out onto the

161

floor. I don't know what noises escaped, nor what other signs I may have given. I was oblivious to all else for the duration. Everything centred on the storm within. Fireworks and rockets and lovely warm waves that went on and on.

Eventually I washed up on the shore of the sea of passion, as they say in the romantic novels. My surroundings gradually came back into focus. Bill and I were at the centre of a small circle of admiring guests who had drawn aside to give us room. Howard was among them. For a moment I was afraid I had made him angry by my public display, but he was smiling broadly and, it seemed, appreciatively. I sagged against Bill in relief and then jerked away again as I came into contact with his erection. I felt a hot flush wash over me. I knew I must have been a bright pink all over, just like the nervous virgin encountering the demon sex for the first time. There was a wave of laughter, and I realised once again that I was among friends who thought and acted much as I do. But it's very difficult to shake off one's early toilet training.

Bill steadied me as the circle broke up and dancing became general. I recovered my equilibrium largely unnoticed. Howard came over to reclaim his baggage and asked If I was having fun. I suppose he was not jealous because he knew that I would respond to him in the same way. I had been doing so for some time now. Sexual response for me is regulated mainly by energy. If I'm not too tired I respond. And I'm not often too tired. Nor do I have frequent headaches. I don't believe I have to ration my sexual responses in order to demonstrate my superiority to base, that is, male desires, or to enhance my status *vis-à-vis* the man in the scene. Using sex, or I should say rationing sex, so as to achieve one's desires is a dirty trick which all too many women have been taught to use all too often.

Only a blind person would deny that society is both male-oriented and male-dominated. That may or may not change. I simply refuse to use sex as a means of bringing about that change. Sex should be fun. You turn it into a weapon at your peril. One could argue that by putting myself in the power of others I had surrendered choice as well. But I would not have 'given' myself to Howard, or to any one else, if I didn't enjoy what I was doing. Furthermore, I know that Howard would 'free' me at any time I demanded. I choose not to demand. I will live with my choice for as long as I enjoy it. Fortunately, I am showing no signs of getting tired of the arrangement.

Harriet had arranged a diversion of her own in order to keep it from becoming a one-woman show. She had chosen Victoria as her victim according to a system of her own. The choice was not wholly whimsical, as I knew that Victoria was due to spend a week or so *chez* Harriet. And, as we all knew, our Vicky is nothing but a low masochist and exhibitionist, and no better than she should be. When Harriet judged the time was right she rounded up Victoria and led her to the stage on which I had stood earlier. Harriet ordered her to strip, and when she was nude Harriet tied her wrists together and hoisted her up tautly to an overhead hook, of which *Schloss* Harriet had many. Victoria was a truly stunning figure. She doesn't sag anywhere, and I felt a momentary stab of jealousy as she became the centre of attention.

When she was satisfied with her handiwork Harriet asked Tom to bring her a riding crop, with which she laid into Victoria's bottom and thighs. At the first blow Victoria jumped and then tensed herself for the next. She strained to look over her shoulder to see when it was coming. She hadn't long to wait. The next blow drew a gasp from her and the indrawn breath was a soft hiss of pain. Harriet continued to lash her regularly, and soon the gasps and hisses formed a steady background to the tableau. Harriet's grunts of effort sounded like a Wimbledon champion serving up an ace. There was a growing network of red stripes criss-crossing Victoria's backside and she was beginning to sweat gently from Harriet's labours.

Harriet herself was slightly red in the face and panting gently from her labours. She has a heavy hand with the crop when she wants to. I didn't think she was exerting all her strength on Victoria this time. One might almost call it light entertainment. She was putting enough into her swing to make Victoria jump when the crop landed on her straining backside or legs with an audible slap. Victoria's hiss of pain as she was struck indicated that she was feeling the blow, but she was very far from the full-throated screams you might expect from someone being heavily lashed. This was by way of a warming up exercise to prepare actors and spectators for the main show. When she judged that Victoria was ready for more strenuous exercise, Harriet paused to blindfold her so that she could not know when the next blow was coming.

Turning to the rest of us, Harriet gestured toward Victoria and asked if anyone else would like to have a go at her. There was a moment of silence as we all took in the spectacle of Victoria stretched tautly and waiting for the next stage of her ordeal. Tom broke the tableau by stepping up onto the dais and taking the crop from Harriet. He moved over to stand behind Victoria, who waited tensely for the next development. Tom landed a full-armed swing across the backs of her thighs. Victoria's scream blotted out the sound of the blow. She seemed to jump straight up into the air in surprise. When she landed she drew in a deep shuddering breath that displayed her tits to advantage and stood waiting for the next blow.

Instead of using the stick again. Tom decided that it was time for the carrot. He stooped down to the right level and thrust the crop between her legs from behind and ran it backward and forward in the central groove. Victoria let out a yip of surprise and then began to cooperate wholeheartedly when she grasped what was being done to her. She spread her legs and thrust with her hips in time with the rod's movement. We watched appreciatively as she began to warm through. Her breath became more rapid and at the same time more ragged. The tense waiting stance had given way to a looser and more rhythmical movement. Little gasps of pleasure escaped her as the crop found an especially sensitive spot.

Tom abruptly withdrew the crop and moved around to stand in front of her. He began to tease her with light flicks

164

to her belly to let her know where the rod was. Victoria arched her back and thrust her hips forward as she tried to make contact with it. Tom drew back and dealt her another heavy blow across the fronts of her straining thighs. Victoria screamed in pain and her body assumed its tense waiting stance. Once more Tom thrust the crop between her legs, taking her by surprise again. He was facing Victoria this time, and the crop found her spot (as the Victorians called it) at once. She gave a gasp of pleasure and once more began the rhythmic thrusting of her hips. Making love to the lash, it's called in all the best manuals of sadism. The phrase was apt. Tom paused from time to time to withdraw the rod and give her a teasing flick on the belly or across her straining tits. Judging from the reaction, these were far from painful.

But Tom gave most of his attention to the area between Victoria's legs, returning there after only a few teasing lashes to other parts. He continued until she was once again on the verge of orgasm, gasping and moaning as she strained for the next peak. She was oblivious to the spectators and the surroundings, concentrating on inner matters. She must have reached the top of the hill if one were to judge by the noises she was making: 'Yessss! Ohhhh God! don't stop.' Positive proof, if more is needed, that some people would benefit from being gagged before engaging in sexual exercises.

With marvellous timing, Tom withdrew the crop just as Victoria went over the top and gave her a real whack between the legs – upwards, right where the action was. She threw back her head and gave a long-drawn scream that shuddered through the room. But from where I stood she seemed to enjoy the pain as much as the pleasure. She strained toward the crop whether Tom was lashing her about the breasts and belly or thrusting it between her thighs. Our Vicky was by then quite out of control. The lashing and the sexual stimulation became one. Her screams were as much agony as ecstasy. Out where she lives there is no difference.

Not even the most inveterate masochist can go on forever, and so Victoria finally ran out of steam. Her knees sagged, her head fell forward and she hung limp and sweating from her bound wrists. The lash fell with a dull crack on her flesh. She jerked and grunted but made no effort to stand. Seeing that she was out of it, Tom stepped back and handed the crop to Harriet. Victoria was left hanging to find her own way back to the land of the living while attention shifted to other things. Audiences are so fickle, but that's show biz. If it's any consolation, Victoria got at least one more dose of her favourite medicine before Howard and I left. Her capacity for public suffering and sex seems limitless.

During the entertainment Howard and I had been standing together. After the performance he turned to me and said, 'Before we go off to do our own thing there are a few more things to do here. Janet has a present for you which I'd like you to see now. We can open the others later.'

He led me over to where Janet stood with a gift-wrapped box in her hands. As we came up, she smiled and held out the gift. 'Howard asked me to give this to you now. I'll open it for you if you like. Or would you like to do it, Howard? No? Well, then I'll go ahead. I hope you like it.'

She stripped off the paper and held the opened box for me to see the gift. It was a soft black leather helmet which was designed to cover a person's entire head. Mine, in this case. It was intended to fit tightly, and there were laces at the back to adjust it. The hood was a combined blindfold and gag. I knew that such things were available from illustrations appearing in catalogues of bondage gear. But this was the first one I had seen close up. It was a thoughtful gift.

Janet held up the hood so that I could see some of the finer details. There were foam rubber pads intended to cover my eyes and a foam rubber lining in the region of my ears. I guessed that this was to deaden outside noises. The nose-piece was rigid enough to allow my nose to remain open for breathing. And of course there was the gag. It was a pear-shaped piece of hard rubber which would fill my mouth and muffle any noises I might make in the throes of passion.

'Let's see how it will look on you,' said Janet. She produced a pair of ear plugs from the box and inserted them one at a time in each of my shell-likes. The party suddenly seemed to recede into the middle distance. 'Open wide, please,' said Janet. When I did she popped the gag into my mouth. Then it was time for the hood itself. Howard smoothed back my hair and held it out of the way as Janet held up the mask. I bent my head for her to fit it on and she made sure that my eyes were covered and my nose went into the right place. While Howard continued to hold my hair Janet smoothed the hood into place over my head and ears. The noise of the party receded even further when my ears were covered.

Between them they laced the helmet tightly on my head. A strap fitted over the top and under the chin and jaw. When this was pulled tight my mouth was held closed around the pear and I couldn't dislodge my gag. I couldn't see or speak and I wasn't hearing very well either. The psychologists call it sensory deprivation. It's supposed to cut you off from the outside world and force you to focus inward – though what you're supposed to find there isn't very clear. We call it fun and just get on with it. It's not possible to silence a person completely with a gag except in novels. One can always make grunting or throaty noises. The same is true of hearing. Even with my ears plugged and covered I could still hear muffled party noises going on around me. But I was completely blind. Not a glimmer of light got past the eye pads. And my whole head felt delightfully confined.

It's bewildering to be blindfolded at any time but in a crowd it's doubly so. You never know who will bump into you, or vice versa. I had been hooded while standing in a relatively quiet corner. The rest of the room was filled with moving bodies and (since this was Harriet's place) with posts and other uncharted obstructions in the floor. Even if my hands had been free I would have been reluctant to try moving about blindfolded in strange territory. At home I could manage well enough so long as I didn't lose my orientation. But not here.

167

I heard Janet excuse herself and move away. As far as I could tell Howard was still there. But he too might have stolen away. I stood rooted to the spot until a hand (Howard's?) took my elbow and guided me toward some unknown point in the room. Another hand stroked my bottom as I passed, making me jump nervously. My guide stopped and then spun me in a stumbling circle three or four times as children do in the game of blind man's buff until I was completely disoriented. Then the hands went away and I stood alone. Noise came at me from all sides, giving me no clue as to my whereabouts.

Once again I grew roots. I didn't know which way to move even if I had had a destination in mind. I imagined people all around me, staring at me as I stood exposed and helpless on a brightly lit stage. Like an actor facing a darkened theatre, except that I had no lines to speak or part to play.

But I wasn't alone. I was reminded of that when a pair of hands reached out of the darkness in which I stood and drew me into an embrace. Music began, distantly. We danced. We might have been alone, or the others might have been dancing as well. I couldn't know. It was dreamlike. I was held and moved by someone but I couldn't tell who it was. Other hands touched me, claimed me. I was passed from unseen partner to unseen partner. The hands explored me and I was helpless to stop them – not that I particularly wanted to.

Still other hands appeared to take me; they continued their exploration of the *terra cognita* which was me. I was passed around the room from hands to hands, male and female (as I guessed from the perfume I could smell). Someone fondled my breasts. The nipples obediently rose up taut so that I could feel once again the pins through my flesh. A pair of hands travelled down my body from waist to belly and found their way between my legs. There they toyed with my cunt lips, still held invitingly open by the tie wraps around my thighs. Another anonymous pair of hands cupped my tits from behind me. I got damp. And warm. And short of breath. More touches and strokes here and there. Mostly there, though here and elsewhere got their share of attention!

And as I was danced from guest to guest I got hotter, and wetter, and shorter of breath. I'm terribly predictable, aren't I? Just tie me up and stroke me and I begin to heave and pant.

But there was more to come. As in all good bondage fantasies, the hands disappeared suddenly. I almost said 'without warning', but what warning would hands give before disappearing? I was standing alone once again. Not for long. A lash materialised from the circumambient darkness and found my bottom. I gasped and jumped away, but nearly fell as my leg-irons came taut. As I struggled for balance another lash – or maybe the same one – cracked across the fronts of my thighs and my belly. I could feel that even through my basque. My breath, already coming in short pants, left me in explosive nasal grunts as I was struck again and again.

Then the hands reappeared and I was dancing again. And soon enough I was heading once again for that old familiar brink of ecstasy. My helplessness and vulnerability were working their old familiar magic. I began to make the low-pitched purr which is the usual accompaniment to my arousal. I was held in a pair of arms and danced through the dark. A voice murmured in my ear, 'If I said you had a lovely body, would you hold it against me?' Those indistinct 'ummmffing' noises coming, apparently from me, were probably meant to be, 'Yes!' or 'please, more!' or both. It was almost orgasm-time again. I was just going – or coming – over the top when, with exquisite timing, the hands and body vanished and the whips found me again. I was struck from all sides. I didn't know which way to turn. I staggered and almost recovered but tripped on my leg-irons and fell heavily to the floor. The fall knocked the wind out of me and the whips continued to sting my exposed body as I flung myself about on the floor.

Someone, probably Harriet, was filming my performances with the by now ubiquitous video camera. It's just as well because at about that time I was losing track of events.

169

What I saw, after the fall if you will, was a woman in a black leather hood wearing a basque and stockings, rolling and thrashing about on·the bare floorboards. Her hands were handcuffed behind her back and she was wearing leg-irons and a steel collar. Of course it was me, but no one could tell that. It was like watching a stranger being lashed with riding crops by a group of men and women who took turns to strike her as she vainly sought to escape.

A naked man – Howard – approached the hooded stranger/self from one side. The whips stopped their lazy rise and fall as he lay down beside her/me. He rolled her/my body over onto him. He guided himself into her/me and she/I began to jerk wildly on the impaling cock. The whips began to lash her/me again about the bottom and thighs and calves. She/I became frantic. The sounds coming from behind her/my gag were continuous and indicated a quite shattering climax. I can confirm this last from internal evidence.

About then I lost consciousness. I blacked out; swooned with desire, however you like to put it. A doctor would doubtless speak of an over-stimulation of the pleasure/pain centres and an oxygen debt. The French would talk of *le petit mort* and smile knowingly. The psychic crowd would liken it to an out-of-body experience. And me? I enjoyed it, and like the heroine in the romances I fainted afterwards.

Howard gently lifted me off him and laid my body on the floor. The spectators were smiling and applauding. Howard stood up and made a half-mocking bow to the audience. With a sweep of his hand he directed their approbation at his erstwhile partner. He didn't try to upstage me just because I had fainted for the nonce. In the crowd I could detect more than one pair of bulging trousers and heaving bosoms. I took that as a compliment.

He stooped to lift me to my feet and helped me to stand while I recovered. Then he led me away to get into my going-away outfit. Just as before, Janet and Helen had appointed themselves to help me. Howard gave them the keys to my chains and we went upstairs to the house part of

Harriet's place. A quick visit to the loo for a wipe-down did wonders for my appearance. My two helpers then unlocked my 'marriage chains' and brought my travelling outfit. Since they didn't take my hood off, I didn't have much to say about what was being done to me. They didn't take off my basque or stockings either. When they helped me into the leather coat I had worn earlier it looked like a replay of my entrance.

Janet tied my hands and brought the rope up between my legs and tied it to my waist belt. Helen buttoned the coat for me and I was ready to be transported. They guided me back downstairs and out to the car. As we passed the door leading to the basement I caught a wild scream which suggested that attention had shifted back to Victoria. Janet and Helen led me on, opening and shutting doors as we went. At length I guessed we were in the enclosed courtyard behind Harriet's place. One of them opened the car door and helped me get in. They buckled the seat belt for me all legal and proper and according to British standards for transporting a girl on her honeymoon. Helen tied my legs together at the ankles and knees and wished me bon voyage.

The car door closed and I waited in darkness for Howard to claim me and drive me away. Their footsteps receded and I was alone. Once again as I sat helplessly in a car ready to travel I fantasised about being abducted by a stranger who would just happen by and see the car with me tied up inside. The door would be jerked open. The stranger would leap in beside me, start the engine with a roar and screech away into the night. I would be unable to plead with him. In my mind's eye I saw myself straining wildly, vainly against the ropes that held me prisoner. With a low, cruel laugh he bore his captive away to ...

By now the more discerning readers are asking if there is anything that doesn't turn me on. Of course there is. For example, I don't go in for dressing in men's clothing. Nor do I enjoy having someone pee all over me (what's called a golden shower by the *cognoscenti*). And sex with dogs and horses and such is a turn-off. Sex with children isn't on the menu either. I obey the old actors' rule about never going on with animals or children. So you can see that I'm not a completely abandoned woman. By those standards, I'm quite proper.

7

HONEYMOON

In the event it was Howard who got into the car with me. 'I was saying cheerio to the others and didn't realise you had come down already. Sorry about the delay.' So much for fantasy!

He started the engine and we drove away sedately. It wouldn't be a good idea to get stopped for a traffic offence. We drove for some time and I nodded off several times before we reached the cottage we had taken for the 'honeymoon'. We had thought of using the cottage in Wales, but our friends weren't ready for a spell of city life just then. In addition, Wales was a bit too far to transport a bound female. So we needed a place nearer to London and yet secluded enough for the kind of frolics we enjoy. Howard had rented a cottage near Lambourne which was within our range and near enough to several large towns so that we could have a day out if we grew tired of dalliance. When we arrived Howard unbuckled me and untied my legs so I could get out of the car. He helped me into the house and steered me to the loo. He knows my habits quite well by now. While I was doing my thing he went out to the car to bring the cases in.

When he got back he wiped me dry and led me into the bedroom. There he untied my hands and took my coat off. Next came the hood and gag. I worked my jaws to loosen the cramped muscles while my eyes adjusted to the light. I saw that it was now dark outside, so I had been tied up in one way or another for almost nine hours. Time flies when you're having fun. My mouth felt stale after the gag. I went to rinse out and clean my teeth while Howard pulled back the bedclothes. Still in my tart's outfit I went back into the bedroom. I was tired and hoped Howard would not insist on the traditional first night frolics. I wouldn't have refused (do I ever?), but it had been a long day. I started to take off my gloves but Howard stopped me.

'If you can manage it I'd like you to wear your outfit to bed. You make a pretty package and I don't want to spoil it just yet,' he said.

I replied, 'Why, thank you, sir. We aim to please. How about my boots? On or off?'

'Off, I think. I don't want you to be too uncomfortable,' he said. 'You sit down and take them off and I'll get some rope.'

I sat. It looked like being one of those nights, I thought as he tied my hands behind my back. He knelt to tie my ankles together and then pushed me gently onto the bed.

'Lie back and think of sex,' he said as he drew the covers up over me. He went to put out the light and then came to bed himself. He pulled me over to him and fell asleep while absently stroking me in the right places. Somewhat later I slept also, though my sleep was more broken and fitful. I kept having these dreams.

When I awoke we had another sunny day on our hands. The birds in the country, I thought, are rather less considerate than their city-dwelling cousins. Surely this row wasn't strictly necessary. But I was awake now, and raring to go; first to the loo and then later for the other. If you're wondering how I can spend the night tied up and still wake up with sex in mind, the best I can do is quote Popeye: 'I yam what I yam.' I have never found a satisfactory explanation for the phenomenon. With me it's as easy and natural (and as frequent, I cynically think) as the headache which entirely too many women develop as soon as the subject of sex comes up. Since I don't want to convert these people, perhaps I shouldn't patronise them either. They are non-consenting adults and must decide for themselves what they don't do with their bodies. I just don't get headaches.

In the immediate case, the only thing making me un-receptive was the urge to pee. Fortunately that was easily dealt with. I called Howard and he came at once to untie me. I went about the business of toilet and toilette and he returned to the business of getting breakfast. Thoughtful of him. Here I'd been lazing around all tied up and he had been slaving away over a hot stove. Midway through brushing my hair he brought a cup of coffee in for me. He leered at me in the mirror and went out again. When I was done I joined him in the kitchen. The table had been laid, and there were omelettes and toast and butter all waiting to be devoured. Catching sight of me, he said, 'I see that we also have tart for breakfast!'

We had a leisurely and comfortable breakfast, which probably describes the bond between us. We felt comfortable with one another, and our mutual desires were well catered for within the relationship. Like most English people, we don't find it easy to talk about feelings. Don't want to talk it all away, as Hemingway laconically put it. Even our sexual encounters are often approached non-verbally. There are times when one or the other of us will say outright that it's time for a hump: 'Barkis is willing'. But more often the signs are unspoken. Howard may leave a pair of handcuffs or a pile of rope where I am certain to go, so that I know he is in the mood. Or I may dress provocatively (as at our breakfast) to indicate my readiness. And sometimes we discuss our fantasies and help one another to act them out. After all, good sex, even without our particular kink, requires some planning. It doesn't *always* just happen – except in romantic novels. There are just so many tides of passion available to sweep one away. And the trouble with being swept away is that quite often some important things get left undone.

At other times we approach sex jokingly, as a way of putting distance between the desire and ourselves. Aes-thetic distance, as the philosopher put it. That's part of it. But equally important, if you're half joking a refusal (not, I repeat, that we often refuse), it is less devastating to the ego. A sense of humour and of the ridiculous is sometimes a great help.

175

I have taken what I call the 'purple prose approach on several occasions. Later that same morning as we were deciding 'which way to walk/And spend our long love's day' I put on my romantic heroine face to propose some more athletics.

'Oh, sir,' I cried, on a rising note, 'I cannot stand it any longer. I must feel your hard, rough accountant's hands upon my helpless, quivering body, driving me frantic with desire! I want to struggle against my bonds, rolling and jerking wildly upon the sweaty, disordered bed. See, already I am breathing heavily; panting with desire in fact. Can't you smell the warm woman-odour rising from my perspiring body? Take me. Bind me, gag me! Whip and ravish me!' I pleaded.

Howard (sadistically, I thought) shook his head, no.

'What kind of man are you?' I wailed. 'I am an adult female, not unattractive by your own admission. I will be bound and helpless and wholly at your mercy. Rip the clothing from my young (well, youngish) and tender body and work your evil will upon me. I cannot resist your caresses, your hands exploring . . . uh, probing my secret places and driving . . . er, forcing me to ecstasy! My body, traitor that it is, will leap and buck beneath your cruel touch, loathsome though I find your bestiality toward your willing . . . er, helpless captive.'

'What, again already?' asked Howard. 'I thought you had had enough to last you for a day or so.' Falling into character, he continued, 'I'm beginning to wonder just what sort of woman you are. Before we were married you were shy, maidenly, proper; restrained in your behaviour. Now I am confronted with a wild, orgiastic Bacchante. I had no idea you harboured such base desires, nor that you would so lose control of yourself as to express them so graphically. I confess that I find myself shocked by your brazenness. You really must learn to control yourself. Besides, I wanted another cup of coffee. If you will abase yourself before me on your knees and then bring me the coffee, I may find it in my heart to forgive your late outburst.'

176

'Behold,' I continued, sliding to the floor in front of him,

> 'I beg of you on stockinged knees
> To ravish me and not to tease.
> For I am burning with desire;
> Tie me up and quench my fire!'

'Kinky broad,' remarked Howard. 'Not now. I have a headache. There is still plenty of time for you to enjoy your own brand of perversion before we settle down to what is loosely called wedded bliss. That usually means no sex and lots of rows, but we will try not to fall into that trap. But to change the subject: how did you like Janet's gift? You tried it out thoroughly. Was it comfortable?'

'Yes,' I replied. 'And exciting. And arousing.'

Howard said, 'Everything excites you. But I think I'll keep you anyway. I've got used to having you around. But to return to the subject of wedding presents. There are more of them for you to look at. Yesterday you were too busy to appreciate them. If you'll get up off your lovely knees, I'll go so far as to handcuff you while I open the presents for you. Afterwards we can decide between sex or sex.'

I was upon the horns of a dilemma. Which way to go? In the end we decided to open the presents. We could always open me later. The presents all turned out to be like Janet's: restraints of one sort or another. And all for me. They were all much better than the usual three toasters and thirteen baking dishes people usually get on such occasions.

From Helen and James came a pair of bondage mittens. These are leather mittens with no thumbs. The whole hand goes in and they lace up to the armpits. There are locking straps around the wrists with several 'D' rings for attachments. Mine had another strap attached to the end which buckled to the wrist band and brought the fingers up to form a fist. When the mittens are buckled and locked on the wearer cannot use her fingers. The effect is very much as if you had no hands. If you were left alone wearing nothing but these mittens you would have a hard time doing anything. Howard sometimes puts the mittens on me and hobbles my ankles. And even though I'm only hobbled I can't get free: no fingers to untie the knots, you see.

Harriet gave me one of her own inventions: a set of shoe locks. There are actually two types which can be used singly or in combination. There is the strap that goes under the arch of the shoe and crosses over the instep before being taken around the ankle and locked. The other sort consists of two straps for each foot and works only with high heels. Since I seldom wear anything else, they are best for me. One strap has a loop in the end that goes around the heel of the shoe. It extends up the back of the leg to join a second strap which goes around the leg just above the calf. Unless you've got two left legs, these straps can't slide off over the bulge of the calf. The long strap is taken up the leg, drawn tight and buckled behind the knee. In use this one draws the heels up and points the toes downward, like a ballerina doing a toe stand. And since most of us – including me – can't do a toe stand, walking or standing is impossible. All of the straps lock.

Peter and Janet had given me a leather body bag. It was basically a sack into which the victim is fitted feet first. It reaches to the neck where there is a draw-string to pull it closed. Once inside you are helpless. Your hands are useless because you can't reach the draw-string. These sacks are supposed to be a good place to keep your partner overnight or for longer periods. If you fancy extra security you can tie your partner's hands and feet before putting him or her into the bag. Mine had two rows of grommets which could be used to lace the bag tightly to my body and make it form-fitting. There were also loops through which poles could be inserted to keep the prisoner rigid.

The last of the presents was from Howard. He looked on with interest as I opened the large box to see what I thought of it. It was a copy of Janet's electric body suit made to my measurements. I discovered later that he had gone to considerable trouble to have it made for me. He had taken Janet into his confidence and they had gone together to the discreet saddle and harness maker who does a sideline in bondage gear. She had modelled it for him, and Howard had supplied my vital statistics for the copy. I wondered briefly if Howard had taken Janet directly home afterwards. The saddler had noted the details and together he and Howard had made some improvements. There was a rigid leather collar sewn onto the garment which could be locked with a padlock if desired. The waist belt had also been modified with a lock. There were several 'D' rings at strategic points for attaching me to various things. The last modification was to fit the electric bits for remote control via a radio transmitter/receiver not unlike those used in remotely controlled garage doors or model airplanes. It was a thoughtful touch. I was looking forward to trying it out.

In fact I was looking forward to trying out all the presents, but now the honeymoon was in prospect. Like the 'wedding' it was as much symbolic as actual. We had told the world (or as much of it as mattered to us) that we were a couple. Now on the honeymoon we would get down to some serious coupling. To that end I stood up amid the debris of wrapping paper and empty boxes in my tart's outfit. I struck a pose and said, 'See anything you like?'

'Well, I might if there wasn't a tart standing between me and the coffee pot,' he replied. 'Go change your clothes before I lose control and tip you into the bed and have my way with you.'

'Oh, would you, sir? Please? I fancy it like mad.'

'I know that, you kinky broad. It seems you're always on the boil. Just this once I'll humour you, but don't get the idea that I'll do it all the time just because we're married. We'll go for spontaneity just now. Help me carry this gear into the bedroom and we'll get you into something you won't get out of in a hurry.'

In the event we went into the bedroom where the late morning sunlight slanted in through the curtains across the bed. We put down the presents and turned to one another. My clothes began to evaporate as we turned in the shaft of light coming through the trees and in at our window. I felt as if I were standing in a golden haze. In fact I was standing in nothing more than the golden shields on my nipples which were erect and alert. We got into the bed and into each other. Things dissolved into soft focus except for the places where the focus was extremely sharp.

Making love in the late morning has a flavour all its own. There is an edge to it which comes from the guilty knowledge that the rest of the world is at work and that we are enjoying ourselves out of hours. Afterwards we lay and watched the sunlight changes in the room, still playing truant from the rest of the world. One of the best things about holidays is that you can take the time to give each day its own shape. You don't have to hurry from one task to the next. Howard idly drew circles with his fingertips around my shielded nipples and my breasts as we were cooling down. Evidently he was taken with my ornaments.

We got up eventually to shower and dress, and presently got into the car for a drive to the village. It was a market day, and the sun shone relentlessly on the crowds of people. We strolled into the town centre from the car park trying to look nonchalant and normal. We succeeded marvellously. No one in all that crowd suspected that here were the notorious sex-and-bondage freaks who had descended upon their quiet village for a week's frivolity and perversion. True, I still wore my shields, and my rings were once more locked together. But no one could see that. Nor could they guess at our thoughts, which at the moment ran more to fruit and veg than to riot and debauchery in any case.

We bought what we needed, listened to the street musicians and idled the time away until the thought of a drink and a late pub lunch was very welcome. Afterwards we drove contentedly back to the cottage with our hoard. Put everything away then made coffee.

Does it seem strange that there should be quiet and contentment in a relationship that must seem bizarrely torrid? I assure you that we have as many quiet moments as anyone else. One cannot always be on the boil. From what I have said it must appear that our life is one unending round of sexual frenzy. But I am only telling you about one aspect of our lives. I am leaving out the parts that resemble everyone else's because everyone already knows about the commonplace.

There was nowhere we wanted to go the next day, so we could devote whatever time we wished to satisfying our particular tastes. We expected no visitors or distractions except maybe those to which we would drive one another.

It would be nice to be able to say that Howard had me for breakfast the next morning, but the actuality was more prosaic. We prepared and ate the things most mortals eat before beginning another day. We even washed up and put the dishes away instead of piling everything into the sink and heading impetuously for the bed. We are sometimes capable of almost superhuman restraint. The subject of what to wear for the rest of that day didn't even come up until the last things had been tidied away. That is not to say that I wasn't the least bit tingly with anticipation. Or that my other half had not given some thought to the matter.

Madame made her toilette. I guessed it would be some time before I had another chance. Monsieur, meanwhile, had dragged the bondage gear from its hiding place atop the bureau. When I returned to the sitting room it wasn't hard to put two and two together and come up with fun. Howard glanced at me as I made my entrance and struck a pose which was intended to be provocative.

'I suppose there'll be no peace until I've pandered to your low tastes,' said he. 'I hope you appreciate how difficult all this is for me. I console myself by thinking I'm laying up treasures in heaven by making others happy.'

Seated as he was amidst a heap of our recent gifts and other bondage gear, Howard did not sound as convincing as he might otherwise have done. It was obvious that he had given a lot of thought to how I was to be packaged that day. He had laid out my 'wedding dress' for starters. I thought that was a good beginning as I fitted the basque on. I turned so that Howard could do up the laces behind. Next came a new pair of stockings to replace the ones I had worn (or worn out) on the day. Then my waist belt, drawn tight and locked on. Instead of my lace-up boots Howard had chosen a more ordinary pair of high-heeled shoes. As we dressed me, I enjoyed the attention and Howard enjoyed the effect, if I was to judge by his erection.

Then it was time to tie me up. He chose the bondage mittens which had come from Helen and James. He fitted them over my hands and laced them up to the tops of my arms. They fitted tightly, and I enjoyed the sense of confinement. He buckled and locked the wrist straps and had me clench my fists so that he could fasten the strap from my finger ends to the wrist bands. When he was done it was if I had no hands.

While I was savouring this new sensation, Howard eased my feet into the shoes and applied the shoe locks. First came the straps under the arch and crossed over the instep. Howard drew them around my ankles and locked them. Then came the heel straps, hooked over the heels of my shoes and drawn up the back of my legs to join the bands buckled above the swell of my calves. Howard pulled the straps tight, drawing my heels up and pointing my toes downward. Instant ballerina. I wouldn't be walking far!

Of course I could still crawl, but Howard had thought of that as well. Janet's hood with gag and ear plugs came next. When Howard had fitted it over my head it was sensory deprivation time again. Before leaving me Howard drew my hands behind my back and fastened the mittens to the ring at the back of my waist belt. I was once more as helpless as my heart could desire.

Howard then left me to my own devices, as he has done so many times. Those devices consisted of very little. I could sit as I was, or lie down on the sofa, or I could heave and bump my way to the floor, where my choices would be the same as before. I sat and waited for Howard. He hovered about on the periphery. I knew that he was letting me concoct lurid fantasies while I waited for him to do something. Obediently (automatically), I concocted busily. And of course he enjoyed watching me.

He did not leave me completely alone. As on the earlier

visit to the country cottage, he came to toy with me from time to time. As I sat he came to cup my breasts or rub the shields against my nipples, which (surprise, surprise!) erected themselves so that I could feel the prick of the tiny needles. He moved the gold caps gently and the pins pulled at my engorged flesh. My tits felt once again as if they would burst. I began to pant tensely. My heavy tits rose and fell rapidly under his hands.

Then he dropped everything and let the sensations subside. He did this several times, always judging the moment so that his repeated touches drove me closer to orgasm while never letting me reach it. This kind of play could have only one logical ending. Once more Howard returned to fondle me. Ever the trouper, I was soon well into my panting act. This time he moved on to other areas. Spreading my legs, he began to explore my cunt with his fingers and tongue. He took my clitoris between thumb and forefinger with a gentle kneading action which did very little to calm me. I added the odd heave and shudder to my panting act.

When Howard judged that I was ready, he lowered me to the floor where he had me kneel astride him as I had on the day before at our do. He made the necessary adjustments and then, with a hand on each of my hips, he guided me down onto his erection. In one long plunge I was home (though far from dry). Fulfilment, if you'll pardon the pun, was complete. There were a few more pants and gasps of pleasure from 'Yr. Obd't. Servant'. It was a longish ride. And a lovely liquid one. Long swoops and dives; lots of peaks to climb; much groaning and thrashing as we galloped for the finish line. When we were done I collapsed forward and lay on his chest. The exhausted swimmers (to mix the metaphor still further) lay on the beach gasping for breath while the tides of passion ebbed.

After a time we disentangled from one another and Howard helped me to a seat on the sofa. Since he gave no signs of wanting to untie me, I guessed that he enjoyed looking at me. The display aspect of bondage is important to him. I sometimes suspect that he is no better than a common voyeur.

There were muffled domestic noises as Howard went about the house looking after things. Since he wanted to keep me tied up, he had to do the things I normally take care of. I saw (when he took my blindfold off later on) that he had put away the breakfast dishes and had tidied up the clutter of discarded clothing and unused wedding presents. From time to time he came over to fondle me so that I didn't feel too neglected or lose interest in the proceedings. Being what I am, I managed not to become too bored.

It was getting on toward noon when Howard untied me and let me get at the bathroom for a splash. When I emerged, he wanted to know what I thought about a shopping trip to the nearest large town. We were about equidistant from Reading and Newbury. I didn't know anything about either one at first hand and so it was a toss-up as to where to go. In the end we went to Reading, perhaps because I had at least heard of it in connection with Oscar Wilde. I always feel an excitement about shopping in a new place because I think I'll come across something new, and I am almost always disappointed to find the usual chain stores and supermarkets. Maybe there is nothing new under the sun. But there was one unexpected find in the neighbourhood of Reading. We ran into Phyllis Martineau. She had apparently extended her usual hunting grounds to the west.

I mentioned Phyllis earlier; and now I must say more about her because she figures in our honeymoon trip. Phyllis Martineau has rape fantasies (don't we all?), but she runs great risks in realising them. My fantasies had been satisfied by those tame intruders. Phyllis' required strangers. As a consequence she is constantly in danger of falling into the hands of a violent or murderous person. We have tried to lessen the risks she runs by taking her into our circle to a certain extent. One or another of the men will surprise her with a raid on her house and person. She usually enjoys these visits, but she still misses the suspense of being taken against her will by a stranger. Several of us have tried to warn Phyllis of the danger, which I am sure she understands. Nevertheless she continues to seek out chance-met men to help her act out her favourite scenario. She is a consenting adult and no one can prevent her from doing as she likes short of locking her up. We try to watch out for her as far as possible to see she stays out of major trouble. We came to meet her precisely because she had got herself into trouble in a small way.

It was small because the newspapers are still shy about reporting anything to do with bondage. I have already said that gays and lesbians get regular publicity. So do prostitutes, and so do all sorts of crime. But the moment any suggestion of bondage appears they all take refuge behind stock phrases and bland generalities. I am in two minds about this attitude. As a bondage freak myself I want to know more about what went on. And at the same time I wonder if too much publicity and social acceptance might not destroy the forbidden fruit effect.

Against this background Phyllis found her way into the local newspapers. Howard came across the story one evening and showed it to me. A young woman had been found in a disused barn by a hunter, or more accurately by his dog, whose behaviour had alerted the man. The 'attractive woman' was in her 'early thirties' and lived near the place where she had been found. All this business of 'being found' suggests that she had been mislaid previously. When found, she was 'nude from the waist down', and the rest of her clothing had been 'seriously disarranged' by her 'savage attacker' in his 'frenzy of lust'. You can see how the language hots up gradually as it circles the subject at a safe but fascinated distance. After noting that the 'attractive blonde had been left bound and gagged by the sex-beast who had so savagely attacked her', the story then made the usual plea for any witnesses to come forward. The writer then lost himself in the (to me) inexplicable rapture which newspapers adopt when writing about dogs. So much was made of the 'courageous' and 'devoted' aspects of dogs in general and the hunter's dog in particular that I began to have serious doubts about the reporter's sanity. Thus we were steered determinedly away from any speculations the story might otherwise have raised.

185

The next day went by without much further news. That was a slight disappointment to those of us who had had their curiosity piqued by the bondage aspect of the case. We were assured, however, that the police were 'working on several promising leads' by the usual tough and tight-lipped local sheriff. The woman (still not named) was 're-covering at home'.

If the second day's news left something to be desired, the story that came out on the third day made up for it. Someone at the newspaper was interested enough in the story to keep tabs on the victim as well as on the more usual police work. In the story we were told that 'a man had been seen lurking near the barn' several hours before the 'attractive blonde, Phyllis Martineau, 33, had been found by the alert dog Sheba'. This time there was a picture of Phyllis. I don't know how the reporter managed to restrain himself from reprinting a picture of the dog. Howard recognised the picture because he had seen her several months before, beside the road with a broken-down car. He would have stopped to help if there hadn't already been another motorist helping.

Things went quiet for a week or so and then Phyllis' picture reappeared with a summary of the case under the heading, 'Bound Beauty in Barn'. Nice alliteration, isn't it? Pity he couldn't work in the 'blonde'. This story informed us that 'a man had been helping police with their inquiries' but had been released without charge after the victim had refused to identify her attacker. 'Refused' seemed out of place in this context, but there it was. And there it re-mained. There was nothing more from the police or the newspapers.

The story would have died for good if we had not seen Phyllis once or twice about the town. Although we were curious about her, I could think of no plausible way to meet her. We couldn't just go up to her and ask her to tell us all without being impertinent or revealing our morbid curiosity. Then one day some weeks later Howard was rather late getting home. It was a rainy day and I was getting worried about his non-appearance. When he did

186

get home he announced that he had solved the mystery of Phyllis Martineau. He had seen her at the roadside with her broken-down car looking both helpless and appealing. This time Howard was first on the scene. So Sir Galahad stopped when he recognised her and asked her if he could help. It turned out that her car was not broken down at all. This was merely the way in which she met strangers to help her live out her fantasies.

Anyway, he stopped. They talked. He mentioned that he had seen her picture in the newspapers and asked if she had quite recovered from the experience. This was the opening she needed to tell him what she wanted him to do. She dived in. It can't be easy to just blurt out to an utter stranger that you want to be tied up and ravished. Yet this is just what Phyllis had been doing for some time. I don't have that kind of nerve or courage, but then I am more easily satisfied than Phyllis. Howard's opening no doubt made it easier for her, but this can't have been so easy or convenient in the past.

Even though he had been half-prepared for it by the newspaper stories, Howard was a bit taken aback when she had explained that she wanted to be abducted and raped. Well, abducted is not the right word. If you're going to be abducted, you need a place to be abducted to. These are not so easy to find as you might think, and a good abduction is rarely *ad hoc*. But he didn't hesitate very long. It was settled that Howard would follow her home while she pretended to be unaware of her sinister shadower. Before driving off she handed Howard a carrier bag with rope in it.

In this case Phyllis had fallen in with the right man. But she could not know beforehand what kind of a person these chance-met strangers were. She was taking a big risk, but that is one measure of how strong her fantasy is. Unfortunately our society is not very good at satisfying such needs – or indeed any but the narrowest sexual needs – in any safe and regular manner. And I don't think it will ever change. Phyllis might argue that for her the danger was part of the fantasy: no danger, no pleasure. In any event, Howard followed her home in the gathering dark, hoping that there were no news photographers hanging around to do a follow-up story on Phyllis.

When he knocked, Phyllis immediately let him in. She was flushed and breathing unevenly, Howard said. Obviously excited. It was not the sort of encounter that called for small talk, or indeed any talk at all. It had all been said beside the road. Howard began immediately, as a proper ravisher should. He pushed Phyllis back from the door and down onto the sofa. He used the rope she had given him to tie her hands behind her back. Her token resistance ended when she was tied. Howard raised her skirt and took off her pants. He used them, to gag her, with a few turns of rope to keep the wad in her mouth. Then he pulled Phyllis to her feet and propelled her up the stairs with a grip on her elbows.

Phyllis had now got herself into the situation she desired. She remained quite passive, Howard said, as he led her into the bedroom. Still playing the part, Howard flung Phyllis down onto the bed and began to take his clothes off. She twisted herself over onto her back so that she could see what he was doing. Her eyes, he said, had gone all soft and languorous. Bedroom eyes. She was breathing heavily, her breasts rising and falling rapidly as she anticipated the 'rape' to come.

Howard too found the situation exciting. Sex with a stranger is itself a pleasant experience. Sex with an attractive woman who begs to be tied up and had is even more pleasant, at least for someone with Howard's inclinations. I hear the gnashing of feminist teeth in the background, but I shall ignore them. Howard said that in this case the newspaper's description of Phyllis was exactly right; she was indeed 'attractive'. He rearranged Phyllis on the bed and pushed her skirt up above her waist. Underneath she wore stockings and suspenders, exactly like the girls in the ads for sexy lingerie do. Howard was pleased.

He pulled her legs apart and tied her ankles to opposite sides of the footboard. This excited her (and him) even more. He unbuttoned her blouse and, supporting her, reached round behind and unhooked her brassiere. Since

188

this was supposed to be rape – albeit rape by prior consent
and arrangement – Howard entered her without further
ado. The effect, he said was electric. Phyllis went off into a
series of spasmodic heavings, most of them of the up and
down variety, and most of those centred on her hips. For
his part, Howard held on tight and rode out the storm. He
reckons that she is a screamer. As far as he could judge
from the noises getting past her gag, she would have had
the neighbours pounding on the doors if she had not been
tightly stoppered. Then they might both have featured in
one of those frequent stories in which the neighbours claim
to be annoyed by the sexual noises of passionate people. I
suspect that they complain because they don't have so
much fun.

When the royal fireworks display was over, Howard
withdrew, leaving Phyllis dishevelled on her sweaty and
disordered bed, as they say in the best romantic novels.
With mock savagery he growled, 'I'm going to search the
place for cash and you'll be for it if I can't find what I
want.'

He then went downstairs to make some coffee. He took
some time at it so that Phyllis could either recover or work
herself up again. In the event she did the latter. Her motto
might well be, 'Don't let a good attacker escape without an
encore.' When he got back to the bedroom, she was twisting and jerking in her bonds and breathing heavily once
again. Her reset time was apparently quite short.

Setting down the cup of coffee he had prepared for her,
Howard turned back to attend to Phyllis. This time, however, his approach was more leisurely. He was feeling
somewhat constrained by his own recovery time. Therefore
he engaged in more extended foreplay. Pushing aside her
blouse and bra, Howard began to stroke Phyllis' bare
breasts with one hand while the other made its way down
between her legs. Phyllis responded to this new attack
much as she had to the earlier one. Not to put too fine a
point on it, she was wildly aroused once again. Howard
prolonged the preliminaries until he was once more erect.
This time she came at once. And kept on coming, the

189

whole act being accompanied by the most extravagant gyrations.

When it was all over for both of them, Howard untied Phyllis and went to make her another cup of coffee. The first one had gone cold, unnoticed on the bureau, during the second act. This time he was a bit quicker, having found what he needed on the first foray. When he got back to the bedroom, Phyllis accepted the cup and focused her attention on it. She made no attempt to pull her clothes together, nor did she say anything more than a low 'thank you.' It could have referred to the coffee or the earlier gymnastics.

Howard didn't have much to say either beyond a polite 'are you all right?'

Phyllis nodded but said no more. They were after all strangers to one another and both felt constrained by the circumstances of their meeting and their coupling. Now that it was over, Phyllis seemed both satisfied and embarrassed. Howard judged that it was time to leave. He told her that he had her phone number and would call when he got home to see if she was all right. She nodded. Howard let himself out and went back to his car. When he got home, he told me about the encounter and about Phyllis' behaviour. I thought it would be rather interesting to meet er, but the chance never came until we encountered her on our outing. I still don't know what she was doing in that area. Did Howard mention our coming trip to her at their last meeting? He could have done. He was not averse to a *menage à trois*, as I well knew.

As may be, we were on our way back to the cottage when we both noticed the blonde woman standing beside her car with the bonnet up. No prizes for guessing who it was. I recognised Phyllis from the newspaper photos. Howard slowed and stopped. She *was* rather attractive, I thought with a slight stab of jealousy. Longish fair hair and a tiny waist that emphasised two other dimensions that didn't need emphasis. Long legs and ankles rather better turned than my own. She recognised Howard of course, but she couldn't very well say so in front of me. We had not been introduced, and in the awkward silence I thought about the toast concerning wives and girl friends.

Howard performed the introductions and when we had been formally acquainted he gave me a 'should we?' glance. I could think of no reason not to. In any case, I was curious to learn more about the competition. Knowledge is power. I nodded. Imperceptibly, I hoped.

Howard grinned at me and turned back to Phyllis. 'Get the rope from your car,' he ordered her.

She seemed dismayed by the abruptness of his approach. She hesitated and sent a questioning look in my direction.

'Get it,' Howard repeated. To me he added, 'You keep a lookout.'

With a shrug Phyllis opened the boot of the car and got out a carrier bag full of rope. While I glanced nervously up and down the lane Howard was busy tying her hands together behind her back. Anyone coming upon us at that moment would naturally assume that an abduction (at least) was in progress. Awkward inquiries would surely follow. But I couldn't help noticing when Howard raised her skirt and took her pants down. She was a natural blonde, I noted. He used her pants and a scarf to gag her.

'Get into the boot,' Howard ordered Phyllis. Awkwardly, helped by Howard, she did so. He arranged her in the space and used more rope to tie her ankles. He bent her legs at the knees and tied her wrists and ankles together. When she was secured, he closed the boot lid, locking our captive inside.

'Follow me back in our car,' Howard said to me. He got into Phyllis' car as I went back to ours. As we set off I thought it was appropriate and exciting that Phyllis was being transported to her fate in her own 'hijacked' car. We arrived at the cottage without further incident. Howard made no move to get Phyllis out of the car. In response to my silent question he remarked that he wanted to let her stew a bit.

I retorted that she would indeed 'stew a bit' if she were left in the boot with the car standing out in the sun.

'You're right,' agreed Howard. 'I think the stewing will

have to be a bit less literal. I want her to have some time to wonder what we're going to do with her and to get a bit more anxious. I think I'll drive her about a bit so that she's really disoriented before bringing her back here. Get me another scarf from your things if you don't mind so I can blindfold her. While you're getting that I'll open the boot and give her a bit of air before we turn out the lights.'

I went to get the scarves and Howard went to inspect Phyllis. When I returned he had the boot lid open and was looking inside. I felt another little stab of alarm: what if he preferred the competition to me? But I said nothing. He took the scarves and blindfolded Phyllis. She was lying mainly as we had left her, but I thought she had struggled against her bonds because her wrists and ankles were rubbed and red and her skirt was rucked up above the tops of her stockings. Howard arranged a blanket for her to lie on and rolled up her coat as a pillow before closing the boot lid once again.

'Want to come along for the ride?' Howard asked me. 'Or I could leave you tied up here while we're away.'

Was there the least bit of reluctance on Howard's part when he asked me to come along? I concluded that there were some things I didn't want to know. And the second alternative seemed equally attractive. I'm so predictable. We went inside and I led the way into the bedroom. I lay face down on the bed as Howard tied my hands behind my back. He tied my ankles and knees with more of Phyllis' rope and bent my knees as he had hers so that he could tie my wrists and ankles together with a short length of rope. He gagged and blindfolded me as he had Phyllis. When he was done he left me lying on the bed. I heaved myself over onto my side and waited for developments. There were muffled noises as Howard moved about the house and the room. Then he came for me. He lifted me and carried me to the closet, where he laid me on the floor. He had arranged a blanket or quilt for me to lie on, and had provided a pillow for my head. Before leaving he pulled my skirt up to my waist and gave me a thorough fondling. Just to be getting on with, he said. Then he closed the door and

I heard the key turn in the lock. There was the sound of receding footsteps. A door opened and closed. The car started up and drove away and I was alone and helpless in an isolated house. Little prickles of excitement ran through me.

I wriggled a bit to settle myself more comfortably and to test the ropes that held me. No slack there. I had no way of predicting how long I might be locked up in that closet. As usual, I felt a short stab of fear at being helpless and abandoned. There was also the chance that Howard might have an accident and be unable to release me. And there was always the chance of an accident which left Howard unscathed but resulted in the discovery of Phyllis tied up in the boot of her car. There might well be another of those 'Beautiful Blonde Bound in Car' stories to titillate the locals. Very awkward. Such thoughts add their own piquancy to our bondage scenarios.

I exercised my active imagination by putting myself in Phyllis' place, helped by the fact that Howard had left me in a similar situation. We were both bound and gagged and locked in a small space. A small shiver of sympathy and anticipation ran through me. The occasional draught that found its way into the closet and chilled my bared thighs caused a different sort of shiver. To my sharpened hearing each creak and rustle in the empty house sounded preternaturally loud. There were no traffic or city noises to break the silence in which I lay. I was alone and quite defenceless and for a time I jumped at every sound.

I appreciated anew Phyllis' fantasy. Even as I lay in the closet she was being driven to an unknown destination by her abductor. Though she probably had a good idea of what was going to happen (after all, this was not her first meeting with Howard), she could not know any of the details of how, when or where. She was completely in the power of another; one of the nicest things about bondage games, at least for me.

Thus between drowsing and fantasising I passed the time until the noise of a car being driven up brought me fully awake with a renewed fear and relief. It had to be Howard,

I thought. But hard on the heels of that thought came the reflection that it might not be. It could be the kind of intruder that Phyllis dreamed of. The cottage was isolated and might thereby attract a thief. Although we had seen no one lurking about, there was no guarantee that there wasn't someone casing the joint as they used to say in the American gangster movies. I began to feel very vulnerable – the price one pays for an active imagination.

I heard footsteps on the gravel drive, coming closer. I lay quite still, listening for some clue as to the identity of my visitor. The door opened and closed again. The footsteps came nearer, and then receded again, as if someone were exploring the house. Was it an intruder, or just Howard playing cat-and-mouse with me? He is quite good at that. I tensed again as the footsteps came into the bedroom and approached the closet. There they stopped. What to do? Should I lie still, or make frantic muffled noises through my gag and drum my heels on the floor? Better lie quietly, I concluded. Wait for developments. I had no way to guess who it was or what he (or she) would do. My active imagination supplied several scenarios based on the discovery of an attractive woman (though I say it myself) bound and gagged in a deserted house far from the listening crowd. Think positive, I always say.

I heard the key turn in the lock and felt a stronger draught as the door was opened. The question of what to do was resolved when I felt hands rolling me over onto my stomach. I assumed that Howard had come back for me, but I was not completely sure it was him. Whoever it was untied the tope connecting my wrists and ankles and then untied my legs. Leaving my hands tied, he helped me to my feet and led me out of the closet and over to the bed, where he sat me down. He unbuttoned my blouse and pushed it as far down my arms as it would go. My bra went next, then my skirt and petticoat melted away. Except for my stockings and suspenders, I was nude under the gaze of my tame intruder. Delicious, but there was more to come.

I was by now almost sure that my tame intruder was Howard. After all, there are certain stylistic details that a girl gets to know very well. But there was just enough uncertainty to increase the tingle factor. Anyway, I'll call him Howard. He pushed me over backwards and drew my legs up, bending my knees and crossing my ankles, which he again tied together. He brought the tail-end of the rope from my bound wrists down under me and tied it to my ankles. When he was done, he arranged me artistically on my back with my thighs spread wide and everything on display. Served up on a plate, if you like. It didn't take too much imagination to guess what was coming. Me, I hoped. But I wouldn't mind if Howard joined me.

His hands did, at any rate, stroking the insides of my thighs as they ascended to the centre of things. The hands were joined by a mouth that planted warm moist kisses on my belly and breasts. After only a few minutes I was purring, arching my back like a cat that was being rubbed the right way. He continued and so did I. The excitement had been building the whole time I was alone in the closet, so it didn't require much more foreplay to arouse me fully. So far as my limited freedom of movement permitted, I began to thrust against the hands, trying to increase the sensations they brought to my relevant areas. Less delicately, you could say that I was close to bursting point and was heaving and thrusting against the hands that roamed over my naked and helpless bod. Up and down they went, while I went mainly up sky-rocket fashion.

The entry, when it came, was most welcome. The bucking and heaving and groaning became more frenzied. From what I could feel and hear, Howard was enjoying himself too. Up until the moment he entered me, I could not be absolutely sure that my intruder was a man. Harriet was quite capable of doing what he had done so far, and would have enjoyed the work. It was right up her alley. But I could tell from what was right up *my* alley that it wasn't Harriet. I came repeatedly, jerking at my ropes and generally playing the role of the captive female to the hilt. Howard was playing the captor to the hilt as well. Byron was quite wrong about the sword outwearing the sheath. With me (and a lot of other women if we are to believe the recent surveys of sexual behaviour) it is usually the other way round. I was almost indecently sated by the time Howard reached the point of no return and suffered withdrawal symptoms; but I was not worn out.

Howard left me on the bed and went away to do whatever he does when I'm tied up. I settled down to recover and imagine what else he would do to me. As it turned out, I had less time to wait than I had anticipated. But what was being done was not being done to me. Shortly after Howard left I heard two sets of footsteps and the sound of the door opening. There was a muffled 'Nnnnngggghh' as Phyllis – it couldn't be anyone else – caught sight of me. Howard had obviously brought her back to our rented cottage and kept her on ice. It was gallant of him to do me while his other captive waited her turn. She may have been kept in the next room, hearing what was being done to me and knowing that she was next. I wondered what effect my presence would have on Phyllis' fantasy.

I knew that her presence was having a reviving effect on my own fantasy. I felt a stirring of the familiar excitement as she was led into the room. Apparently Howard wanted her to know that there were other women who enjoyed being tied up during sex. He parked Phyllis somewhere nearby before coming over to remove my blindfold. After such a long period in darkness, my eyes were dazzled by the sudden light. When I could see clearly again, I saw that her hands were still tied behind her back and she was wearing a bright all-over pink blush. Very becoming. We nodded at one another. Even in those bizarre circumstances we still observed the civilities.

The introductions over, Howard led Phyllis over to the dressing table and backed her up against it. Her bottom rested against the edge and propped her up as Howard got busy with the second part of the programme. He knelt in front of her and spread her legs. She didn't resist. I wouldn't have either in her place. When he buried his face between her thighs, I knew from my own experience what he was doing. Phyllis shuddered at the first contact and her rosy hue deepened. Her knees sagged ever so slightly and she moved her hips so as to offer herself more openly to Howard's busy lips and tongue. She must have been aroused by the hours she had spent as Howard's captive and had had plenty of time to imagine what he was going to do. Phyllis began to moan softly. Her nostrils flared widely as she fought for breath and her shoulders shook as she became more and more aroused. Howard's tongue was apparently right on target. From the way her arm muscles flexed I guessed that she was tugging against the ropes that bound her wrists behind her arched back. Had she been able to free her hands, I am sure they would have flown like released birds to hold Howard more tightly against her centre.

Phyllis had probably forgotten I was there. She was lost deep in her own pleasures. But I hadn't forgotten myself. The sight of Phyllis going through her paces had the usual effect on me. I was feeling warm between the legs and was doing my own writhing on the bed as I watched Howard and Phyllis. She was by now completely out of control, thrusting with her hips and rolling them from side to side. Howard was holding her firmly by the bottom to keep himself from being flung off by the wild motion. Her moaning was almost continuous and her breath rasping in her nose. Then she stiffened and began to jerk wildly in Howard's grasp. This, I judged, was the moment of truth. Or one of them. If the earth didn't move for her, it was because she was already moving so much herself. Any more motion would have been superfluous. Howard had said that she was a screamer. I could see – or rather hear – why. The amount of noise which was getting past her gag was impressive. I wondered where she found the breath.

Phyllis was not the type to pass out, but her knees did sag noticeably as she came. Howard was supporting her and he lowered her gently to the floor. They finished up with him lying on the floor and Phyllis kneeling astride. She began to cooperate wholeheartedly when she saw that Howard was guiding her down onto his erection. When things were lined up she impaled herself eagerly on the member for South Howard. The effect was entertaining if

197

you happen to be a voyeur, which in part I am. It was also exciting if you enjoy sex yourself, which I do. And quite frustrating if you are tied up on the sidelines, as I was. I had to content myself with watching the gymnastics.

Phyllis stiffened as she sank home, and then began to move vigorously up and down on the sword between her legs. She occasionally lost her balance and had to be steadied by Howard, who was clearly enjoying himself as well. A little too clearly, I thought from my position on the sidelines. I could use a bit of attention myself. It's too bad that they haven't worked out a satisfactory way to deal with two women simultaneously. Phyllis meanwhile continued her steady rise and fall, becoming more and more frenzied. She was making that steady moaning sound I had noticed earlier, almost a hum, rising in pitch as she approached another climax. Howard was cupping her bobbing breasts and teasing the erect nipples. Occasionally one hand or the other would stray down her rib cage to stroke her belly when she rose on the up-stroke. Her own hands were white with strain as she struggled against the ropes that bound her.

Her swoops subsided as Phyllis bore down on the cock inside her. She sat bolt upright astride Howard and squeezed her eyes shut. She appeared to be holding herself in a tight bundle, the better to enjoy the sensations spreading from her belly. Then there was a series of muffled shrieks as she came. Phyllis sagged in Howard's arms and he eased her torso down until she was lying atop him. She shuddered occasionally while recovering her equilibrium. What the seismologists call after-shocks. I wondered what her climax would have registered on a sexual Richter scale. Howard held her against his chest as she came down from the heights of ecstasy, as they say in the purple prose department downstairs. When she was breathing more normally, he rolled over and eased her to the floor. I didn't know if Howard himself had reached his climax or if he was still recovering from his encounter with me. I liked that idea and wriggled with pleasure.

'Contain yourself,' Howard said. 'I'll be back for you

soon enough. In the meantime I'll leave you two to get acquainted.'

'Mmmmmff?' I said through my gag.

'I'm coming to that. Hang on a moment.' He bent over Phyllis and untied her gag. She pushed the gag out and croaked, 'Water.' Howard nodded and helped her to her feet. He steadied her into the loo. There were peeing noises, flushing sounds and swallowing gurgles. Presently they emerged and Howard led her to a chair near the bed. He waited while she found a comfortable seat before tying her ankles together – to prevent the patter of tiny feet, he said.

Howard came over to me and removed my gag. Then he left us alone to get acquainted. To begin with, Phyllis maintained an embarrassed silence, due partly to the fact that Howard and I were a couple and she was the third side to the triangle. I pointed out that I had witnessed her dramatic performance and that there wasn't much of a secret about what had happened. When it became apparent that I was neither jealous nor angry, she opened up a bit.

In the course of the subsequent talk it emerged that Phyllis viewed bondage solely as an adjunct to sex. The necessary foreplay which would allow her to enjoy her rape fantasy. She seemed quite single-minded in her approach to sex. She didn't seek bondage situations for the thrill of being tied up or (as in my case) being left helpless for indefinite periods of time. I enjoy the uncertainty and the absolute freedom from responsibility almost as much as I enjoy the sex that almost always follows. I didn't try to change Phyllis' orientation or preferences. She seemed quite happy with her fantasies, and that is rare enough to keep me from meddling. I merely suggested that she might exploit the uncertainty factor for greater pleasure.

The conversation was full of uncertain pauses. Conventional attitudes certainly had much to do with that. She probably thought I was secretly angry because Howard had had her right in front of me. Most women would have felt very threatened by the knowledge that their man had another sexual partner. I told her that I was aware of Howard's encounters with her and other women, and mentioned that I had done similar things, but she was still a bit uptight.

Phyllis admitted that she was obscurely ashamed and embarrassed by her fantasies, and I guessed that she was suffering from the conventional attitude toward sex: if it's fun it's bound to be sinful. I think she used the bondage and rape fantasy as a means of avoiding the guilt many of us are made to feel about our sexual drives. If I'm tied up and raped, the argument goes, I can't be responsible for or guilty about what happens. Of course that argument is full of holes. If you're not responsible or guilty, by the same token you're not supposed to enjoy the experience. And you should certainly not put yourself into the kind of situations that could lead to abduction and rape. But the mind has ways of disguising things we'd rather not face. Phyllis had found a way to deal with her hang-ups which itself made her feel embarrassed; but she had no intention of abandoning her practices.

These are just guesses on my part. I'm not a psychiatrist, nor did I have any desire to explore the fantasy with an eye to making her more 'normal'. I am well aware that my own fantasies are not 'normal', but I enjoy them too much to give them up. Nor would I be justified in trying to talk someone else out of something they enjoyed. Pots and kettles, you know. If I'm crazy, I don't want to be 'sane'. But if I insist on going ahead with what I like, I become a threat to the rest of the people who believe that their own attitude toward sex is the only correct one. So I keep it dark. They once hanged witches in this green and pleasant land, you know!

I can think of yet another reason for Phyllis' reticence. She had realised her fantasy in a most satisfactory manner and must have found her continued helplessness irksome. She probably wanted to leave the scene of the crime as unobtrusively as possible until the next time. On the other hand I was still enjoying my fantasy and was in no hurry to be untied. Phyllis' fantasy depends on being abducted by a stranger. It does not include talking to him (or her) afterwards. That's how strangers become acquaintances, and then friends. If she stayed on Howard would have to come into the conversation and his value as a 'stranger' would be lost. So I was glad that Howard came back before the silences got too awkward. He untied Phyllis and she fled to get dressed. Howard left me tied up while he went to make his farewells.

When he came back he set about me once more – which was just what I had been hoping for. He isn't a superman and so his attentions were mainly limited to what his hands and mouth could do for me. I was not disappointed. I had been warming through while he did Phyllis and was glad of the opportunity to let off steam. When I came back to the present, Howard untied me and went out to make some coffee and sandwiches. I spent the time refreshing myself in the loo and was waiting in bed for him when he came back. We watched the telly for a while and then drifted off to sleep, tired out by the day's activities.

8

BICYCLES AND HORSES

Helen likes to do her thing outdoors. She is into bicycling and horseback riding and has taken her taste for sex and bondage into her sport. Even so, I have to take partial credit for one of the ideas which Helen developed and used extensively for her own pleasure.

When I spent the weekend at *Schloss* Harriet, I had witnessed Janet's encounter with the exercise bike. I thought that the idea could be adapted to an ordinary bike and might provide some interesting rural rides (though not of the type William Cobbett had taken). Helen is not into electric shock therapy, so it wasn't necessary to do anything drastic to the bicycle to make it fit for what she wanted to do. Basically it was only necessary to modify the seat.

I got the original idea from a trashy and utterly fantastic story about an American motorcycle gang's bizarre method of discipline for their women who stepped out of line. Leave it to the Yanks to run a good idea ragged. Whenever there was an infraction (by one of their women, of course) of one of the obscure rules which govern the behaviour of bikers, a member of the gang would set about preparing a special punishment bike. This consisted primarily of fixing a dildo of suitable proportions to the seat of the motorbike. The offending female was set astride the contrivance and, suitably penetrated, would have her hands and feet chained to the bike so that she could ride naked as Godiva through the Californian night to her death.

The victim would then be herded by the others at high speed down a coastal highway, going out of her mind (we are told) with pleasure from the vibrating spike inside her. As they approached the chosen spot the outriders would lash her onwards, braking at the last moment as she drove over a sheer cliff into the ocean. The writer depicted her going to her watery grave chained to the throbbing motorcycle and still experiencing her monster orgasm, shrieking in ecstasy as she plunged into the depths. That's how they treat love and death in the American novel. The gang would then ride back to their den suitably chastened and uplifted, where the mechanic would set about preparing another bike for the next offender. We are assured that she was already contemplating how she could break the rules so as to reap the reward. As I said, utter trash, and a sheer waste of bikes and broads, as the Yanks say. We planned to be more conservative in both.

I presented the idea to Helen and James and they set about realising it. James bought an extra seat for Helen's bicycle and fixed a suitable horn to it. He thought it would be easier to put the new, modified seat in place whenever the fancy took them. It simply wouldn't do to leave the rampant seat in place all the time. It might frighten the horses or alert the vigilant gendarmerie. The original seat was saved for ordinary outings. Waste not, want not. Like most new ideas, it didn't work out the first time. In fact there were several trials. Helen and I alternated as guinea pigs in these scientific experiments in a noble spirit of self-sacrifice. The whole point of experiments is their repeatability – a principle applicable to scientific as well as sexual experiments. We didn't want to run a destruction test as the American bikers in the story did. If they didn't mind using up bikes and women, we had to be more sparing of both. But *autres payes, autres moeurs*. And they have more of everything.

Part of the equipment James prepared was a waist belt for attaching the rider to the bicycle. It went on under the clothing and was fastened to the seat with short chains so as to keep rider and steed from parting company. The rider would have to wear a full, rather than a tight, skirt so that it could be raised when seated. That would allow bare bottom to meet bare seat and lend all sorts of erotic overtones to the affair. And, incidentally, would serve to conceal the connections between rider and bicycle. Another requirement that became apparent early on was that the rider wore no tights unless they were of the crotchless kind. Stockings and suspenders were all right if you wanted to be provocative and provoking.

A final requirement was some sort of mounting block so that the rider could get into the saddle and get the saddle into her. The height of the seat could be adjusted to suit the individual and allow her to come to a stop in the usual manner by resting one foot or the other on the ground. However, she could not dismount, and it would be as well not to fall over. But all mechanical contrivances have their limitations. We just do the best we can!

If all this sounds terribly strained and artificial, the same could be said for almost all the other things I have been describing at such length. Pleasure, no matter how you take it, is almost always carefully prepared. There are rare instances where everything comes together as if by chance and the world moves for you. But it doesn't always happen, and so you have to have something else up your – er – sleeve. Our games require careful preparation, but the preparation is part of the game and part of the pleasure. If this preparation still sounds like too much trouble, there is no compulsion involved. Being a bondage freak doesn't mean you have to like all sorts of bondage games or even try out all the things I have been speaking about. I am telling my own story in the form of a menu, and plain fare is one of the choices on offer to those who prefer it. The important thing is that you get a choice.

For the trial run Howard and I made a foursome with Helen and James. We met at Janet's place because their property is large enough to ensure a certain degree of privacy. In addition their barn would be a handy place to get the bike and rider ready for the cycling party. Janet and Bill were going to be away that day, but they didn't mind if we used the place as a staging area. 'Just don't do anything scandalous while we're out. I'd hate to miss it,' Janet said when we told her of our plan. We promised to be discreet and to give her a full report when next we met.

We arrived a few minutes before the other two so we had time to get our bicycles sorted out. I had brought along a picnic hamper in case the day stayed fine. If all went well, Helen at least would have a hearty appetite. When she arrived, Helen was looking flushed and excited. I was a bit excited too. This was mainly my idea and I wanted to see it road-tested. James and Howard unloaded their bikes and put Helen's over against the mounting block. The ordinary seat was in place but James brought the modified one from the car and set about making the change while I helped Helen get into her waist belt. She was wearing a full skirt which she raised above her waist so I could fasten the belt on her. She took off her pants after the belt was locked around her waist. The short chains dangled front and rear.

James had finished fitting the rampant seat to the bike and it was time to mount up. The dildo jutted up quite aggressively. Helen got up onto the mounting block and positioned herself above it. James helped guide her down onto the spike and she slid home with a small sigh. Once again Helen raised her skirt so that the chains could be fastened to the seat. She was arranged artistically on the seat with her bottom divided and slightly pendulous. We could see the shaft on which she was impaled. Its base was fixed to the seat and the shaft was just visible among her pubic hair before it disappeared up inside her. James fastened the chains to the rings on the seat. 'Lift up a bit if you don't mind, Helen,' he directed.

She obligingly lifted herself from the seat until the chains came taut. The dildo slid part way out and then back in again as she sat down with another sigh. Helen's face was flushed and her breath gave a catch now and again. She was ready for action.

James lowered her skirt and said, 'That'll do you, I think. As you were.' Helen wriggled a bit on the seat as she settled herself. In his best Texas trail boss accent he said to us, 'If you all want to mount up we'll head 'em up and move 'em out. We'll form up behind the lead heifer so's we can see what she does.'

Because she looked set to have the most fun on the ride, and because her bicycle had a carrier, Helen got to look after the picnic basket. It was sunny and cool as we set off with Helen in the lead. She would set the pace. James had mounted a speedometer on the handlebars of her bike so that she could see for herself what speed gave the best results. He joked about marking the dial in orgasms per mile, but he said it would take some time to gather enough data to mark it correctly. Helen replied that she would be glad to cooperate, which suggested that she was already enjoying herself. If nothing else she was the centre of everyone's attention. Not bad for anyone's ego.

There was very little traffic using the farm track we were on. In the green hedgerows along both sides the birds were nesting and singing. A flock of starlings was following a plough to squabble over whatever insects it turned up. It was all very peaceful and very English. But Helen didn't seem to be taking very much interest in the scenery. She was pedalling at a brisk pace and seemed to be enjoying the ride. We kept up as best we could. I reflected that she was having all the fun. We were only getting marginally fitter.

For a moment, watching Helen's flushed face and pumping legs, I thought of the tale of the motorcycle gang. I imagined her going on and on until she dropped. And I began to feel a little bit of excitement myself. Therein lies the appeal of those sex-and-violence stories. The interweaving of sexual arousal and death lies somewhere deep in all of us. Deeper in some than in others. It's probably no accident that the French call extreme sexual orgasm *le petit mort*. They would have us believe that they are the only ones capable of such transports of delight despite being a largely Roman Catholic country. We northern Protestants are not allowed such fun, more's the pity. A little ecstasy between the legs is good for what ails you, in spite of what churches and theologians say. But there – I'm preaching again. A bad habit. Back to Helen and the great bike ride.

The leafy hedgerows were flashing by at a good rate but Helen didn't notice that. She was concentrating on what was happening between her legs. The full skirt had lifted in the breeze and there were those occasional glimpses of stocking tops and bare thighs that are the reward of those who like to watch ladies on bicycles. She didn't try to spoil the effect by steering with one hand and holding her skirt with the other. No spoil-sport, she. Or maybe she was just too busy with other things to notice. From the outward signs, our invention looked like being a success. Helen was clearly teetering on the brink of her climax. And when she fell over the edge there were little gasps and squirmings that told us she had.

But our Helen is nothing if not game. She stoically kept on pedalling because we had not yet come to a suitable picnic place. Of course she was not even considering a re-peat performance. She did slow down for a bit to catch her breath. She even tried to make some bright but totally dis-jointed remarks about the lovely day and the lambs in the fields, tra la. But her thoughts were clearly somewhere else. You could say she was miles away, but she wasn't. Her attention was once again concentrated on the centre of things. It wasn't too long before she was showing signs of warming up once again. I began to wonder if we would have to go on and on, passing every picnic place because Helen was in the throes of yet another orgasm. It *would* be cruel to stop her for something as mundane as lunch. When she came there were some quite indecorous gasps and shudders. She managed to keep her eyes open and to retain control of the bike. That was just as well. A crash isn't the best way to end a lovely experience.

James must have thought that it was time for Helen to have a rest. Or maybe he was just getting hungry. At any rate, he caught up with her and asked her to slow down so that we could find a place to stop. We had ridden some four or five miles by then – most of it uphill for Helen. She had reached some lovely peaks on the way, but a rest wouldn't do her any harm. So she slowed down and we kept our eyes open for a likely spot for a picnic. She showed a marked tendency to squirm on her seat even at slow speed. I wondered whether she was trying to find a more pleasant position, or merely a more comfortable one.

After another half mile or so we came to a shady spot by the roadside and pulled over. There was a good cover in the trees and we found a suitably sylvan (and secluded) glade in which to rest. Howard and I kept look-out against the chance pedestrian or car while James got Helen unfastened from her bike. After he had raised her skirt to unlock the short chains, he rested his hands on her thighs and she leaned forward to give him a long thorough kiss. Her way of saying thank you for a lovely ride, I guess. I can think of worse ways. We averted our eyes decently.

When they had untangled themselves, James lifted Helen off the seat and set her on her feet. She seemed a bit wobbly for reasons left as an exercise for the class. It wouldn't do to leave Helen's bicycle in plain sight with that aggressive looking saddle horn in place. James laid it on the ground and laid his jumper over the more *outré* bits. He laid his own bike atop hers and we laid ours close by for added camouflage. I took charge of the picnic basket and Howard spread the blanket for us. Helen was wearing a happy smile as she helped me to lay out the picnic things. She tipped me a broad wink and said, 'You'll like it a lot. I did.'

'I can see that,' I replied. 'I'm looking forward to my turn. I'll let you know how it goes. Bon appetit.'

Conversation, at first desultory, gradually became easier as we ate the sandwiches and drank the wine. The obligatory ants arrived as we were into the cold potato salad. Over a second bottle of wine we lazed about for an amiable hour. I can see why the siesta is so popular in less hectic lands. As I drowsed, I was turning over in my mind the coming ride. Helen had enjoyed her turn. Soon I would see for myself how my idea had worked out. No amount of food and drink and lazy talk could drive that idea out of my mind. By the merest chance, you understand, I had chosen a full skirt over stockings and suspenders for our outing. Always prepared, that's me.

But no one else was ready for another hour or so. The shadows lengthened toward mid-afternoon before James stirred himself. He asked Helen to stand up so that he could remove her waist belt. As he raised her skirt to unlock the belt she joked, 'Avert your eyes for a moment. I'm really a very modest woman.' You could have fooled me, but Howard and I got busy clearing up the debris of the picnic. While I repacked the basket he went over to the pile of bikes and extricated Helen's. He wheeled it over to a handy rock so that I could use it as a mounting block. James came over to me with the belt he had taken off Helen. And suddenly it was time for the main event. I raised my skirt so that James could lock the belt around my waist.

He guided me down to a soft landing while Howard steadied the bike by holding the handlebars. The chains were fastened to the seat and I wriggled a bit to find the best position. To lighten the atmosphere I put on my damsel in distress persona as they secured me to the seat. Turning to Helen, I said, 'Oh, save me! These two villains will have their lustful way with me unless you remonstrate with them.' I clasped my hands and rolled my eyes heavenwards. 'They intend to strap me to their evil machine and then gloat as I writhe in helpless ecstasy – er – distress.'

James picked it up at once. 'Siddown like a good goil, sister. Dis won't hoit so bad if ya kinda – uh – cooperate. Yeah, cooperate. Dat's a good woid, ain't it? I like long woids.' It sounded as if words with more than three letters counted as long words – woids!

Howard smiled as he continued to hold the bike upright. I could tell from the bulge in his trousers that he was upright too. He enjoys my purple prose. He calls it my 'hysterionics'.

Helen joined in. 'Yes. Sit down as he says. Trust me, you'll love it.'

'How can you say these vile things to me? How can you watch as he treats me so rudely and makes these immodest

suggestions to me? I thought you were my friend. I thought
. . . Oh God! He's forcing me onto that horrid horn. Help!
Help! Oh, help!'

James growled, 'Hey, I like dose long woids she uses:
"immodest suggestions". Only dey ain't suggestions, lady.
So siddown an' shuddup unless ya want to git hoit. Yeah,
a real lady. It's too bad we got to do dese things to ya, but
orders is orders. A waste. I coulda put her to better use.'

'Oh, how horrid!' I wailed. 'I would far rather suffer the
worst your beastly machine can do to me than submit to
your base desires. Is there no one among you with a shred
of decency? Why must you treat a helpless woman so cruelly? Save me,' I implored of the trees in general.

My pleas did not go unanswered. A man dressed in farm
labourer's clothing strode out of the woods into the clearing. I judged him to be in his early twenties, and wearing
an expression in which bravado and consternation struggled for supremacy. He was carrying a pitchfork in an aggressive manner as he advanced towards us. I had seen him
first because he had emerged nearly opposite me while the
others had their backs to him. I sank down quickly on the
impaling horn and twitched my skirt down to cover it. I
was still showing a lot of leg (which he eyed both nervously
and with appreciation), but I couldn't help that now. My
sudden subsidence caught Howard by surprise but he
caught my weight and held the bike steady. I was about to
whisper a warning to him when young Lochinvar made
that unnecessary.

''Ere, you lot. What are you doing to that lady? I heard
her askin' for help and I come on you three actin' roight
suspicious like. You just let her go or I'll be callin' the
police. I've a mind to call them anyway.'

The others were surprised, but Howard rose to the occasion quickly. Turning to the man, he asked (with every
appearance of curiosity and interest), 'Did it really sound
that good? We were hoping to work on the rape scene a
few more times before opening night. Tell us how it looked
to you.'

The young man added a look of bewilderment to the

other two fighting for possession of his face. Clearly, things had taken an unexpected turn.

'Did we sound convincing when you heard us?' I asked, muddying the waters still further. To hear the ostensible victim speak about sounding convincing gave him pause. I continued, 'You see, we're putting on a play in a couple of weeks' time and were using the clearing to rehearse one of the scenes.'

'A play? You mean one o' those things where folk get all dressed up, like, on a stage?'

'Yes,' I replied.

'Oh. Well,' said he. 'I don't know about convincing. I heard something about horns and bodies that sounded queer and dangerous to me. What kind of play is it then?'

'It's a melodrama', James replied.

'A mellow what?'

'A melodrama,' James repeated. 'Our play pokes fun at an earlier set of ideas and style of acting. It's about the Greek myth of Europa and the bull.'

'Is that the one about the Spanish bullfighter?' he asked.

'No, I think that's *Carmen*,' I explained. 'The story we are dealing with has to do with a woman called Europa who is carried off and raped by a bull.'

'What'd she want with a bull?' he demanded incredulously. 'That'd be dangerous, that would. Most bulls ain't good company. And wouldn't that be too heavy for her? Have you ever seen a bull mount a heifer?'

'Not if it were a feminist bull and he let her get on top,' Howard interjected lightly.

'Feminist bull?' There ain't no such thing. Bulls is all male. Don't you know nothin' about animals?' he asked scornfully. 'And besides, it wouldn't be natural, like, a bull and a woman fu – I mean, doin' that,' he finished lamely.

'I was only joking,' Howard said. 'Anyway, it's only a story.'

'Well, it ain't the kind of story we country folk tell. 'Tain't decent. We don't hold with mixin' people with animals. 'Tain't natural, like I said. And this woman, what's her name? Europe? Sounds foreign to me. They get up to

211

funny things in foreign parts. Let 'em get on with it and not trouble us, I say.'

'Ah, to be in Scotland, where men are men and all the sheep are nervous,' Howard put in.

'We're decent folk around 'ere, so don't you go making your bad jokes. We don't need those animal sex and animal rights people comin' around.' He had gone red in the face and was brandishing the pitchfork menacingly in Howard's direction.

Howard let go of the handlebars and raised his hands in mock surrender. Good job I was self-supporting or I'd have gone down and done myself an injury. Or fallen off the horn of my internal dilemma and given the game away. To defuse the situation I hastily spoke up. 'We weren't actually planning to use a bull on the stage. As you said, that would be too dangerous. We thought we'd use a bicycle like this one to represent the bull. If you loosen the handlebars and swing them around so that they point forward, they resemble a bull's horns. Anyway, you needn't worry about me. I'm not in any danger. But thank you for coming. Not too many people nowadays would have.'

'Well,' he said doubtfully, 'if you're sure you're all right then, I'll be off. But you folks be careful with play-actin' in public. Maybe I'll come see your play if you come this way.' He was eyeing my legs as he backed away and he had doubtless put me down in the class of scarlet (though interesting) women: actresses and such.

'I'd be pleased if you did,' I said. 'Goodbye.'

He moved off and the other three began to grin like idiots. 'Don't start laughing, for heaven's sake,' I warned. 'Our rustic hero might be listening from the shelter of the sylvan shade. He might hear you and get angry. Good job he didn't ask where we were playing. Still, it *was* nice of him to come to my rescue. But now I am in the hands of fiends again. Do your worst.'

I waited on my bike as the others finished gathering up the rest of the picnic things. It was getting towards late afternoon and we had about two hours' ride before we got back to Janet's place. Eventually the others got on their bikes and we started off homewards. I noticed immediately a vital difference between my bike and an ordinary one: I was feeling each bump and irregularity in the road much more acutely than I normally did. On we rode as I waited for the rising tide of ecstasy to wash over me. I tried squirming about on the seat and felt some agreeable sensations from between my legs, but the world refused to move. If nothing else I wanted to give my invention a thorough road test before turning it loose on an eager public, so I pedalled a bit faster as Helen had done and felt the increased juddering of the seat both inside me and against my bottom. It was pleasant enough but hardly overwhelming.

Where Helen had enjoyed the ride thoroughly, I found myself waiting for something which never happened. I think I know why. Helen's fantasy seems to be based mainly on doing her thing outdoors. She is aroused by penetration to a much greater degree than I am, and she is aroused by the risks in arranging to have sex in places where others are more or less likely to go. She enjoys bondage most when she is outside. On the other hand, I am mainly interested in bondage, whether indoors or not. Most of my activities occur indoors because I like long sessions where privacy is essential. There was not enough of the bondage element in our experiment to feed my fantasy. Gag me, tie my hands and feet and plug me with a vibrator and I'll go off like a bomb. But there just wasn't enough restraint in those two chains to make me feel helpless.

When we got back to Janet's place she was waiting for us with tea and questions. She wanted to know how the experiment had gone. Like me, she is interested in new ways to enjoy the oldest sport. I listened while Helen turned in her report and was struck once again by the differences in our two approaches. The invention was a howling success from her point of view. It takes all kinds. When it was my turn I told Janet why I found the bike less than ideal. Faced with our two different accounts of the experience, Janet was unable to make up her mind about trying her own rural ride. Helen promised to leave the bike (or at least the seat) with her so she could do her own field trials. Janet thought that was a good idea, and we passed to other subjects.

Before we all went home, James arranged with Janet for them to come over next weekend for some other field sports. Janet invited them to come to lunch if they wished. They could set off afterwards. Janet and Helen are both horsy types. Janet likes to ride. Helen to be ridden. She goes for the pony-girl aspect of bondage. She likes it because it lets her combine the two main elements of her fantasy. Because of the acute lack of suitable venues, Helen doesn't get much chance to practise her particular kink. She enjoys pulling James (or anyone else he decrees) in a trap of the kind used in Ireland and America for harness racing. She says that she would like to do a bit of harness racing herself (the thrill of competition, you know), but it is even harder to find competitors than it is to find a secluded stretch of track long enough to stage a race. It isn't the kind of event that would go down well at Ascot. For one thing, Helen doesn't like hats. The Queen would not be amused, nor is it difficult to imagine the reaction of the general public. The rabid feminists would insist on seeing Helen as yet another woman subjugated by those horrid males. It is tempting (continuing the equine metaphor) to imagine them wearing a sort of mental blinkers which allow them to see every encounter between the sexes as an 'Us versus Them' contest. Janet's place offers their best chance of a run, but she does not own miles and miles of land. Mainly Helen has to content herself with a short trot against the clock.

Helen has her own pony-girl outfits which she wears whenever she has a chance to do some horsing around. Like most bondage gear, it is quite revealing – the next best thing to being entirely nude. No sense in hiding your assets, I always say. Both of her outfits use a head harness made of stout leather. The head harness has blinkers and a bit to go between her teeth. The bit also serves as a gag. The reins lead from the ends of the bit back to the driving seat so that James can control her. It is basically the same

214

arrangement one finds on horses, but as horses don't say much as a rule, the bit is just a bit. If the day is cool, or if James fancies it, Helen wears a tight black leather corselet with a waist belt for fastening her to the traces of the cart. With this outfit she generally wears tights, since her relevant areas are covered up anyway. If he wishes, James can add dildoes or vibrators to suit. The crotch strap of the corselet holds them in place.

In more clement weather Helen operates the nude mode. The head harness is retained, but the corselet is replaced by a leather body harness. The harness consists of straps that go over the shoulders and cross between the tits. There is a waist belt with D-rings to fasten her to the traces. Another strap leads between her legs and is taken back to the driver's position as a sort of third rein. This latter strap is normally used to hold a dildo inside her. There is a rubber pad with 'fingers' on it to cover her modestly and massage her gently in a sensitive spot. By pulling on this rein James could drive her wild. The game was sex and speed.

The harness leaves her boobs and buns free to jiggle in an interesting way. As a concession to verisimilitude (of course there was no other motive involved) there is a plume of horsehair which gives Helen a bushy tail. It is attached to a vee-shaped rod, one end being a dildo which goes up her arsehole and the other being the bushy bit. The business end and the hairy end, she calls them. Whenever he wishes to encourage Helen, James can use a whip on her backside.

As I have said, they mainly had to content themselves with a stretch of woodland track on Janet and Bills' property. When it was time for a run, James would convey Helen to the barn in which I had undergone my first encounter with the electric bodysuit. There she would be kitted out in the uniform of the day and harnessed to the cart or sulkey, as I think these lightweight traps are called. Her hands were usually tied behind her back before she was led out to race the clock (there being no regular stable of pony-girls near at hand to provide competition. Like most specialists, Helen finds herself in a class of one.)

On the prearranged day Helen called Janet. She said that

she was feeling horsy. Would Janet mind awfully if . . . 'Of course not,' Janet replied. 'Come right ahead. There's plenty of hay out in the barn if you feel like rolling about in it afterwards.' It was arranged for Helen and James to come over at about lunch time for some refreshments before the frolic. Janet added that the open-air run would help the digestion and burn off the calories if nothing else. 'But I know you're really interested in the something else,' said Janet.

Janet prepared sandwiches and salad which she planned to serve on the patio. It was a good day for an outdoor meal. And for Helen's run. She never picked bad weather for a run. She said she was a pony-girl, not a masochist. And besides, if there was the chance of a good satisfying fuck while she was still glowing with conscious virtue from her exertions, who wanted a damp cold day for it? There was usually a good fuck to be had. Otherwise Helen would not be nearly so eager to run naked, or almost so, through the woods pulling James behind her on the cart. In Helen's scheme of things carrots were much more important than sticks. And a lot more fun. Helen and James arrived as Janet was putting the last of the lunch things on the table.

When she heard their car drive up, she went around to the front of the house to meet her guests. 'Welcome to the nude pony-girl and equestrian centre,' she said in greeting. 'You look positively radiant, Helen. Looking forward to the run, or just to the bit that comes afterwards?'

'More to the afterwards,' Helen replied. 'You don't think I'd put up with all this work if there was no reward, do you?'

'Of course you would,' Janet said. 'You love being harnessed to the chariot and whipped up to speed.' According to Janet they sat down to lunch with the prospect of sexual games to follow for an added sauce. The best sauce there is next to actual hunger.

After lunch they all adjourned to the barn to prepare Helen for the outing. Since it was a fine day, sunny and quite warm, James decided that Helen would operate in the nude mode, that is, wearing as little as the job called for.

216

Helen called it her Number One undress uniform. They had left her things in the barn. Since there was virtually no other place they could practise their peculiar sport, there was no sense in carrying the gear backwards and forwards. It was only necessary to get the equipment from the storage box in the tack room. While Janet and James collected the gear, Helen got undressed down to the bare essentials.

Helen unbuttoned her blouse and shrugged out of it. She laid it carefully on a bench. Reaching behind her, she undid her bra next and laid it aside. Her nipples (Janet said) were already erect and crinkly with anticipation. If this were one of those purple-prose porno novels, I'd have said that her breasts were engorged and her nipples erect with desire. But as it's not . . . Helen took off her skirt and stood before them in shoes, stockings and suspenders. This is the stuff sex fantasies are made of. Attractive woman starkers in a deserted barn. Stockings and suspenders right out of a voyeur's dream. Her bare breasts heavy and full, breath shallow and rapid. It is only necessary to imagine a bestial rapist lurking in the shadows as his eyes devour his intended victim.

James stood in the tack room door with the harness. 'You look fantastic,' he said. 'Let's be having you over here for the rest of it.'

Helen stood her ground momentarily for effect before going over to the others. James began to fit the harness to her. The wide waist belt came first. There were straps from the belt that crossed between her breasts and went over her shoulders to fasten at the back of her waist. They would ensure that the harness would not slip down when she was pulling her hardest, and would help spread the strain. At the sides of the waist belt there were D-rings to fasten her to the traces. There was a third ring at the back. Helen stood docilely as she was buckled into the harness. When all the straps were tight she posed for them and said, 'My God, the things we do for fun!'

James fitted the head harness next. This consisted of a strap around her forehead and another that went over the top of her head and buckled under the chin. This was fas-

217

tened loosely for the moment so that James could put the bit in her mouth. With the bit in place the chin strap could be drawn up tightly and would keep her mouth closed. 'Any last words?' James asked her as he prepared to put the bit between her teeth. Helen shook her head. 'Open your mouth then,' he continued. When she did so, he placed the steel bit between her teeth and pulled it back until it distorted her face into a grimace. James buckled the strap behind her head, pulling the bit deeply into the corners of her mouth. Unlike normal bits of the type used on horses, Helen's incorporated a flat metal plate which rested atop her tongue and effectively gagged her. When James pulled the chin strap tight she could only grunt.

To complete the transformation of his wife into a pony-girl, James attached the blinkers to either side of her head harness. Then he fastened the reins to the ends of Helen's bit. From their box of tricks in the tack room he brought the dildo with the flattened rubber base I mentioned earlier. The third rein went through the ring in the base and up between her legs. By using this rein judiciously, James said, he could bring about a quite startling decrease in Helen's performance. 'She can't worry about going when she's coming,' he joked. Finally came the horse hair plume. James greased the inner (or Helen) end and spread her buns. The device went in all the way and when he released her the cheeks clamped the plume and kept it from falling out. Helen was looking definitely horsy. James tied her hands behind her back with a leather thong and fastened them to the ring at the back of her waist belt.

James led Helen by the reins to the rear door of the barn, where he hobbled her ankles. He left her there while he went to fetch the sulkey. This was a very light affair and was easily managed by one man and pulled by one woman. Janet helped to manoeuvre Helen between the traces and attached her to them by the rings on the side of her belt. Everything was now ready.

Before leaving, however, James turned to Janet and told her to take off all her clothes. She hadn't expected anything of the sort but she did as he asked, laying her own dress

218

and underwear on top of Helen's. When she was nude, Janet stood with the light breeze flowing around her and between her legs while James went to get some rope from the store room. With this he tied Janet's wrists together in front. He tied another length of rope to her bound wrists and made her raise her arms over her head. James bent her elbows so that her hands were behind her head before leading the end of the rope down behind her back. He pulled it tight and tied the end around her waist.

'You can amuse youself by struggling if you want to,' he told Janet. With an arm around her waist he guided her over to the ladder which led to the hay storage in the loft. He helped her to climb up, steadying her from behind as she made the slow journey. The steadying hand gradually shifted until James was caressing her cunt as she climbed. When she reached the top Janet stepped carefully onto the flooring of the loft, acutely conscious of the hand between her legs. She was careful not to stumble. James came up behind her with more rope and a roll of masking tape. While Janet waited with her hands tied behind her head, James arranged several bales of hay into a barrier so that she wouldn't fall over the edge of the floor. He sat her down on a bale of hay and gagged her with the masking tape, using long strips that covered her mouth and went back past her ears on either side. He also taped her eyes shut. She didn't resist.

As she sat in darkness, Janet could hear James moving about nearby. The stems she sat on poked her in the bottom and the backs of her thighs. Suddenly she felt his hands on her shoulders, gently forcing her to lie back on the hay. When she was lying on her back, the hands shifted to other, less neutral areas. Not to put too fine a point on it, James was fondling her bare breasts and rubbing her clitoral area with practised hands. If being tied up while Helen waited to go for her gallop was unexpected, this attention was even more unexpected. But most definitely not unwelcome. Janet relaxed and enjoyed it. Her breath became shallow and rapid and she was groaning as loudly as her gag permitted.

As James continued to arouse her, Janet began to thrash about. She pulled at the rope that held her prisoner but got nowhere. James continued to tease her. The two hands were joined by a pair of lips and a tongue which strayed from her swollen nipples down her stomach and between her parted legs and on into the eye of the storm. She struggled more wildly as she felt her climax building. James was doing his best, but just then Janet wished that he had four hands instead of the usual two. However, the English have a long tradition of making do with what is available. Janet made do. She gasped and shuddered when her climax took her. It was turning out to be a very nice day. The unexpected pleasures are often the nicest.

The hands and mouth went away without warning, and Janet could hear the sound of clothing being removed. Since she was already nude, it didn't require a great mental effort to figure out who else was getting that way. James reached for her and she let him help her down to the floor until she was lying on her back with parted legs. Janet said that she was looking forward to the next bit, but James made her wait while he returned to the attack with mouth and hands. She felt as if her skin were on fire as his fingers trailed over her belly and down between her thighs. She was sure that Helen could hear the action from where she stood waiting for James to return for the main event of her day. But Janet didn't waste much thought on Helen's state because she was beginning to heave and pant once more herself.

When James entered her, she forgot all about Helen, and indeed everything else. If a stiff prick lacks a conscience, an aroused woman can also be indifferent to the finer social niceties. Janet concentrated all her attention on the tiny explosions occurring between her legs. She became more frantic as James moved in and out. He was holding her hips and pressing against her breasts with his chest. Janet said that she almost fainted when they came together. They call that a roll in the hay. She was sweaty and warm when he withdrew and lay beside her.

She gradually came back to earth and James stood up

220

and helped her to her feet. He untied the ropes around her waist and led it up between her legs, tying it once more around her waist from the front. Now the rope rubbed on a rather sensitive spot. Janet began to be aware of all sorts of interesting possibilities in her altered situation. She tugged experimentally on the rope and was rewarded by a tingle in her crotch. James took no notice of her action. Once more he guided her to a seat on a bale of hay, where he tied her legs together at ankles and knees.

When he was done, James said, 'I'll be off now. You can struggle a bit if you like, Janet. But be careful not to get too close to the edge. I'll be taking the ladder away and nobody will know you're here. Enjoy yourself.'

Janet heard the sound of his retreating footsteps and shortly afterwards the scrape of the ladder as it was taken away. Then she heard a slight creak as James mounted the cart. The whip cracked on something – probably Helen, because she let out strangled shriek – and the noise of wheels retreated. Janet was alone and powerless to help herself in a profound silence that stretched out around her. She knew that James and Helen would be back, but she had no idea when that would be. But James had arranged things so that she could amuse herself if she wished. The time need not hang too heavily. She should be grateful for small favours, she thought. And she was, as soon as she had wriggled a bit on her perch. That rope between her legs was really well placed.

I've already described how us avid bondage freaks amuse ourselves while we're left alone. No need to go into that again. Suffice it to say that Janet spent the time agreeably enough. Some indeterminate time later, Janet knew she was no longer alone. The sound of wheels on gravel told her that the cross-country run was over. Footfalls on the barn floor came closer. There was a scrape and a thump which she guessed was the ladder being replaced. Then she felt hands lifting and turning her. They untied the rope at her knees and ankles. They peeled the tape off her eyes, and there was James grinning at her. He peeled the tape away from Janet's mouth and untied her hands.

'I hope you enjoyed yourself today,' was his first remark. 'When you're ready, come down and help me with Helen. She's had a good run and needs a rub down. I'll get started on that right away,' James said with a broad wink. He went back down the ladder.

From her lofty perch Janet could look down over the lower floor. Helen stood in her harness near the rear doors of the barn. Her hands were still tied behind her and she was flushed and sweaty. James was nowhere in sight, but she heard the sound of running water. Janet walked over to the ladder and climbed down. James was drawing warm water in a bucket, presumably to use on Helen. Janet splashed water on her face and spent a few minutes picking bits of straw off her body. James enjoyed the show. Lucky him, Janet thought. Two nude women to choose from. But there was no need to choose when he could have both. Perhaps had already had both. At that point Janet didn't know what had passed between James and Helen on the run, but there was a good chance that the exercise had been interrupted for an exercise of a different sort. Helen was dressed for the part.

Janet went to dress herself while James carried the water over to Helen and started to wipe the sweat from her body with a damp towel. If he lingered a bit on certain parts, Helen didn't seem to mind a lot. When she was dressed, Janet went to help him and together they got her cleaned up and unharnessed. Janet left them in the barn while Helen got dressed. She said that there would be coffee and refreshments at the house when they were ready. All in all it had been an eventful day, she reflected as she walked up to the house through the gathering dusk.

9

REMOTELY SHOCKING

Victoria Sims and Bill Mason have gone further than anyone else toward making their house a bondage freak's version of the ideal home. They have been clever about it – not obvious, I mean. They haven't fitted hoisting gear on the ceilings or turned the spare bedroom into a torture chamber. They don't even have a mirror in the ceiling over their bed. However, there is an unusually large number of potted plants hanging from unusually stout hooks, and the newel posts of their stairway run from floor to ceiling. They have hidden their torture chamber discreetly in the basement. The visitor wouldn't even know it was there unless they knew him well enough to display it. Their cellar resembles Harriet's in intent, but it is done on a much smaller scale. This is due partly to a lack of space, but the size also reflects the fact that it was designed with only one victim in mind.

I suspect that Victoria is nothing but a low masochist. You know what I mean, one of those perverts who derive pleasure from pain and public humiliation. And would you believe she's into bondage as well? Personally, I can't understand someone who likes to be tied up and whipped, or who enjoys being shackled in awkward or suggestive positions for hours on end. She even enjoys having sex while tied up. The things some people get up to! So this is a cautionary tale, designed to make virgins go hot and cold all over. Maybe that's the test. If you go hot, you're not a virgin.

Between themselves, Victoria and Bill have worked out

223

a *modus vivendi* guaranteed to make a dyed-in-the-wool feminist froth at the mouth. He works and brings home the pay. She spends most of her time at home in bondage – a bird in a gilded cage, she calls herself. She regularly does her housework in chains. He lets her out whenever he decides she deserves it. She loves it, or says she does. He seems satisfied as well. It works for them. Or it has so far. I don't know what they will do if they ever have children. Or if the feminists find out.

Victoria is under virtually permanent house arrest, much like Hilary had been. The difference is that Victoria and Bill knew what they wanted to do from the outset, and did not need a push from the law to fall into bondage as Hilary had. When she is not tied up or chained, Victoria may be locked into the basement cell. In any case she is locked inside the house. Or she may be nude, or dressed so scantily or provocatively that she dare not venture out even if she was able. Her clothes are locked up so that she can't get at them. Bill carries an impressive ring of keys with him when he goes out. Owning a slave is not all a bed of roses. Even a willing slave is an obligation.

Victoria also subscribes to Harriet's weight reduction programme. That involves long confinement and what we groupies call 'stringent discipline' for those who do not attain their goals. There's also a certain amount of submission and humiliation involved, which she laps up. Victoria really doesn't need to lose weight, but she enjoys what Harriet does to her. So she submits herself to the routine every so often. One of her standard openings is to announce that she is getting too fat. That is the signal for Bill to take her in hand himself, or turn her over to Harriet if they can arrange a convenient schedule. If the announcement occurs on a weekend it is easier for him to begin the process before arranging for Harriet to take over later.

He begins by dressing, or undressing, her to taste. There's no reason for sex, pain or domination to be unaesthetic unless you're a complete Philistine. Next he secures her hands behind her back with rope or handcuffs so that she can't feed herself very readily. He may gag her as well

224

if he wants to make eating impossible. Alternatively he may give her a hearty meal (bringing to mind the old chestnut about the condemned man and the hearty breakfast). This serves as a reminder of what she is renouncing, albeit temporarily, and (she says) it heightens the sense of deprivation.

If he wants to be more subtle, Bill can lace her last meal with a laxative and a diuretic so that she soon loses what she has eaten. Victoria says that there is an added dimension of humiliation when she cannot control her bodily functions. The sense of imprisonment is augmented when she knows she dare not get too far from a toilet. With her hands tied she has to be helped with her most private acts. And there is the added *frisson* of a possible accident before she can get to the loo. These masochists are strange people.

If there is an accident, he has to clean her up so long as he keeps her tied. If Harriet is in charge, Victoria may get a whipping with the riding crop to remind her to be more tidy. Or she may get a lashing from Bill when the fit takes him. If he doesn't feel like cleaning up the messy bits, he can always untie her and make her clean up after herself. There's no obligation for him to treat her fairly. She likes being treated as a slave and the 'humiliating posture' she finds herself in gives her added pleasure. It's a matter of choice. Her choice and his.

A variation of the laxative routine, and much more humiliating according to Victoria, is what she calls her 'incontinence belt'. It is her version of the mediaeval chastity belt, and indeed it serves the same function, though that is not its main purpose. When she is locked into the belt, she cannot be penetrated in either of the usual places. But its real purpose is to keep her anal and urethral sphincters dilated so that she can't control them. In the case of the urethral sphincter, there is a catheter arrangement which is inserted before the belt goes on. The belt holds it in place and prevents her from removing it. There is a semi-rigid tube which is inserted up the back passage past the sphincter which serves to keep it open. Victoria can't get at either of these devices to remove them without removing the belt. Bill keeps the keys to that.

225

When she is wearing her belt Victoria has to be very careful if she is to avoid a messy accident. So she wears it mainly at home. She told me that she had worn it, or been forced to wear it, for as long as two days. During that time her constant companion was a bucket. She said she felt like those diplomatic couriers who have their attaché cases handcuffed to their wrists. She was as careful about her bucket as the courier is of his briefcase. She jokingly called the bucket her 'close friend' and seemed to enjoy the experience.

Occasionally she is made to go out while wearing her belt. That, she says, is both humiliating and exciting at once. On those occasions she has to wear a long coat to conceal the plastic bags attached to her body to contain any accidental spillages. When the bags get full she has to go to a public toilet to empty them. She says there is a faint odour of piss and shit which others sometimes notice. But she likes to suffer. So she seeks out such experiences. When wearing her belt in public, Victoria says that she feels 'exquisitely violated'. *Chacun à son paradis.*

Another of the devices they have adopted is what Bill calls her electronic lead. It consists of a pocket-sized transmitter which he carries, and a receiver connected to a battery-powered shocking device which Victoria wears as a collar around her neck. Of course she has to wear a high-necked top to keep the secret a secret. It is an adaptation of the electric or electronic dog training collar which our American cousins have developed and which caused the RSPCA no end of anguish. Victoria's has been modified so that the shock can be sent to areas other than the neck, to put it politely. These devices are available in this country in case the idea appeals. But anyone wanting one had better hurry before the bleeding hearts succeed in banning them.

Victoria mainly wears her electronic lead in public. For those occasions she has a leather panty-corselet which holds the anal and vaginal plugs inside her. There is a network of wires in the cups which makes contact with her tits. It resembles my electric body suit in purpose, but her

226

arms are left free. When she is in public, none of her electronic enhancement shows. With the tight leather garment under her clothes she merely looks like an attractive woman with an exceptionally taut and shapely body. If anyone were to touch her, it would be obvious at once that something about her was different. But unless someone took all her clothes off, it would only seem that she was wearing a stout corset. Unusual these days, but not unknown.

But then there is not much danger that a woman would be accosted in the street and disrobed -- worst luck! If any evidence of her bizarre underpinning is ever discovered, it will only be as the result of an accident requiring immediate hospitalisation. In that case there might be some awkward questions from the hospital staff, but they could do nothing if she clammed up. She might be unable to control herself in public if Bill pressed the button at the wrong time. Victoria says that the shock can be strong enough to stagger her and drive her to her knees, but Bill does not use so much current as a rule. At full strength the shock causes her muscles to spasm. She would almost certainly fall as her knees give way. And she would almost certainly let out a full-throated shriek which would be sure to attract attention. Even when the shock is mild she has to exercise strong control so as not to give a yip of surprise or jump too high.

According to Victoria, shopping in this rig can be a real experience. She is in a continual sweat from knowing what could be done to her by remote control and without warning. Her corselet has a locking zipper up the back so that she can't remove it or get at the plugs inside her. It wouldn't do any good to slip into the nearest toilet or changing room and try to remove her corselet. It only comes off with the proper key, and even then she needs some help in peeling the leather 'skin' off. So once locked into the garment and out on the street she has to try to act normally while being quite abnormally stimulated.

Bill uses the electronic lead to control her spending. A touch on the button is enough to let her know that she has spent enough money or time in the shops. When she feels the short shock she knows she will have to drop whatever she is doing and go back to him, just as a dog knows it's time to go when the lead is tugged. She is reasonably sure that she won't get a full strength jolt in a public place because that would give the game away. But there is always the uncertainty. What she knows is that he can give her as much as he likes when they get home if she does not obey him. Or merely if he feels like it. And she loves it.

Once when Howard and I called round Victoria answered the door in an obviously agitated state. She was fully dressed but her blouse was clinging to her in damp patches. Her skirt was wrinkled and she was sweaty and trembling. Her hair straggled in damp tendrils. It was obvious to the *cognoscenti* that she was in the midst of one of her 'at-home' sessions.

Alert as always, I completely misread the signs. 'You look awful. What's the matter? Are you all right?' When the truth finally dawned I asked, 'Have we come at an awkward moment? We can call back later, or tomorrow if you like.'

Victoria shook her head and mouthed the words, 'Come in,' but no sound came out. She stood aside to let us enter. As we went through the hall I asked her, 'Laryngitis?'

'No, diffenbachia,' Harriet answered cheerfully as she emerged from the sitting room with a flask of colourless liquid in her hand. 'We're trying it out to see what dose is required to keep her quiet for a couple of hours.'

Victoria's throat worked but once again no sound emerged. I noticed that she was wearing a leather collar locked about her neck. So she must be on her electronic lead.

Harriet said unconcernedly, 'I think we've overdone it just a bit this time. The original idea was to keep her quiet for about two hours, but it's been over three hours since we gave her the stuff and she's still quiet as a mouse. I'm beginning to wonder if it'll ever wear off.'

Harriet didn't seem to be too worried, even though Victoria shot her an anxious glance. I reflected that as a nurse

Harriet should have some idea of what she was doing. I had heard of diffenbachia before. It's also commonly called dumb cane or mother-in-law's tongue. It is a poisonous plant whose juice (properly measured, of course) could render one speechless. Too much could kill, but like all plant poisons, the concentration had to be pretty strong for that. I had once toyed with the idea of trying some myself, but I didn't really know what I was doing. My common sense had overruled that impulse. Besides, I enjoy the sensation of being gagged and so had no compelling reason to try this other method. Now, however, seeing its effect on Victoria, I felt a renewed interest. What would it feel like if I could not make a sound? What couldn't be done to me if I were literally speechless?

'We're putting her through her paces,' Harriet continued. The equestrian metaphor seemed to be habitual with her. 'I do the chemistry and Bill does the electrics. He's in the basement at the moment fixing something up. When he's done we'll carry on. In the meantime I'll ask Victoria to get us some coffee. You won't mind, will you, dear?'

She nodded and made her way towards the kitchen. She still looked shaky so I followed her to see if she wanted any help. Once again I asked Victoria if everything was all right. She nodded and gave me a wan smile. It wasn't my place to stop her. Nor would I seek to dissuade a consenting adult once I was sure there was actual consent. So I dropped the subject and helped with the coffee.

While we were busy in the kitchen, Harriet and Howard were talking in the sitting room. Harriet was saying something about going on holiday soon and the conversation turned to places to see and places to avoid. Victoria seemed tense and subdued but as she couldn't speak I couldn't question her. We took the coffee pot and the cups through into the other room. Harriet was saying that she rather fancied an outdoorsy holiday. She had no patience with pre-digested package tours. Probably because someone else was in command, I thought.

Harriet rose as we entered and helped with the cups.

Victoria poured a cup for each of us but none for herself. From the stiff way she was holding herself, I guessed that she was wearing her leather corselet and didn't want to drink anything that might make her want to pee. When she sat down she held herself stiffly erect. An occasional low, ominous creak came from her leather skin whenever she shifted position on the settee.

There was a step in the hall and Victoria's eyes turned quickly towards the door. It was obvious that she was expecting a shock at any time and was preparing herself as best she could. Bill entered the room and nodded hello to us. In his hand he held a small black box which was obviously the control device for Victoria's electronic lead. He set it carefully on the coffee table where she could see it. This was a form of psychological torture for her, not knowing when he would pick up the box and switch it on. Her eyes followed his hands nervously. She relaxed only slightly when he took a cup of coffee.

'I thought I heard voices when I was downstairs,' Bill said to us. 'I was just replacing the battery in the control box. I'm glad you dropped in. Harriet and I were just putting Vicky over the jumps. Maybe you'd like to watch.' To me he continued, 'I remember how you handled Janet that night at your place.'

'All compliments gratefully accepted,' I replied while thinking again how easily the equestrian metaphor came to them. Maybe they thought of us as horses. Howard made the usual noises about not wanting to intrude, but I was intrigued by what I had seen so far and wanted to see more. How predictable I am! I was glad when Bill assured us that we were welcome to stay. I don't get many opportunities to see a real masochist in action at close range. Victoria is not one of those milk-toast types who use pain just to enhance sexual pleasure. She is deeply into pain for its own sake. You could say that we are all alike in method, but the ratio of pain to pleasure is different in every case. In Victoria's case the ratio was about 70:30 in favour of pain. I like it about 30:70 the other way. You could say that she likes a bit of food with her spice, while I prefer lots of food with a touch of spice.

230

Bill never asked Victoria what she thought about spectators. In their relationship he gives the orders and she obeys. I knew this already but still didn't feel comfortable. The relationship was between Bill and Victoria. Third parties added another dimension. Since she couldn't tell us what she preferred, I caught Victoria's eye and looked a question at her. She smiled and gave a small shrug and a nod which I took to mean we could watch if we wanted to. We, or rather I wanted to. Howard went along because he knew I was interested. I was hoping to learn a thing or two by watching others do their thing. Or by watching as Bill did Victoria's thing.

Harriet got things moving by rising to her feet and announcing that we had wasted enough time on talk. Action time had arrived. She rummaged in her handbag and came up with a handful of tie-wraps. You'll never catch our Miss Jones without the right stuff no matter what the occasion. She moved over to Victoria, who stood up stiffly as she approached. Harriet moved around behind Victoria, forming a loop in the tie-wrap as she went. Without being told Victoria brought her hands together behind her back. Harriet slipped the loop over her wrists and pulled it tight. With a pair of cutters she snipped off the protruding end. The whole thing took less time to do than it takes to describe. It's easy to see why the police and the bondage freaks have taken so readily to this handy device.

Somewhat to my surprise, Harriet then came to me with another tie-wrap already looped and ready in her hands. I had planned merely to watch, but that doesn't often happen with Harriet in charge of anything. Or even when she's just there. She really likes tying people up. If people like her didn't exist, people like me would have to invent them.

But there is no time for philosophy when Harriet is approaching with bondage in mind. Sighing elaborately, I submitted to having my hands secured behind my back with the tie-wrap. It seemed to me that Harriet pulled it extra tight. She knows all about the trick of clenching one's fists to provide a little slack in ropes and had compensated for that. When I relaxed there was no slack. She clipped off the end with her cutters.

231

I thought that would do it, so I was caught completely off guard when a hard shove from her sent me staggering backwards. The arm of the settee met the backs of my legs and I went sprawling in an undignified heap with my legs in the air and my skirt hiked up around my hips. She was on me in a flash, and before one could say 'Jack Robinson' (though why anyone would want to say that escapes me), Harriet had another of her tie-wraps around my ankles and was pulling it cruelly tight, as they say in the S and M magazines.

Harriet looked down at me. I lay in an untidy heap where I had fallen. 'Positively disgraceful', she said. 'Skirt over your head and everything on show.' However, she made no move to help me up. Instead she turned to Victoria with a cheerful, 'Let's be having you.'

She picked up the control box, which was in fact a miniaturised radio transmitter tuned to the frequency of the receiver on Victoria's collar. That receiver in turn was connected to two electric probes in two rather intimate places, and to a fine network of wires which fanned out to cover the bottom, belly and breast areas of her corselet. In this respect the corselet resembled the electric body suits which Janet and I both enjoy so much. The chief difference was that Victoria's garment was designed solely for inflicting pain. There was no compensating arrangement for giving pleasure to the wearer. Bill and Harriet were using the corselet as an obedience trainer: do as we say or else.

Now it was being used to torture Victoria. Nothing was asked of her except to suffer. But that may be an over-simplification, if not a misnomer. She suffered, but willingly. And she was willing to suffer because, in the manner peculiar to masochists, she derived pleasure from it. I don't pretend to understand how she did this, but she obviously managed it. Nor do I know how or why she came to be as she is, any more than I can account for my own preferences. But there was no denying that she had chosen this course as I had chosen mine. Part of the inducement (as in my case) was the linking of sexual gratification with pain. There we were alike. We differed in the amount of pain we were prepared to tolerate, her tolerance being much greater than mine.

No doubt there are those who would see Victoria as a sick woman requiring treatment – the treatment ranging from psychiatric counselling to public stoning, depending on the sexual morés of the person advocating it. I have spoken to her at length on several occasions, and she seems quite sane to me. Of course I am not an unbiased witness, because my own sexual preferences would at least cause the Mrs Grundys of the world to call me kinky (kinky in this case means anything you yourself are not into). And many of the reactions woud not even be that tolerant. There is a general agreement in our crowd not to make judgments of that sort. Pots and kettles shouldn't discuss matters of relative blackness. But I must add that no one I know is molesting children, or even committing axe murders in their spare time.

Harriet moved one of the switches and Victoria stiffened where she stood. 'Ah, good. It's working again.' And she set to work without further ado. Harriet held down one of the switches for several seconds. Victoria jerked erect and rose up onto the balls of her feet as if trying to escape the shock by rising into the air. She expelled the air from her lungs in an explosive gasp while the tendons in her neck stood out with her effort to scream. Her mouth gaped open but no sound emerged. Behind her back her hands were twisting. Harriet switched to another circuit and Victoria's knees buckled. She fell to the carpet and her legs thrashed wildly. It reminded me of Janet's performance. I had probably looked the same way when it was my turn.

Victoria's contortions continued as Harriet switched from one circuit to another. Her back arched and then straightened and she rolled from side to side on the floor. Sweat burst out all over her straining body. I remembered from my own experience that sweat spread the current to areas it ordinarily never reached, as the beer advert has it. It seemed to be doing the same in this case. Victoria's contortions became wilder as she jerked and bucked. She was beyond conscious control and couldn't hold still. It was all happening in an eerie silence except for the thumps Victoria made as she flung herself about. At one point she rolled onto her back and her heels drummed wildly on the floor.

Harriet switched off abruptly and Victoria slumped, seeming to shrink as her taut muscles relaxed all at once. Her breath came in great sawing gulps and she was covered in her own sweat.

The whole performance couldn't have lasted more than five or six minutes, but it must have seemed much longer to Victoria. Harriet went over to examine her charge. She felt the carotid pulse and bent close to check her breathing. She rolled Victoria over onto her stomach and examined her wrists. They were red from her struggles but still securely tied. Those tie-wraps don't give at all. When she was satisfied that Victoria would recover, Harriet straightened her legs and looped another tie-wrap around her ankles. As she pulled it tight Harriet said, 'She'll be all right in a bit. Let her rest. If you two men don't mind, you can give me a lift home.'

Bill nodded and they all went out to collect their coats. The front door opened and then closed again. I heard the key turn as we were locked inside. From outside came the sound of car doors, and then the engine started. The noises diminished as they drove off, leaving us bound hand and foot in the silent house. Victoria lay where she had finished, on her stomach and with her face turned away from me so that I couldn't see her expression. She may have been unconscious but she was breathing normally. At any rate Harriet had been satisfied, and she should know about these things.

When Harriet had tied me up I had not made any attempt to get free. I had been much too interested in what was going to happen to Victoria. Now that the show was over and I turned my attention to my own situation. I pulled at the band on my wrists but there was no slack. Nor was there any in the strap around my ankles. Those tie-wraps are tremendously strong and I knew there was no chance of breaking loose. Harriet had taken the cutters away with her. There might be, in fact there probably was, another pair in the garage with Bill's tools. But they may as well have been on the moon for all the good they were to us. All the doors were locked and both of us were powerless.

Time passed. Quite a long time. There was still no movement from Victoria, nor any sign of the others' return. They had gone to drop Harriet off, but there was no guarantee that they would return immediately when they had done so. She would probably offer them a drink or a coffee when they got to her place. Who knows, she might even offer herself. So, what to do? When you've been left tied up you have to let your imagination entertain you. Enjoy your helplessness. If you're made of the right stuff you'll be all right.

At length Victoria stirred and moved from her position on the floor. She rolled onto her side and her eyes focused on me. I could see her throat working as she tried to speak. 'Hello,' she husked. Evidently the effect of the diffenbachia cocktail was wearing off. 'Sorry I got you into this.'

'I don't mind,' I replied. 'When Harriet's in the mood to tie people up she's hard to resist. And I enjoyed the show. Anyway you know me – when you can't escape, relax and enjoy the experience.'

Victoria whispered, 'Come closer. I can't talk properly yet and we might as well pass the time in conversation or something. I'll soon be myself, I expect. Sorry about the smell.'

I wriggled and twisted until I could lower myself to the floor. Then I could propel myself across to Victoria on my bottom. In the process my skirt rode up over my waist but I couldn't do anything about it. Victoria, I thought, eyed this development with approval. When I got closer I veered over to the settee so that I could sit more comfortably with my back braced against it.

'Are you all right?' Victoria asked.

'I should be asking you that question,' I replied.

She reassured me that there was nothing wrong with her. 'I'd like to make this up to you,' continued Victoria. 'You

235

must think I'm an awful hostess. I couldn't welcome you when you got here, and then I got both of us tied up. To finish off, I thrash about and then pass out.'

As she spoke Victoria was performing her best imitation of a snake as she wriggled across the floor in my direction. I thought I detected something more than concern about her failings as a hostess in Victoria's remarks. When she arrived at my side her head was in the region of my crotch and she was eyeing the territory intently. As usual, I was wearing no pants and so everything was on display. When Victoria lowered her face into my lap my darkest suspicions were confirmed. Not that I minded, but my conscience was telling me that I shouldn't just accept passively from her. As it turned out, my acceptance was anything but passive, but that came later.

'It's not fair,' I said to her while I was still capable of coherent thought. 'Let me lie down and we can do a sixty-nine for one another. You squeeze my head and I'll squeeze yours.'

'No good,' she said. 'My corselet is as good as a chastity belt. It's stiff and tight. Relax and enjoy it,' she said in a stronger voice.

So I did. Victoria shut up and put her lips and tongue and teeth to better use. Better use at any rate from my point of view, which was just above and behind the head that was moving about in my lap. I opened my legs as widely as I could and Victoria got as deeply between them as the space allowed. That was deeply enough for her purpose, and for mine. Things got warm and fuzzy around the edges. At some point I heard a voice, mine, no doubt, as Victoria's was not fully recovered even though her mouth was quite busy, crying out loudly. It, rather I, was saying, 'Ooooohhh' and 'Aaaahhh' and making other sounds even less articulate than that but still clear in their meaning. It was my turn to thrash about. Victoria was having a time holding me down. When next I began to take an interest in my surroundings Victoria was lying on her back with her head in my lap. Her hair trailed between my parted thighs and tickled gently. She asked me if that had been 'fun'. I nodded, though 'fun' was not the word I would have used. Much too weak, I thought.

'Did I stop too soon?' she asked anxiously. Apparently she was still worried about 'entertaining' me. I assured her that I had definitely arrived and she settled back with a relieved smile. 'Good,' she said. 'We can talk now.'

Victoria resembles the protagonist in *The Story of O*, the classic tale of slavery and suffering. The protagonist of that story is simply called O, because that is what she seeks to be, a zero, a cipher. She has no character save what her lovers or owners impose on her. She accepts without question or demur whatever they do to her. And some of the things they do are pretty horrendous: branding, whipping, rape, erotic piercing, bondage. Through it all she is totally passive.

And through it all she is handed from one man to another as she works at effacing herself and becoming what they wish her to be. At the end of the tale O is taken to a party dressed as an owl, or at any rate she is given an owl mask to wear. This suggests that she has achieved wisdom or self-knowledge, and the sum of it is this: she is nothing in herself and exists only as a reflection of the will of her owner. According to one version of the story she asks her owner to kill her – the final act of self-effacement.

In Victoria's case the suffering and humiliation she undergoes is aimed at achieving sexual gratification rather than self knowledge. Subjugation and pain are the means to an end rather than an end in themselves. Like O, Victoria is passive. So am I to a certain extent. Indeed this is true of most bondage freaks. At one point O says that she enjoys a grand sense of freedom from responsibility when she is helpless. I can understand that well enough. When I am tied up I am powerless to influence what happens to me. Everything must be done for me or to me. I have no duties or responsibilities or tasks. All decisions are made by others. Victoria has spoken of similar feelings of freedom, paradoxical as the whole thing sounds. Like O, Victoria and I, indeed all of the people in our group, have chosen to do what we do. To paraphrase Orwell, bondage is freedom.

While we laid about waiting for the men to come back, Victoria and I talked. We exchanged stories and compared notes. I told her some of my experiences – only right that I should contribute something to the conversation. But I learned more about her and her own bent. Most of it was new to me and so quite interesting. She and Bill had devised some new routines to satisfy her particular fancies. She told me that quite often Bill would put her up the pole. No, not that way. They didn't want any children for the same reasons I've already spoken of. Their method was intended to immobilise Victoria and to remind her of her subservient role at the same time. 'I'm nothing but a sex object to him,' Victoria said with a smile as she described her confinements.

Bill had designed and built an impalement device, for want of a better term. Like most bondage gear, it had to be built at home because it wouldn't do to advertise what one was about too widely. The friendly neighbourhood wrought-iron shops could hardly fail to ask some questions, if only to help in the fabrication of whatever they are asked to make. If you know what something is supposed to do, it may help you to build it.

Bill had read a newspaper account about an American woman who was divorcing her 'brutal and selfish' husband. In itself that's nothing new. But the nature of the 'brutality' was. According to the woman, her husband was fond of going out drinking while she stayed at home. In order to make sure that she stayed there the husband had taken to leaving her tied up and – this was no doubt the 'brutal' bit – he had 'fixed rods inside her vagina and rectum so that she couldn't sit down' until he came back to release her. Our American cousins sometimes do the strangest things. The newspaper was vague about the method of 'fixing' the rods, shying away as usual from anything to do with bondage and sex but unable to conceal the fascination I described in the case of Phyllis.

After some thought Bill had showed the article to Victoria and she (predictably) had expressed some interest in the idea. But there was no hint about how to go about the

238

mechanics of it. It was up to them to get over that part. In the end Bill came up with a working variation of the vague idea that did more or less what they wanted. He began by cannibalising the telescoping rod that supports the screen used for showing home movies. The old cine-camera has been replaced by the video camera anyway, so there was no reason to keep the old things about. What he wanted was the screw joint that controlled the telescoping rod. The rod itself was too flimsy for what he had in mind.

Armed with the joint, Bill set about welding a stronger steel pipe to it to form an extendable pole, the length being determined by intricate calculations and careful measurements of the ground clearances of the intended user. There was some interesting by-play during this stage of the design, but I needn't go into that here. If you want to know all the vulgar details of someone else's sex life you'll have to ask someone else. Bill welded the bottom of the pipe (vertically, of course) to a steel plate. It all looked terribly phallic and threatening at this stage, Victoria said. To the top of the pipe he welded a U-shaped piece of flat bar (more careful measurements here as everyone has a slightly different radius in that area). The purpose of this bit was to prevent Victoria from slipping down and doing herself an injury.

He also made two steel dildoes to fix to the flat bar. They could be used either together or separately and required the most careful down-hole measurements, as they say in the oil business. It was all a bit reminiscent of the work James had done on Helen's bicycle saddle. Because he is most thorough, Bill wire-brushed the whole thing and coated it with zinc oxide primer before spray painting it a discrete scarlet colour.

When it was all good and dry, Victoria was summoned to the basement to admire the finished product and try it out. '*Pour moi?* Oh, how nice of you, dear. But you really shouldn't have gone to such trouble,' she remarked.

Bill was more succinct. 'No trouble. Skin out of those clothes.'

Without any further urging Victoria got undressed.

When she was nude Bill sent her to put on the highest heels she owned. Victoria came back wearing her four-inch spike-heeled shoes with stockings and suspender belt. 'I don't like to wear these shoes without tights or stockings. They hurt my bare feet. Somehow I knew that tights wouldn't do for this occasion,' she explained when she returned. 'You approve, dear?' Another rhetorical question, but it was part of the submission ritual she enjoyed.

The same ritual called for Bill not to pay her any superfluous compliments, so he merely said, 'You'll do'. But the bulge in his trousers said a great deal more as he helped Victoria to mount the pole.

As she stood over the pole Victoria reached over and patted Bill's tent pole. 'Is this for me too? How gallant. Maybe we can put it to good use later.'

Bill planted her feet on either side of the steel pole and loosened the screw clamp so that he could raise the rod between her legs. He paused just before the dildoes penetrated to lubricate them with hand cream. Then he slid them into Victoria's body. As they went home she gave a little gasp of delight and squirmed a bit on her perch. Bill lengthened the pole until she was standing erect with her full weight on her feet. The U-shaped flat bar fitted snugly into Victoria's central groove. You could say that she was firmly in the saddle. When Bill tightened the clamp to hold the rod in place, she was unable to dismount without help. The screw clamp was out of her reach and she could not stand on tiptoe and so get off the dildoes inside her. That's why Bill had put her on her high heels. Nor could she bend her knees and gather herself for an upward spring.

Bill stepped back to admire his work. Victoria stood erect on the basement floor with the rigid scarlet pole between her legs. It wasn't necessary to tie her or fasten her in any other way, though that was a possibility for later. Victoria was up the pole and could only stand there until someone released her. Well, she didn't have to stand *absolutely* still. Nor did she. She squirmed even more when Bill got a short strap with which he lashed her back and bottom. Victoria being what she is, she enjoyed the whipping and the impalement equally.

At subsequent sessions they tried several variations on the first run. Bill added rings at the base of the pole so that Victoria's ankles could be chained. At the top end he could handcuff her. He added a ring to either end of the U-shaped bar so that her wrists could be chained either in front of or behind her. And of course they could substitute rope for the chains if desired. And sometimes it was. She's really kinky.

At a still later date Bill wired the pole up to Victoria's electronic lead so that he could offer her a more shocking impalement. He tied her legs together with the pole between them. The current then flowed through her legs before reaching the steel spikes inside her. That caused some interesting muscle spasms and a good deal of noise. The noise of course could be reduced with a proper gag. And sometimes it was. Victoria could be left atop her perch for almost any length of time. During that time she could amuse herself by knitting, reading or just fantasising and squirming. All of which she did, though not too much of the first two!

I once asked Victoria how she got into submission and suffering and how they are related to her sexual practices. She had no clear answer. I have often tried to analyse my own preference for sex and bondage with no more success. The urge to be tied up is certainly not something my parents discussed with me when I was becoming aware of the delicious differences between boys and girls. In fact, like most parents, mine told me as little as they could. If my parents (or even my friends and acquaintances) were aware of bondage as a sex game they never let on to me. But I got the urge from somewhere, even though I didn't do very much to develop it until my friend suggested the rings and padlock to me.

Victoria suggested that my urge to be tied up and her urge to suffer pain and humiliation stem from the paranoid way in which our society views sex. Ah, yes. It always comes down to sex, doesn't it? We are all made to feel guilty about sex; indeed about most things that are enjoyable. It's the old puritan ethic: if it's fun, it's sinful. She argues that

241

if we can't resist, then we can't be guilty of anything. We become victims of others' lust and remain innocent ourselves. The only trouble with that argument is me. I enjoy sex. I enjoy it even more when I am playing bondage games. If guilt is the basis of our actions, being tied up should make me more guilty, not less so. The other problem is that I don't believe sex is anything to feel guilty about, no matter what you actually do in bed (or out of it). So I am no closer to an answer. If anyone can come up with a satisfactory explanation for my urges, be sure to tell me about it. In the meantime I shan't lose any sleep through worrying about the way I am.